Lan SKELI

Lancashire County Library
Bowran Street
Preston PR1 2UX

www.lancashire.gov.uk/libraries

DONKEY PUNCH

DONKEY PUNCH

A Cal Innes Book

Ray Banks

First published in Great Britain in 2007 by Polygon.
This edition published in 2008 by Polygon,
an imprint of Birlinn Ltd
West Newington House
10 Newington Road
Edinburgh
EH9 1QS

9 8 7 6 5 4 3 2 1

www.birlinn.co.uk

ISBN 10: 1 84697 021 0
ISBN 13: 978 1 84697 021 4

British Library Cataloguing-in-Publication Data
A catalogue record for this book is available on request from the British Library.

Typeset by Hewer Text (UK) Ltd, Edinburgh
Printed and bound by Creative Print and Design, Wales

To my wife Anastasia,
for preferring bloody violence to bloody sex.

What matters most is how well you walk
through the fire.

CHARLES BUKOWSKI

PART 1

Letter from America

ONE

'So, Callum, how are things?'

'Things are fine, Mr Burgess.'

Derek Burgess is another in a long line of people with a feigned interest in my mental health. He's about my age, he's never heard a decent song in his life and it shows. I've been seeing him for the past thirty months, and he's worn the same outfit to every appointment: that dull grey suit – jacket on the chair behind him – the white shirt, dark blue tie that doesn't quite match. He looks like a probation officer. Which is precisely what he is.

'All this time, you still don't call me Derek,' he says. His fingers are normally in a state of motion. This time is no different; he's bending a paperclip out of shape, smoothing it into a straight metal rod. Normally he'll bend it back to its original shape, but he's set it aside for a purpose.

'Think of it as a sign of respect,' I say.

'Or a sign of distrust.' Burgess uses one end of the mangled paperclip to dig some unseen dirt from underneath his fingernail. The faint clicking sound makes my teeth itch.

'Either way, it's a little late to start getting pally now, isn't it?'

'Mmm. I suppose so.'

Burgess lays the paperclip on the desk just so. Then he scratches at a razor burn above his collar before he looks down at my notes. Our early appointments were textbook examples in how to knock the ex-con down a peg or two. I came out with a proper prison-hard attitude and Burgess had all the condescension to combat it. As we progressed I dropped the sneer – it required too much energy to maintain – but Burgess stayed as patronising as ever. It's the curse of the civil servant. They find a behaviour that works, they'll stick to it come hell or high water. All the better to keep that line in the dirt clear: I am the one in charge here, and you are the criminal. So I've kept the formality, calling him Mr Burgess while he addresses me by my court name. Gives Burgess the power trip he needs in a thankless fucking job and it lets me sit here without suffering bullshit questions.

'You're still working for Paul Gray?' he says. Still nose-deep in my file. I wonder what they have in there, apart from my record. Vital statistics. Whatever probation officers doodle while they talk.

'Paulo,' I say.

Burgess looks up. 'Sorry?'

'His name's Paulo. And yeah, I'm still working for him.'

'How's that going?'

'Fine, good. As well as can be expected, y'know.'

'It's steady employment?'

'As a rock.'

I'm not lying to him. The PI days are over, if they'd ever been there in the first place. I've been concentrating my energies on caretaker work, whatever errand Paulo needs me to run. Sweeping floors, picking up the focus pads, grunt work. Whatever pays the bills and keeps me clean. Because God knows, being on licence isn't all it's cracked up to be. Probation's a barbed wire leash. And I've already felt it dig into my throat once before.

No, all I need now is for people to leave me alone, let me get on with the simple life and stop questioning me about my state of mind. Since I got back from Newcastle, that's been the hot topic with Paulo and it's got so I'm second-guessing myself. That'll lead to full-on senility if I let it. So sack that.

'You plan to keep working at the boxing club?' says Burgess.

'Man plans, and God laughs,' I say.

'Excuse me?'

I smile. 'Yes, I plan to keep working at the boxing club, Mr Burgess.'

'Okay then.' Burgess plucks the paperclip from his desk, drops it into a metal bin. From the sound of it, the bin's empty. Burgess is a stickler for cleanliness. 'You're sure you're doing fine. You're okay.'

Keep the smile going. 'I'm doing dandy, Mr Burgess.'

Burgess gazes through me, like he's trying to read my mind instead of asking me straight out. Probably thinking that if he did ask something, he'd get a fistful of lies in return. Some blokes I know, that stare puts the shits up them, makes them paranoid. Others just take it as a confirmation of their recidivism, makes them think their record marks them like a bad dose of acne, that they haven't got a chance in the outside world. And that's what they call a self-fulfilling prophecy. I start thinking that if Derek Burgess hadn't gone into the probation service, he'd have made an excellent psychopath. Maybe he was anyway. It doesn't matter, but that stare of his doesn't do anything to me but make my back ache.

'Okay,' he says. And refers back to his notes.

I sneak a glance at my watch. Right on cue, it's time for another pop of codeine. But I'm not about to start necking prescription pills in front of my PO. For one, he doesn't know about my time in Newcastle. If he did, I'd be in Strangeways instead of his office. Secondly, if painkillers come into the equation, that's me fucked. Prescription medicine on the fly spells addiction in day-glo letters to these blokes, an arrow pointing straight to rehab and therapy and God knows what else.

So I wait.

'That's about it then,' he says. 'How do you feel?'

'How do I feel about being a free man? Pretty good.'

'You don't have any . . . anxiety.'

'I've been thoroughly rehabilitated, Mr Burgess. I've been eased back into society. No anxiety whatsoever.'

'Glad to hear it.' Burgess pulls a form from one of his many pigeonholes and smoothes it out on the desk between us. He moves the plastic holder with his name on it and looks up at me. Then he pushes the form across the desk as if he can't bear to touch it. 'If you'll read this through, sign where I've marked, that'll be it.'

I pick up the piece of paper and start reading. Or pretend to read, looking at it for enough time to make him think that I've scoured every last word. I can feel the sweats start, know that the pain in my back's only going to get worse.

Burgess does what he always does: asks me if I understand what I'm reading.

'Yeah, I get it,' I say. I grab a biro from his desk and slash my signature on the dotted lines. Push the form back to him.

Burgess doesn't touch the paper. 'So.'

'Yeah.'

I get to my feet, fight a show of pain. Burgess picks up the biro between two fingertips. No final handshakes, no stirring words of encouragement, certainly nothing in the way of tearful farewells. This time we've spent together, it's been forced by a court of law. I didn't tell him anything but the bare essentials and he didn't care enough to push. With Burgess' caseload, that's the safest option. Besides, he probably thinks he'll be seeing me again soon enough. Definitely no love lost, and I don't think either of us has come out of this thing any the wiser. But what the fuck. Not everything has to be a learning experience.

So I nod to him, head for the door.

As I walk out of there a free man, I'm sure I hear the biro hitting the bottom of the bin.

TWO

The last person I expect to see when I get back to the Lad's Club is Mo Tiernan. And what I really don't expect to see is Mo Tiernan come flying out of the club. But there he is, tumbling through the double doors and rolling into the road.

I slam on the brakes. Instinct, even though he's nowhere near me. And then I think about speeding up. Instead, I get out of the car and light a cigarette. Take a moment to bask in the bastard's pain.

Paulo comes storming out the door. His face is bright red, fists balled at his sides and there's blood on his shirt. A quick glance at the pair of them, and it's definitely Mo's blood. Mo's taken a proper battering, his Berghaus jacket ripped at the collar. He struggles to his feet. His right leg gives out, but Mo wraps himself around a lamp-post and hangs on, spits blood at the ground.

'What did I tell you, Mo?' says Paulo.

Mo spits more blood.

'I told you, I saw you around here again, I'd put my foot in your arse.' Paulo slows as he crosses the road. 'And I know you fuckin' heard us, because you were there when I said it.'

Paulo peels Mo from the lamp-post and short-jabs him in the side of the head. Mo twists, his hand up over his face, then drops. I take a drag off the Embassy and start walking over. Part of me thinks it's great to watch Paulo kick the shit out of Mo Tiernan, but enough's enough. Paulo's got a face on that means a red mist is falling.

'Paulo,' I say. 'Leave it.'

'Where've you been?' he says, not looking at me.

'Had an appointment with my PO.'

Mo groans, pulls himself up onto his knees. Paulo makes a move to put the boot in, but I get in the way. Hold up my hands, smoke blinding me. 'That's enough, mate.'

'This fucker's a dealer,' Paulo says, leaning round me and pointing at Mo.

'I know he is. Fuck you doing round here, Mo?'

Mo shakes his head, tries to grin.

'He was dealing is what he was fuckin' doing. We got to take this to your dad, Mo? Your dad want to know what you're doing in *my* club?'

'Fuck off, nonce,' says Mo, his voice thick.

Paulo pushes past me, kicks Mo full in the head. Once, hard. I put my hands on Paulo, ease him back. 'C'mon, mate. You're gonna fuckin' kill him you keep that up.'

Mo rolls over onto his back, makes a choking sound. He's smiling, one hand extended to make a wanker gesture at Paulo.

I push Paulo back into the club. 'Don't play to it, man.'

'He deserves it. Me and that little twat had an agreement. He comes back in here, I got every right to knock him into a coffin. I got every right to *stomp his fuckin' head into the ground.*'

'Get in the office, mate. Come on . . .'

Paulo points over my shoulder as we head to the office. The other lads have stopped sparring, talking, whatever they were doing. Standing around watching the floor show. 'You. Simpson, you little bastard, you're *out*. Don't give us none of that shit about not buying, I know it was you, I saw you buy, you're out. I got no time for them what don't want to be helped, you know that. You *all* know that. I warned you the last time, you bring it in my place, you're out and I'll be having words with your fuckin' social worker.'

I kick open the door to the office, push Paulo inside. He pulls himself away from me, shakes his hands out. His shoulders hunched, breathing still heavy. And the colour's yet to drain from his face. Bloke's a mess of aggression and he can't seem to shift it.

'You need to calm down, mate. You're about to turn green and start smashing shit. And I don't want to see you with your clothes ripped up, alright?'

'I'm calm, Cal.' Paulo runs a hand over his head. 'You do me a favour, will you? Make sure that prick's packed his bag and gone. I don't want to see him when I get back out there, know what I mean?'

'You going to be alright in here?'

Paulo slumps into a chair. 'Just make sure he's out.'

I watch Paulo for a second, just to make sure he's settled, then head back into the club. The lads are still standing about, caught in a freeze-frame of shock, heavy bags and speed bags either swaying or hanging still. They've seen Paulo lose his temper before, but not to that degree. I have to say, it kind of scared me, too. And then there's Ewan Simpson, standing all alone but giving it some with the righteous indignation. Fronting like a fucker, Ewan's a short, fattish bastard with hair brushed forward to hide what I think might be a slappable forehead. As I get closer, I'm positive the lad's balding.

'You want summat?' he says.

I grab his arm, dig my fingers right into the muscle. 'You heard the man. You're out.'

'I didn't buy nowt, man. Gerroff us.' He tries twisting out of my grip, but I pull him towards the door.

'Doesn't make any difference to me, Ewan.'

Ewan ducks. I let him go. 'Yeah, the fuck you gonna do about it?'

The bastard's giving me gyp. Hangs around with Tiernan, he's bound to have a false sense of his own importance.

I just smile at him. 'Fuck am I gonna do about it? Ewan, let me tell you something. You're in enough shite already without picking a fight with me. You got caught buying from Mo Tiernan, that means you're a shit-for-brains—'

'I didn't buy.'

'You want to turn out your pockets? You want me to search you, son?'

He backs up a step. 'You don't search me, you fuckin' ponce. You keep your fuckin' hands off us.'

'You don't want to do that, you're out.'

'I don't have to do nowt,' he says, a step forward and leering. 'Fuck are you, anyway? I seen you knocking back the pills, man. Everyone knows you're a fuckin' junkie.'

'Those are prescription.'

'So's mine.'

'That's why you're buying from Mo.'

'I lost me script.'

'Get out, Ewan.'

'Fuck off, you know what it's like, man. You're a fuckin' pillhead, eh?' He looks around for support, gets nothing. But that doesn't stop him. 'Least your fuckin' smackhead brother knew what he was.'

'You what?'

'You heard. Your fuckin—'

I hit him hard in the middle of the forehead with the heel of my hand. I wanted to punch the wee scrote, but I had to pull it at the last minute. My hand connects sharply, Ewan takes a couple of faltering steps back, water in his eyes. I rub my palm, then scoop him up before he hits the floor, shove him towards the door. He's dizzy, flailing. I keep shoving. He skitters on the tiles in the hall, then holds his hands out to get his balance.

'Out, Ewan.'

He walks a few steps to the street. Mo's still out there, but he's on his feet now, dabbing at his nose. He stares at me, then Ewan. He holds up one hand to the lad and I feel sick. Haven't seen Mo Tiernan since Newcastle, haven't wanted to. And if I expected any change in the bloke, I'd be disappointed. The only thing shifted about Mo Tiernan is that his eyes are glassier than ever. And that doesn't bode well.

Ewan raises his hand to Mo, gives me a filthy look, and heads up towards Regent Road. Mo goes in the opposite direction, doesn't acknowledge me. Six months, and I'm a ghost to him.

I hope it stays that way.

As I cross back to the office, I tell the lads to get back to what they're doing, show's over, fuck are they looking at. Some of the skinnier, smaller lads go back to it slowly. The rest will follow when I've disappeared. Get this place smelling of sweat and leather again.

Paulo's returned to his natural colour. He's sitting in my chair, his hands loose on his knees.

'You want to tell me what all that was about?' I say.

Paulo shakes his head. 'Ewan's a tough kid, but he's not stupid. Thought I wouldn't have to tell him twice.'

'You know what he was buying?'

'I dunno. Could be anything. Mo's a fuckin' chemist.'

'I didn't know he'd been around,' I say.

Paulo wipes his nose. 'I told him to keep away. I can't be doing with that. Y'know, regardless of the fact that he's a dealer, I can't be doing with him hanging around the lads, can I? All it takes is one nosy bastard with an axe to grind and I'm in the middle of a full investigation.' He leans his head back. '*Evening News*'d have a field day: "PROBE INTO GAY DRUG CLUB".'

'Probe?'

Paulo smiles, but his eyes don't match it. 'They always use probe when it's something gay, Cal. Bunch of giggling fuckin' schoolboys, man. Sense of humour in the toilet.'

I fold my arms, look out at the club. Some of the lads are getting back into the swing of things. Sparring's started up again. 'You thought about getting more help?'

'I got no one I can trust right now. Serves me right surrounding myself with young offenders, eh?'

'You got me. You could've told me.'

'Yeah, and look at the state of you recently. Least your medication's prescribed by a doctor and not a dealer.' He frowns. 'It is, isn't it?'

'Course it fuckin' is.'

'Good.'

'You know Mo's not going to take that beating for an answer,' I say. 'You know that's not the end of it.'

'Uh-huh.'

'You want me to have a word for you?'

'You in with the Tiernans now?' he says.

I'm not. I was at one point – in up to my earlobes – but that was a while back. And I don't want to be back in, not if I can help it. But a mate's a mate. You put yourself on the line every now and then if you think it'll do good. Paulo's done it often enough for me, about time I repay the favour.

'Nah,' I say. 'Not in with the Tiernans. Then, way I hear it, neither's Mo.'

'Right enough.'

'Just thought if you wanted, I could have a word is all.'

'Forget it. Mo comes back, I'll deal with the bastard again. Might not take a beating for an answer, but the point'll get through with enough kicking, eh?' Paulo runs a hand across the back of his neck. 'I need a pint.'

'No, you don't.'

'Nah, I need a *shot*.'

'You need a brew.'

'That'll do in the meantime.' He gets up. 'Ewan gone?'

'Yeah. Took some persuading, mind.' My hand still aches, but I'm not about to rub it in front of Paulo. Not supposed to hit the lads. Not that hard, anyway.

'Daft lad. I thought I knew him better than that.'

'Can't save 'em all, mate.'

'Rate I'm going, it's not even half,' he says, clapping me on the shoulder. 'You want a brew?'

'I could murder one.'

Paulo nods, leaves. I go over to my desk, grind out the smoking filter I'm holding and take a pill. Mo Tiernan's still a problem I'll have to deal with.

Maybe later, I think. When I'm not shaking so much. And besides, it's time I got back to work.

THREE

'No, Don. Listen to me. No.'

But some people can't take no for an answer. Don Plummer's one of those people. He's spent so long schmoozing his way out of court appearances, he's somehow got it into his head that he's the Cary Grant of the slum landlord world. Which is why he's now giving me proper earache on the phone. I lean back in my chair, stare at a signed photo of Henry Cooper and Paulo. Cooper's signature, not Paulo's. And it reminds me that this room is now Paulo's office. Not that I've ever given it much of a makeover, but Paulo's stuff is everywhere, his boxing glory days captured in clippings and newspaper photographs dotted along the walls. A filing cabinet with the club's accounts and memberships, the lads' records dating back years. I'm sure I'm in there somewhere. And a photograph on the desk of Keith. I don't know much about the guy; just know that he warranted inclusion on Paulo's tattoo with his Mam and Dad.

'I'm closed for business, Don,' I say. 'I sacked that shite a long time back.'

'Hey, c'mon, Cal. I know you, a couple of jobs—'

'*Bad* jobs.'

'Bad jobs, they'll put the wind up anyone.'

'I mean it, Don. I'm working for Paulo now.'

'You can't live off that.'

'I do okay.'

'Look, Cal, if it's a question of trust—'

'Yeah, Don, because otherwise I trust you about as far as I can sneeze you.' I have to wedge the phone under my chin as I reach for my Embassys. 'And anyway, it's not just the nature of the job—'

'Here, this is legit, Cal. It's completely bona fide, alright?'

'Only Arthur fuckin' Daley uses words like bona fide, Don.'

'I never steered you wrong in the past, mate.'

'And that's another one.' I light my cigarette, grab the phone. 'Don, I go into Moss Side with an eviction notice, I'm liable to get my fuckin' head kicked in. And I'll tell you something, I'm sick of getting my fuckin' head kicked in. Doesn't hold the romantic mystery it once did.'

Plummer sighs into the phone so hard, I have to hold the receiver away from my ear. When I put it back, he's talking again.

That's what Plummer does best: talk. Talks himself into business, talks himself out of jail. He owns a string of properties across Manchester, most of which aren't fit to house a dying dog. But with flat prices being what they are, he still manages to find tenants desperate enough. Asylum seekers, students, down-on-their-luck-and-high-on-their-own-supply dealers. So it's no surprise that some of his tenants don't pay up on time, if at all. And when they don't, it's normally up to muggins here to deliver that piece of paper. At least, it used to be up to me. Too many times, people take offence at the sight of a peelly-wally lad handing them an official eviction notice. They have an allergic reaction, brings them out in vindictive arsehole, makes them reach for the bloodstained baseball bat they keep by the front door.

'Y'know what, you're that worried?' says Plummer. 'You bring along one of Paulo's lads, I'll pay him too.'

'I tried that before, remember? They slammed the door on his fuckin' hand.'

'I don't remember that.'

I flick ash. 'You were on the Costa.'

'It's an easy job this time, though. No threat.'

'Asylum seekers, Don?'

'Uh, immigrants, yeah.'

'So what is it? They didn't pay their rent, or do you still have their benefit books?'

'I don't work like that, Cal. You know I don't. I'm one of the good guys.'

'Then why d'you want them out?'

He pauses. 'Well, you know how it is.'

'You found someone who'll pay more.'

'No, it's the *situation*. With our asylum-seeking friends. I'm not a racist, you know that. I'm like fourth generation Irish, so talk about getting pissed on . . . But I can't take any chances right now, know what I mean? There's pressure on.'

'Oh, I get it.' I sniff. 'They've been handing out literature, buying rucksacks, that sort of thing.'

'No need for that, mate. I'm in a precarious position. Local community's been pretty bloody vocal about the whole thing, let me tell you. I mean, you know me, I'd keep 'em in if they paid, right? Money's money. But there's the big picture to look at, y'know?'

'You been reading those Jeffrey Briggs pamphlets again? "The Big Picture". Jesus . . . Are they even fuckin' Muslim, Don?'

'Here, you don't do it, I'll find someone who will.'

'Yeah, go sniffing on the National Socialist circuit, I'm sure you'll find a couple of skins who don't mind getting their boots bloody.'

'What's your problem?'

'I told you. I'm out of it. You opened your lugs every now and then, you'd know that.'

'It's *legit*. I wouldn't come to you if it wasn't.'

'Don, the Virgin Mary herself could tell me to hand over that eviction notice and I wouldn't do it. You know why? *Because I'm working for Paulo now.* You get that? I am working for Paulo.'

'Look, just keep it mind, Cal. I'll call you—'

I slam the phone down on him. As I move to tap ash from my cigarette, my back flares from ache to full-blown agony. Reach across and struggle with the child-proof cap on my prescription bottle.

'And I thought I was in bother.'

Paulo's standing in the doorway.

'You been there long?' I say.

'Long enough to know you need a holiday.' I thought the club was empty, but somewhere behind him I can hear the thump of glove against bag. ''Bout time you and me had a talk.'

I try to lean back in my chair, but just manage to look uncomfortable. I fiddle with the cap. 'What's that supposed to mean?'

'You're a state.' Paulo folds his arms.

'You blame me? After what happened . . .'

'Yeah, I know. I thought, well, Cal's been through the bloody wringer, I'll let him wallow about until he can get his head from shed. Course, now you're getting on my tits.'

'Yeah, me and everyone else. You're a fine one to talk about being fucked up, Paulo. I saw you today.' The cap doesn't budge. '*Fuck*in' thing.'

'Push down and twist,' he says. 'I know. Tell you the truth, mate, there's been some stress. Not just Mo, either. I need you to do something for me.'

I push the cap, twist. It comes off easily. Dry-swallow a couple of pills and reach for another cigarette. Nicotine should kick in faster than codeine.

'I already swept the floors,' I say. 'I'll wait until your slugger out there's done before I pick up.'

Paulo closes the office door, shutting off the sound of the club. He clears his throat, then hits me straight with it: 'I need you to go to Los Angeles.'

That hangs in the air for a bit. I feel like laughing. Or asking, Los Angeles as in America? But that's a stupid question. Far as I know, there isn't a Los Angeles in Salford. We're not that exotic.

'You're joking,' I say.

Paulo grabs a chair, pulls it over to the desk and sits down. 'There's a kid been coming in for a while, he's a good fighter.'

'Which kid?'

'Liam Wooley.'

I think about it. 'Isn't he the fuckin' head case?'

'He had some trouble.'

'He did an old lady over.'

'That was a long time ago.'

'Took her bingo money with menaces, as I recall. She was in hospital for a week.'

'And he served his time.'

'He's a fuckin' scally, Paulo.'

'Here, did I ask for the lad's CV?' Paulo glares at me. 'He's done his time, just like you did yours. And he got himself straight, got himself focused. Which is more than I can say for some people.'

'I'm straight.'

'And I'm glad, Cal. But mentally, you're all over the bloody shop. You got back from Newcastle and, yeah, things went pear-shaped. But a bloke moves on with his life. You sitting round here, popping pills like they're sweets, it's doing my brain in.'

I shake my head. 'What's this got to do with Los Angeles?'

'I been talking to a guy, he runs this amateur gym over there. Tells me there's this smoker he's been organising on behalf of the Enrique Alvarez foundation. It's not Golden Gloves or nowt, just a comp for a bunch of kids to come together and fight for trophies. But thing is, these smokers, they're a magnet for scouts. Couple of previous winners, they showed enough promise, they turned pro.'

'And Liam can turn pro.'

Paulo shrugs. 'I think he's got it in him, yeah. He's the best I've seen in a long time. But he's not going to make it over here, not with the baggage he's carrying. And normally I'd say, fuck it, that's something he has to work through, but I don't have the time to invest and he doesn't have it to waste.'

'I don't get why I have to go over,' I say. 'It's got nothing to do with me.'

'He's seventeen. I know the lad's mature enough, I could send him out there on his own, but officially, he's underage. He needs someone to go with him.'

'Paulo, I'm not playing chaperone.'

'You don't have to chaperone nowt, Cal. Liam's driven. He

knows he's not going to get many chances like this in his life, and Christ knows I told him exactly how many strings I had to pull to get him considered. So you don't need to keep an eye on him. I don't expect you to. If Liam fucks this up because he goes out and gets hammered, he knows he'll get a thrashing when he comes back.'

'No pressure then.'

Paulo opens his hands. 'Here, he does his best, he'll have done his best. That's all I want.'

'I can't do it, Paulo,' I say. 'I'm still on licence.'

'I been counting the days just like you have. Today was the last.'

'Fuck's sake, man, I'm no good with these lads. What do I have in common with Liam except a record? You go with him.'

'I need to take care of this place.'

'I can take—'

'You can't even take care of yourself right now, I'm not going to trust you with my club. Besides, you're not listed staff, Cal. Anything happens, I'll need to be here. And you need a holiday.'

'I don't like holidays.'

'Then don't treat it as a holiday. Treat it like work. You've been saying you're working for me, well, here's your job. And I already bought the tickets, so you can't get out of it.'

'What the fuck am I going to do in LA?'

Paulo's eyes drop to slits, like he's actually thinking about it. 'Well, let's see. You're going to look after Liam, pep him up when he needs it, leave him alone when he wants to be left alone, look after all the admin like his pass book and stuff and basically let him do what he needs to do. And while you're keeping out of the way, you're going to go to bars or Universal Studios or Hollywood, eat a burger or a hot dog or some Reese's Pieces and act like a bloody tourist. Pretty much anything you want that'll get you out of this funk you've been in.'

'Why didn't you ask me about this before?'

'Because you would've said no.' Paulo gets up, pushes back his chair. 'C'mon, I'll introduce you to Liam.'

I drag a few quick ones off the Embassy before I grind it out and follow Paulo out into the club. He's obviously picked up a few moves from Don Plummer, added a few of his own. Like me not having the chance to turn him down. I promise myself I'll find a way out of it. I'm not well. Got to go to the doctor's tomorrow and get a refill on my script, so I'll get him to conjure up a bogus sick note. My GP's a bastard, but I get the feeling he's corrupt. Because I don't think I'd be able to stand the flight, never mind all the crap I'd have to do in Los Angeles. Apart from my back, which has been murder for months, I'd have to spend time with Liam Granny-basher Wooley.

As soon as I see him, I recognise the lad. He was just a record before, but now his face pops into my memory. A couple of months ago, he'd been a real beast and a bad fighter. Anger issues, not someone you wanted to fuck about with. He had the scally dead-eye to a tee and liked using his forehead instead of his fists.

Now the kid I knew has been stretched to a hair under six foot. His face is long, sallow in the strip light. Liam's sporting a number one and deep shadows under his eyes. As we approach, he's battering the shit out of a heavy bag. For all the force, the bag doesn't move that much.

'Liam,' says Paulo.

Liam laces a couple more rights into the side of the bag before he takes a step back and looks at the pair of us. Gives me the once over and obviously isn't impressed with what he sees. I'm the same, reckon he looks like a thuggish gazelle.

'What's up?' he says.

Paulo points at me. 'This is Cal.'

'Y'alright?' says Liam with a twitch of the chin.

'Cal's going with you to the smoker.'

Liam's eyes flash blue just the once. He almost looks happy. 'You sorted it?'

'Yeah.'

'Ah, sweet.' Liam pulls off one glove with his teeth, offers me his hand, slick with sweat. I take it, shake it. His is a solid-grip handshake with nothing to prove, a direct contradiction to his eyes. It doesn't sit well with what I know about him. 'Nice to meet you, Cal.'

'Yeah,' I say. 'You too. Can I have my hand back now?'

FOUR

I know they're in there. As I pull up outside the Harvester, I notice Baz's pimped-out ride parked up the street. A Vauxhall Nova, Baz is the kind of bloke to spend all his money on a car that's neither fast nor furious. This isn't the country for fast motors, but to Baz it's all Miami waiting to happen. Doesn't matter that the under-lighter he's got on the car probably eats away half the battery.

I feel like putting a brick through the windscreen. Stick my hands in my pockets instead. I'm shaking, don't want Mo to see the tremble in my hands. He might think it's got something to do with him. And that's the last thing I want.

The Harvester's the hyena's den. They want to be lions in here, but there's no chance. Skinny, teeth permanently bared in a whisky grimace, the scavengers of Salford come here to drink when they've been barred from all the other pubs. Mo Tiernan's barred because he kicks off, or he deals. Or it's one of his dad's pubs. Time was, Morris Senior ignored Mo's activities as long as they didn't step on his own, but that time's long gone. Last I heard, Mo'd been dealt a paternal beating that puts him way out on his own. Uncle Morris Tiernan, veteran hard bastard, wants nothing to do with his son. He's out of the family and good fucking riddance.

I push open the door, catch a whiff of beer and urine, stale sweat. Under it all, the smell of yeast, throwing me back to the odour in the air when I stepped out of Strangeways. Thought I was free then. I couldn't have been more wrong.

The landlord glances at me as I step into the pub. He's an ex-bare-knuckle bruiser in the old school tradition, had his face mangled this way and that, but his features still cling stubbornly to his skull. That same mule instinct applies to the décor of the place. The landlord keeps most of the windows boarded up, reckons what's the point in replacing the glass? Bastards in here'd just put it through again.

If I hadn't done time, didn't wear it like a fucking badge, I'd be out on my ear right now, makes me wonder how Mo's managed to stay here so long. Probably his old family ties. News doesn't travel that fast when you're pissed out of your face. Not that maintaining a drunk in here would be easy: the pints are so dirty, you'll shit through the eye of a needle for a week straight, end up with an arse like a chewed orange.

It doesn't matter. I'm not here to sup.

Mo Tiernan's sitting with his back to the corner, just like his dad does. The difference is, Morris does it to keep an eye on the place; Mo's just shit scared someone'll stick a knife in his back. But he's trying to throw a don't-fuck-with-me attitude at the rest of the pub, flanked by Baz and Rossie. Two mates, don't have a brain between them. Baz has put on more weight, sitting further back from the table to accommodate his gut. Rossie's wearing a cracked and battered leather jacket. Last time I saw him, that jacket was brand new.

It's still quiet in here. Things won't hot up until last orders, the desperation for another drink pushing grudges to the foreground, fucking people up for good. I make my way over to Mo's table, wishing I had a gun so I could end this thing right now. My hands still in my pockets, I stand in front of him, say: 'Mo.'

Mo looks up, his face streaked brown with dried blood, his eyes hooded and the left beginning to swell. He sighs. 'Been a while.'

Rossie straightens up in his seat. Baz tries to look intimidating by lighting a cigarette.

'Not that long,' I say. 'Saw you a couple hours ago.'

'Yeah.' Shakes his head. 'Forgot you was there.'

'I need a word.'

'Nah, I got nowt to talk to you about.'

'What're you doing hanging around Paulo's?'

'You heard us, mate? I got nowt to say to you.'

'What about Paulo?'

'What shit's between me and Paulo, it's between me and Paulo, know what I mean?'

'No,' I say. 'I don't.'

Mo takes a sip from his pint, sets the glass back on its beer mat. 'You know what I fuckin' mean, Innes.'

'What've you got to sort out with Paulo?'

He looks at me like I just asked him how to spell his name. 'Cunt's a fuckin' uppity poof, isn't he? He broke me fuckin' finger, broke me fuckin' nose. Thinks he's a fuckin' saint, know what I mean? Cunt needs a smack, bring him back to the real world.'

'You smack him, he'll smack back. You know that.'

'Yeah, and that's the way of the fuckin' world, innit? Fucker smacks me, I smack him back, there we go. Keep going until one of us gives up. Fuck d'you care anyways?' Mo nabs the cigarette from Baz's mouth, takes a drag off it. 'Not like you're his boyfriend, is it?'

'I care because he's a mate,' I say. 'And he doesn't need trouble from a fuckin' scally pillhead, Mo.'

'You what?'

Rossie's hand strays to his pocket. Baz watches him. For a couple of hard lads, they've got a great way of telegraphing every move.

I stare at Mo, say: 'You want to start something, Rossie?'

Mo taps the table. 'Leave it, man.'

'Called you a fuckin' scally, Mo,' says Rossie. 'Come in here shouting the fuckin' odds—'

'I'm not shouting.'

'Leave it,' says Mo.

'Yeah, Rossie, leave it. I came to talk to the organ grinder, not his fuckin' monkey.'

Rossie's face twists. 'You what? Fuckin' monkey, is it?'

That could be a bad move, but it's a calculated risk, winding him up. Testing the water. Knowing that Mo's not going to start a kick-off in the one pub he can drink in. Besides, knowing Rossie, this is all blustery, chest-puffing bollocks. The bloke's packing a knife, yeah, but he needs the nod to do anything. And Mo's not going to give it to him.

'Fuck you doing, taking the piss, man?' says Mo. 'We done all our talking.'

'I'm telling you to leave Paulo alone.'

'That a fuckin' threat?'

'It's a friendly piece of advice.'

'The fuck d'you know about friendly? This is my place, you come in here and you're giving us orders? Fuck gives you the bottle to talk to *me* like that? You know who I am.'

'I know who you were.'

Rossie's hand moves again. I catch it out of the corner of my eye.

'I'm warning you, Rossie-mate. You pull a blade and I'll put your head through that fuckin' wall.' I remove my hands from my pockets. There's sweat on the palms and I hope to God the light doesn't catch it. 'I'm not holding anything, alright? Settle down.'

'Fuck's that supposed to mean?' says Mo. 'You know who I were?'

'You know what it means.'

'Nah.'

'You still in tight with your old man?' I say.

Mo pauses, still staring at me. He scratches some dried blood from the side of his nose. 'So we need a man-to-man, eh? In the bogs, right?'

'Okay.'

He gets up, kicks Baz until the fat bloke moves his chair back.

'Where you going?' says Baz.

'I just said, man, I'm going to the bogs.'

'I wouldn't trust this cunt,' says Rossie.

'Like I fuckin' care. You're not gonna try owt, are you, Innes?'

'You wanted to talk. That's good enough for me.'

'See,' says Mo, holding out his arms, a cracked smile on his face. 'He's gonna do nowt. Have a bluey, man. Calm the fuck down.'

And we walk to the gents, Mo still smiling like we're old mates just catching up.

FIVE

'There y'are, lads. Curse of the prostate, eh?'

There's an old guy in front of the urinal when we step into the toilets. He looks like he's been at it for a while without joy, so I suppose the eye-watering stink in here must be from the other drinkers. One hand spread against the wall to steady himself, the other hanging onto something I don't want to see. Salty-looking stubble takes up most of the guy's face, thickening into a nicotine-stained moustache.

Mo's smile has disappeared. 'Eh?'

The old bloke gives us a knocked-out grin before looking down. 'Size of a bloody walnut, apparently. Bursting for a piss and it's like a fuckin' drip then that's it.'

'Don't give a shit, mate,' says Mo. 'Get out else I'll chuck you out.'

'I won't be long.' The guy sways at the urinal, his bottom lip out in concentration. 'Normally takes a few minutes, but that's all I want.'

Mo looks at me, blinks, then glares a cross-hair at the old bloke. 'I tell you, I'll give you the count of three before I come over there and put your skull in the pisser, you get me, mate?'

'Here, c'mon, eh? I'm suffering here, mate.' He glances at Mo. 'Looks like you know all about suffering, a face like that, eh?'

Mo's arms drop loose at his sides. I step up to the old bloke, lean towards him but keep my eyes averted. 'I'd do what he says.'

'Not you an' all.' When he speaks, there's a stink like stale brandy stirred with a cigar.

'Go on, get out,' says Mo.

'Fuckin' hell.' The bloke fumbles with his zip. 'Can't even piss in peace these days.'

'Out.'

'I'm going.' The bloke moves from the urinal, his feet going in opposite directions. 'Used to be a bloke didn't have to put up with this *shite*. I hope whatever bloke did that to your boat, I hope he finishes the fuckin' job next time.'

Mo watches him leave, his fingers twitching. Even after the door clatters shut, the tension stays with him, knotting him up. 'I should've done him.'

I lean against the one working basin, fold my arms. 'You think so?'

'Yeah, I fuckin' think so. Mingin' old cunt.'

'What'd you want to talk to me about, Mo?'

He frowns. 'You was the one wanted to talk to me.'

'I said what I had to say. Leave Paulo alone.'

'You're in no position to make threats, mate.' He draws a rattled breath through his nose. 'You got nowt on us.'

'I'm not threatening you, Mo. I'm asking you.'

Mo flexes his fingers, stares at the back of his hands. He swallows. 'It's all over the fuckin' place, innit?'

'What?'

'Me and me dad. Like, people know about it an' that.'

'Yeah.'

'You start it?'

'Nah, Mo. I kept my mouth shut like I always do. None of my business, is it?'

He nods. 'I would've left you to go back, y'know.'

'I know.'

'Dad were the one wanted you out and about. He's the one what sent that fuckin' Clayton bastard all the way up to Newcastle.'

'I know.'

Mo shakes his head. 'Know fuckin' everything, don't you?' He coughs. 'You got a ciggie?'

I reach into my pocket, pull out the Embassys. Walk over to Mo, who's standing there, all legs and arms. As I get closer, I swear he has a belly under that tracksuit. Putting on the pounds, getting older. It's a shock.

So's his elbow in my face.

I reached out with the cigarette pack and found his hand clamped on my arm, his other arm swinging hard and wild, caught me high, just above the eyebrow. I jerk my head back. Mo keeps my arm, twists it as I turn, slams me into the cracked mirror above the basin. I let out a grunt, the last breath of air in my lungs escaping. He pushes my arm up my back, forcing my face into the mirror.

'Yeah, you know it all,' he says, his voice low. 'You know it all, don't you, son?'

My face grinds against the mirror. Glass giving way against my skin, tiny stones burrowing into my cheek. I try to struggle against him, but Mo's grip is firm. He's picked up some muscle with the extra pounds. Pushing me further, I'm bent over the basin. My back spikes, feels like my legs are going to give it up.

'Mo,' I say. 'Mo, you're out—'

'You got fuckin' *notions*, threatening me, man. Just cause me dad don't talk to us no more, you think I give a fuck?' He puts more pressure on my arm. 'The fuck I ever got from that cunt, eh? Nowt but a name and a bunch of shite I never fuckin' wanted. Think I answer to him? I don't answer to him.'

I can see him in the mirror. His face is screwed up.

'Nah, Innes, you're looking at a brand new hard case, know what I mean? He cut me loose, I got no fucker to answer to now. How d'you like that? I say a cunt needs a smack, he gets a fuckin' smack and I don't have to get the go ahead from me deadbeat dad to do it.'

More pressure, pushing my arm. Any more, and he'll have my arm out of its socket. I open my mouth, feel crumbled glass cut my lip.

Mo leans right up to my ear. 'I could do you right now, Innes. I could get Rossie to stick his fuckin' butterfly right in your throat. Nobody'd give a shit, neither.'

'You don't have any protection, Mo.' The words come out choked.

'You think I need protection?'

'From yourself, you do . . .'

Mo nudges my head across the mirror, glass dropping into the basin. Then he lets me go. My balance goes for a burton, my numb arm dropping down my back. I stumble, try to grab at the basin, miss. End up on my arse in the middle of the floor. I pull myself out of the way as Mo takes a step forward and spits into the basin. He wipes his hand across his mouth as he looks at his reflection.

'You take it how you want it, Mo,' I say, dabbing at the cut on my lip and struggling to my feet. 'You want to take it as a warning, you want to take it as a fuckin' threat, a joke, whatever the fuck you want to take it as: leave Paulo's club alone. You took one beating already, Mo. Way I left him, he's all set to tear your heart out.'

'I ain't scared of an old poof.'

'You want to push this?' As I steady myself, I feel a wave of nausea. Takes me a moment to fight it back, but I'm still bent over when I say, 'You want to push this, forget we ever had this chat, see what happens. I guarantee you, you do something daft, Paulo'll make sure you do your time up Cheetham Hill. And you won't have your dad or his brief to get you out of it.'

'I don't need me dad.'

'You'll need him, you keep this shit up.' I pick bits of mirror from my cheek. None of the pieces dug too deep. Just another thing to make my face more interesting. 'I mean it, Mo. That's all I came to say.'

Mo sniffs, picks my cigarettes from the floor. He takes one out and lights it with a Clipper. Relaxed now, he chucks the Embassys to me, smoke drifting from his mouth. 'Then you said what you come to say, right?' He taps ash on the floor. 'And I'll do whatever the fuck I want to do about it.'

'You do that, Mo.' I tuck the cigarettes back into my pocket and make for the door.

As I cross out into the pub, I see Rossie getting out of his seat.

His lips move, but I don't hear what he's saying. Shake a finger in my ringing ear and keep walking, the carpet tacky under my shoes. I don't look up again until I'm out of the pub, a cold breeze pulling the breath out of me like smoke.

That could've gone better. And I don't know if I feel better for warning Mo, or worse for showing him I can be beaten. Either way, my hands have stopped shaking and the message has been passed on. He'd be daft to try anything now.

But then, Mo Tiernan's never been the sharpest tool in the box.

SIX

'You all set?' says Paulo.

'Ready as I'll ever be,' I say.

'I was talking to Liam.'

'Right. Course you were.'

Getting up at stupid o'clock in the morning made my brain numb. Stupid to go to sleep at all, considering the night I've just had. First Mo, then picking bits of glass out of my face. As it turns out, it doesn't look I've suffered any lasting damage. The tiny cuts should heal in a couple of days, and there's only slight swelling above my eye. Not so slight that Paulo hasn't noticed it, but he hasn't said anything yet. I'm hoping he'll forget about it.

Declan phoned last night. Sounded pleased with himself. Looks like he's coming to the end of his programme, and he's doing great. He's also got some of his accent back. Amazing how little time it takes to fall back into the speech patterns, though he still sounds a bit like a Manc trying on a Leith accent for size. He's going to move out of Mam's place, got himself an office job, he's sailing towards one of those new flats where the prostitutes used to congregate.

Good on him. Glad to know he's doing okay. I told him about my trip and the awe was thick in his voice. I promised to bring him something back. What, I don't know. I don't think they do sticks of rock in LA. And sometimes I wonder who's the older brother here. But then I just put it down to his newfound lust for life in a pure Iggy Pop sense. Certainly made him talkative – he was on the phone well into the wee small hours, which has left me knackered.

It was Paulo's idea to get to the airport early. Nothing was stopping him driving us there. Of course, with all his planning, he didn't reckon on the M60 being a graveyard.

So we're stranded in an almost empty airport, waiting. Small talk ran out about an hour ago, and we're making do with grunts, short questions and even shorter answers. That kind of slow-down fatigue that precludes any real conversation.

I try to stave it off once the coffee shop opens. Liam's cradling a cup of some kind of speciality tea that smells like fruit and looks like a urine sample. I've had to make do with an Americano. I ask for a couple shots of espresso, see if that perks me up.

Paulo hands me a sheet of paper. 'Here's the reservations at the Ramada. I put directions on there, too. I know what you're like.'

'Cheers, Dad.'

'Hope for the best, prepare for the worst. You got Liam's passbook, the letter, right?'

I pull out the letter from Phil Shapiro, Paulo's contact in Los Angeles. It's a formal invitation to attend the competition. When Paulo gave it to me, it was like he was handing over a signed copy of the Bible. 'I've packed the passbook.'

'Any problems, you've got Phil's number,' says Paulo. 'He's expecting you, but if you get lost on the way to his place, give him a bell, he'll point you in the right direction.'

'Okay.'

Liam sips his tea. He's reading from a leather-bound notebook. 'We'll be good, Paulo.'

'You better be. This is costing me . . . Well, it's costing me.'

'I know,' says Liam, turning a page.

'Just so you do.' Paulo checks his watch. 'Ah, Christ, how much longer do we have?'

'An hour,' I say.

'Right.'

'An hour till check-in. Then we've got a couple more until we board.'

'Gotcha,' says Paulo. He works his mouth.

I've never seen Paulo like this. Normally the bloke's a rock.

There've been times when he's lost it, used his fists or an open-handed slap to the back of a lad's head, but he never went overboard. That tussle with Mo pushed him to places he didn't want to go, made him see parts of himself he didn't want to see. And now, I don't know. Looks like he's veered the other way. This close to clucking like a mother hen.

'Calm down, mate,' I say. 'We're here in plenty of time.'

He raises an eyebrow. 'Look at you. You never flown in your life and you're calm as.'

'No, actually, I think I'm about to shit myself.'

'Don't let him shit himself,' Paulo says to Liam.

Liam looks at the pair of us as if we're nuts.

'I mean it,' says Paulo. 'He'll stink up the plane.'

I yawn, a jaw-cracker. The coffee isn't working. And I'm gasping for a cigarette, but I don't want to leave these two. I pull Paulo to one side and we start walking. Our footsteps echo in the airport. We stop a good way from Liam, who's busy leafing through his wee book. Paulo turns and watches the lad. He doesn't want to let Liam out of his sight.

'Paulo, you going to be okay?' I say.

'What d'you mean?'

'Mo.'

'Mo's a scally. He's not worth getting het up over.'

'That's what I thought. But I wanted to hear it from you.'

Paulo looks at me. 'You think I'm unsteady, eh?'

'I think you've been steadier, mate.'

He shakes his head, turns his attention back to Liam. 'Nervous about the comp.'

'Not just that, though, is it?'

'How's that?'

'You drinking?'

He squints at me. 'You popping pills?'

'You are drinking.'

'Only what I'm used to. A pint every now and then. Not like I'm coming home bladdered.' He licks his bottom lip. 'And who d'you think you're talking to, Cal?'

'I'm just asking.'

'I'm just worried, mate,' he says. Paulo sips his coffee, pulls a face. 'That's foul. I can't believe I paid three quid for that.'

'You're worried.'

'Yeah. I mean, what if Liam goes all the way?'

'What if he does?'

'Well, it's not just his future, is it? It's the club's too. Liam does well out of this tournament, we all do well out of it. Not the cash, mind – that's all Liam's. But if he does this, ends up turning pro, it's like all the shit I put up with for years is worth it.'

'Don't build it up, Paulo.'

'I know. That's what I've been telling myself. Don't build it up. Too many things can go wrong.' He looks around the airport. 'There a bin round here?'

'Took 'em all out, I think.'

'Yeah, bombers everywhere. Least of my worries.'

'About Mo . . .'

'I thought I saw the back of that bastard six month ago.'

'I'm sorry I brought him in the club,' I say.

Paulo looks down at his coffee. 'You didn't bring him in – he brought himself in. Or Ewan brought him in. I dunno. Whoever brought him in, it wasn't your fault. You can't keep knocking yourself in the gut over that. You did your bit in Newcastle, you didn't fuck up my life, you didn't fuck up your own too badly and you'll get over it. That's good enough for me. All we do now is keep you on the straight and narrow, right?'

'Cheers, Paulo.'

'No bother, son.'

I sip my coffee. 'Don't worry about Liam. He'll do it or he won't. Like you said, he does his best, there's nothing to worry about. Either way, you did all you could.'

'Yeah.'

Paulo starts walking back to Liam, his step a little slower. He looks at his watch again, says, 'You lads better get yourselves checked in.'

I nod, grab our bags. 'I'll call you when we're settled.'

'You do that. Want to make sure you get to the hotel in one piece.'

We're about to leave when Paulo puts his hand on my arm.

'By the way,' he says. 'Where'd you get that shiner from?'

'Noticeable, is it?'

'Where'd you get it?'

'I fell over,' I say.

'Shit,' says Paulo, shaking his head. 'All that bonding we just did and you go and lie to me like that.'

'I'll call you from the hotel.'

When we leave, I look over my shoulder. Paulo's never looked so small. He waves at me.

I don't wave back.

SEVEN

Charlotte Douglas.

There was a lass at my school called Charlotte Douglas. She had all the fragile grace of a bin lorry and thighs that rubbed together as she walked. My mam said she'd blossom with age, but all that happened was that Charlotte grew tits. That was enough change for some lads. Every time I looked at her, I saw the mean, fat Charlotte who dunked me in a muddy puddle and told me it was shitwater. And if you got shitwater in your mouth, that was it, you were due a long, slow and painful death. See all them kids in Africa, the ones with the swollen bellies and flies on their faces? That was shitwater did that to them.

It just goes to show, some ugly ducklings don't grow into swans; they grow into ugly ducks. And while beauty's only skin deep, Charlotte's kind of ugly went right to the fucking marrow.

This place could've been named after her. Charlotte Douglas International Airport, North Carolina. If you put a gun to my head, I couldn't point to this place on a map, but here I am. And it feels like purgatory, if purgatory ends up being one giant fucking shopping mall. Sterile. Too much white on the walls, glancing the sun into bleary, jetlagged eyes. Because if I thought I was tired before I got on the plane, I'm dead on my feet by the time we get to Charlotte. We've done a whistle-stop tour of the United States, a clutch of airports that seem as empty as each other. For all Paulo moaned about how much this was costing him, it seems he's done a cheapskate on the tickets.

I want a cigarette. That's a given. I've been on a plane for thirteen bloody hours, got another seven to go, of course I'm going to want a cigarette. But this place is plastered with no smoking signs. I could go outside, but there's no guarantee I'll be able to find my way back in. So I've camped out with Liam at a table outside Canton Cuisine with a pile of food on a plastic plate and a Budweiser on the side.

Egg noodles, sesame chicken, special fried rice. A spring roll that I took one bite out of, noticed black strings under the batter, and thought better of it. The rest of the food has been sitting here so long it's congealed into a greasy lump. In the meantime, cabaret is provided by the staff at Canton Cuisine. There's a tiny old lady perched on a stool, haranguing the two guys on the counter. I don't know Mandarin or Chinese or whatever, but I do know when someone's getting bawled out. The taller guy looked like he was going to say something at one point, but it stuck in his throat.

Good for you. Keep your dignity.

I take a swig from the beer. It's cold enough not to taste of anything. Across from me, Liam's picking at the salad he brought with him, his nose still in that notebook. He didn't trust the airline food, been eating out of Tupperware ever since we left Manchester. The plane meals were chock full of preservatives, he'd said. Might as well eat the seats.

'What're you reading?' I say, stifling a belch.

He looks up. 'Book.'

'Yeah, I know that. What's in it?'

'Stuff,' he says.

'And what's in the box?'

'Carrot sticks.'

'Fantastic. Just what every growing boy needs.'

'You taking the piss?'

'I'm serious. You need your greens. Or oranges.'

'You dehydrate on the plane,' he says by way of explanation.

'And what's the wet bog roll for? Dessert?'

'Kitchen towel. Put it in there to stop the carrot drying out.'

'You're a bright lad.'

He puts the book down. 'When's our flight leave, Cal?'

I check my watch. 'Boards in about an hour.'

'I have to sit with you for another hour?'

'Another eight hours, Liam. Fuck's sake, son, how're you going to handle it?'

Liam doesn't say anything, goes back to his book.

'You finish your carrot sticks and have a wander about if you want to. Go shadow box or something. I'm not bothered. Just don't get lost.'

Liam bites into a stick, then gestures towards my plate. 'You gonna eat that?'

'Nope. Thought I might leave it, see what it turns into.' I stifle another belch.

'It stinks.'

'And I ate on the plane, didn't I?'

'No wonder you've got wind.'

'Tell you what, how about we stop talking? Cause I don't need you pecking my head right now.'

No, what I need right now is a bed, a bottle of duty free and a quiet place to smoke. That sounds like heaven and I hope this spell in purgatory gets me there. The flight was hell so I deserve to work my way up to something.

We were packed in like veal. Liam took the window seat and promptly fell asleep, the B.A. Baracus school of travel. I was wedged in the middle, elbow-to-elbow with a guy who stank of airport soap, had a two-day growth on sagging cheeks and looked like he was about to get stuck into some heavy-duty perspiration. Which he did as soon as we took off.

I spent most of the flight trying to avoid conversation with him. The bloke wore the uniform of the transatlantic businessman: the crumpled suit trousers, striped shirt and tie. He carried expensive-looking hand luggage. Looked like the kind of guy who said, 'I eat fellas like you for brunch.' So I watched a kid's film with only one side of the headphones working until they brought the meals.

That was when he thought it was a great time for a chat.

'Your first time?'

I wanted to tell him to fuck off, but my mam brought me up better. 'What makes you say that?'

He pointed at my lap with a greasy fork, dwarfed in his fat hand. 'Four hours in and you've still got your seatbelt on, I'd say it was your first time.'

I looked at Liam; he was still fast asleep. I unbuckled. 'I'm not a good traveller.'

'You don't say. You left dents on the arm-rest.'

'Well, I don't fly much.'

'Yeah, it's your first time. I fly all the time.'

'Good for you.'

'Part of my job.' He paused, waiting for me to ask what he did for a living. I didn't. 'Doesn't get any easier, though.'

'I can imagine.'

He shoved a forkful of mashed up chicken into the open wound he called a mouth. Acted all delicate by dabbing the corner of his mouth with a napkin, then ruined the effect by talking through his food.

'Your friend isn't eating?' he said.

'Nah, he doesn't eat anything that doesn't come out of Tupperware.'

'He seems pretty easy with travelling.'

'He's easy with everything.'

'Look, I've got something that might help if you're interested.'

'Really.'

The businessman eased himself onto one buttock, fumbled around in his trouser pocket so long I thought he was indulging in a Barclays. Yeah, that was a real stress-reliever, but it'd probably get me chucked off the plane. I was about to ping for the flight attendant when he sat back down with a thump, showed me a wee tin.

'Nah, y'alright, mate. I got gum.'

He set his fork down, popped the lid on the tin and shook a scattering of tiny pills. 'They're not mints.'

'What are they then?'

'Betablockers.'

'Okay.' Like I knew what betablockers were.

'You're wound up, they'll unwind you. Go on, take a couple.'

I pinched two of the pills, washed them down with a swig of Coke and sat there, waiting for something to happen. 'So what do they do? Knock me out or something?'

'No, just take the edge off. Stop your nerves from fraying. I take 'em all the time.'

'They legal?'

'If you've got a heart condition, yeah.' He nabbed a couple of pills with his chubby fingers, placed them at the back of his tongue, swallowed some water.

'D'you have a heart condition?'

'If you don't calm down, I might have by the end of this flight.'

It wasn't my fault. Liam had fallen asleep with the blind up on his window. I didn't want to wake him up by leaning over him, so every time I glanced his way I saw the wing of the plane in my peripheral vision. And it was shaking, almost bending. I had premonitions of it snapping off mid-flight. I had visions of John Lithgow going mental, screaming about a gremlin and William Shatner would be in the back, nodding in recognition.

'You'll know,' I said. 'Is the wing supposed to do that?'

'Yeah. Don't worry about it.'

Don't worry about it. Famous last words if ever I heard them. I wondered if I'd have to end up eating him when we crashed or whether I'd be dead on impact. Then I checked around for the emergency exits.

I don't know if the betablockers worked. I didn't feel any calmer. When the trolley dolly took away our trays, I made a point of throwing away a stack of dollars on half a dozen overpriced drinks. The businessman joined me, vodka and tonics, a couple of Michelobs. Then I took some of my prescription, settled into a snooze that was punctuated by nightmares of DVT and sudden turbulence.

It didn't ease up when we touched down, either. There was Liam, fresh as a fucking daisy, and me doing the ragged refugee waltz, looking like I'd just dropped from the undercarriage. I got stopped at immigration by a woman whose bosom looked like a couple of Rottweiler puppies sleeping on her lap. She chewed gum, very American, and she didn't give a shit. It's always easy not to give a shit when you've got a gun strapped to your hip. I gave her a smile along with my passport.

'How long are you staying, Mr Innes?'

'A week. I think. As long as it takes, I suppose.' I was busy watching Liam sail through immigration, wondered what he'd done for it to be that easy. And Christ, was his officer *smiling* at him?

'Mr Innes?'

'Hello,' I said. 'Sorry.'

'Mr Innes, the United States isn't big on *supposing*. You have up to thirty days. Any longer than that, you'll have to apply for an extended visa, do I make myself clear?'

I did my Tom Cruise, complete with forehead vein. 'Crystal.'

'What?'

She didn't get it. And then I saw her name tag.

Crystal.

Jesus.

Telling the story to Liam now, I get the same look she gave me.

'I don't get it,' he says.

'*A Few Good Men.*'

'Eh?'

'Doesn't matter.'

And Paulo said this lad had it together. What a fucking joke.

EIGHT

When we hit LAX, I have to go through the prerequisite blood-urine-DNA test in order to get a canary yellow lawnmower. There are economy rental cars, and then there's the Geo Metro.

'This the best you could get?' says Liam.

'It's what we can afford. You got some spare cash floating about, I'll upgrade us to a Reliant Robin.' I grab his bag and stuff it into the back seat with mine. My bag's a little heavier now I've visited the duty free shop. Liam's been whinging about that detour, put a face on, but he can get to fuck. My holiday, I'll smoke and drink as much as I want.

Liam gets into the car and I slam the door shut for him as I pass. It bounces open again. 'Fuck's sake.'

'Here, I've got it,' says Liam. He pulls the door shut. Looks at it, pushes it. Seems sturdy enough considering it's about as thick as Bacofoil.

'Good lad.' I get into the car. 'But you might want to buckle up. I don't want you falling out.'

'I'm not going to fall out.'

'Buckle up. I'm not explaining to Paulo how you ended up as fuckin' roadkill.' I make a mental note to call the rental place from the hotel, let them know the car's not up to snuff. I'll be buggered if I pay extra for a shoddy door.

Turn the key in the ignition and the whole car shakes, a high whine coming from the engine.

'Oh, nice,' says Liam. 'Sweet ride. All you need's the furry dice.'

'Shut up.'

The directions to the Ramada Inn are right on the money, which makes up for the fact that I've never driven an automatic before and this country has some suspicious roads. It all seems too easy, too laid out. No roundabouts, no real curves in the road. Like motorway driving, except I'm doing it everywhere. When we finally get parked up and walk into the hotel reception, all that easy driving's calmed me down. I don't even mind that I look shabby as hell compared to the surroundings. There's a bloke behind the reception desk who makes me feel as if he's been waiting for us.

'We have reservations,' I say. 'Innes and Wooley.'

The receptionist taps at a computer keyboard and smiles at us. 'Two non-smoking.'

Liam nods.

'Sorry,' I say. 'Non-smoking?'

'Yes.' The receptionist catches my tone, frowns for a second as he checks the reservations again. 'Two non-smoking queens.'

'You what?' Now it's Liam's turn to get riled up. You want to annoy a scally, intimate he's gay.

'Queen-sized beds, Liam,' I say. Then back to the receptionist. I lean on the desk, give him my friendliest smile. 'I'm a smoker. Any chance of changing the room?'

'Uh, let me just see, sir.'

There's a long silence, punctuated by the tap of keys. Liam stands there looking sullen. Then: 'I'm sorry, sir. All our smoking rooms are occupied at present.'

'Come twenty hours on a plane, Cal. Fuck difference does it make if you don't have a smoking room?'

I don't look at him. 'It makes a difference, Liam, because I'm a smoker. I bought a load of Marlboros at LAX and being a smoker, I'm looking forward to smoking them. They didn't let me smoke in the fuckin' airport, they don't let me smoke in the fuckin' rental car and now they're not going to let me smoke in the fuckin' hotel room. So, yeah, you could say it makes a difference, because I haven't had a cigarette in twenty hours which is almost a fuckin' day. And watch your language, son. We're ambassadors for our country.'

I smile at the receptionist. He says, 'I can let you know when one of the smoking rooms becomes available.'

'That'd be lovely,' I say, grabbing our room keys.

'I'll get you a bellboy.'

'That won't be necessary.'

Liam and I pick up our bags and head to the lift. I check the number on my room key and press the button.

'You want to treat people with a bit more respect,' says Liam.

'Yeah, right. You were all ready to kick off when you thought he was calling you queer.'

'I knew what he meant.'

'Course you did, slugger.'

'Don't call us that.'

'What's the matter, punchy?'

'Paulo never told us you were an arsehole.'

I watch the numbers flick by. 'He's never seen me jonesing, Liam.'

'Yeah, but jonesing for what?'

'Fuck's that supposed to mean?'

The lift doors open. Liam snatches his key from my hand and stalks off up the corridor.

'I said, fuck's that supposed to mean, Liam?'

But he's already slammed his door.

I step out of the lift, my gut twisting. Then I head to my room. Lad's got some issues, that's about right. Play them off like he's sorted upstairs, but he's still got some glitch. What else do I expect from a kid who used to beat up pensioners for pocket money?

My room's decent enough. Nothing swish, but it'll do. A balcony, television, nice big bed and I'm sure if I hunt about for a while, I'll find a well-stocked mini bar. I dump my bag on the bed and check out the en suite. It's pristine, absolutely spotless. When I turn on the light, a fan whirs somewhere in the ceiling. I wonder how long I can go without using the toilet, because this is just sickeningly clean. British hotel bathrooms are clean too, but they're never *this* clean. Like the staff are whispering in your ear at check-in: 'We appreciate you're a guest and all, but don't go thinking we're your slaves, alright?'

I check the toilet. It's gleaming. But it looks blocked, judging by the amount of water in the bowl. I might have to call someone about that if it becomes a problem.

Back in the bedroom, I unpack the duty free. Stick the Marlboros on the writing table and glare at them. I crack open the litre bottle of Smirnoff Black and look around for a glass. There's a couple of tumblers in the bathroom. I pour myself a hefty measure. It stings going down, but the warmth catches up and overtakes.

Drinking in LA. Ah, Mam, if you could see how far your little boy's come.

Course, the trouble with drinking is that it makes me want to smoke. I tear open the carton of Marlboros, slip a pack into my jacket pocket and down the rest of the vodka.

Somewhere in this fucking town there's a place where a guy can light up. And I'll find it if it kills me.

Then I'll phone Paulo.

NINE

'Sir?'

I shake myself lucid, one of the Marlboros hanging from the corner of my mouth. My hand's cupped round a small pink Bic lighter it took me a good half hour to find in a local supermarket. I couldn't bring my lighter, something to do with it being a weapon of mass destruction. The flame burns the tip of my thumb, so I kill the gas. 'Sorry, what? I was miles away.'

'We don't allow smoking.' In case I'm as deaf or as stupid as he thinks I am, the bartender points to a sign nestled amongst the bottles on the back bar. It reads: THANK YOU FOR NOT SMOKING!

You're welcome, I'm sure. And thank *you* for the exclamation mark. Very friendly.

I put the Bic down, look at the bartender. 'This is a bar, right?'

He looks at me like I'm mildly retarded. He's an anorexic Beach Boy in a red waistcoat, his teeth too even and white. Manages to look utterly disgusted with me and smile at the same time. 'Yeah, it's a bar.'

'And you're telling me I can't smoke in a bar.'

He holds his hands up. 'If it were up to me—'

'I got these at LAX,' I say, tapping the Bic. 'I've been everywhere since I touched down and not one single place allows smoking.'

'That's unfortunate.'

'Now why would they sell me these fuckin' things if I can't smoke them anywhere?'

'A cruel practical joke?'

'Tell me about.' I pull the cigarette from my lips, slide it back into the packet. Looks like I'll have to make do with the booze. I take a swallow of Budweiser, crave a full pint of it, but bottles look like the norm over here. 'Is there anywhere I *can* smoke?'

'Outside,' he says.

'In the smog?'

The bartender's smile widens. 'Yeah, it's not much of a choice, is it?'

'Nope.' I tap the Marlboro pack and order an Absolut. I should be more adventurous, but jet lag's crept up and smacked me across the back of the head. Doesn't help that there's a jazz band playing in here. I never could stand jazz. There's no point to it, no emotion in it. Nothing but musical masturbation and nobody likes a fucking show-off. The bartender slides me my vodka on a paper napkin. I stare at the clear liquid, then take a drink. It tastes okay. It'd taste better with smoke in my lungs, but there you go.

'You're British,' says a guy further up the bar.

I look around the bar before I turn to him. Nobody else in here, it looks like, unless there's a party in the toilet I don't know about. He's smiling. They all smile here. Then again, so do rabid dogs. I turn back to my drink. 'If you want.'

'I have a cousin in Birmingham.'

'Alabama?'

'England.'

'Right enough. I think I know him.'

'You do?'

'Yeah. Ugly lad, right? Won't let people drink in peace?'

'That'll be him.'

The guy's ginger, but probably calls himself 'strawberry blonde'. Has that face that looks like someone's taken a chisel to his cheeks when he smiles. He wears glasses with small round frames that seem incapable of staying on the bridge of his broken nose. When he pushes his specs back up, I notice the elbow of his tweedy-looking jacket is frayed. A second glance, and the jacket's a size too small. But what's bothering me is that he looks like someone famous.

'Nelson Byrne,' he says.

'Callum Innes.'

Nelson moves down the bar to shake. When he holds out his hand, I notice how big it is. Scar tissue on the knuckles, calluses on the palm.

'Good to meet you, Callum. What you doing in LA?'

'Babysitting.'

'Anyone famous?'

I crook an eyebrow at him. 'Might be in a couple of years.'

'You must be earning a fortune,' he says.

'Ah, you know, whatever I can steal.'

'Sounds like a guy I used to know.'

'Lawyer?'

Nelson waves his hand and pulls a face. 'Promoter.'

'Promoter?'

He finishes his beer. 'Get you another?'

'Nah, I'm fine thanks.'

Nelson orders another beer, a Heineken. The bartender slides it across, grabs the empty bottle. Nelson tucks a fingernail under the bottle label, starts picking at it. 'So how are you finding the City of Angels?'

'You people really call it that?' I say.

'No, but I thought you guys did.'

'We don't.' I sip my vodka. 'It's okay, I suppose. Haven't seen that much of it, tell the truth. I just got in. I wish there were places I could smoke. Fuckin' Gestapo everywhere.'

'Yeah, it was hard when I smoked.'

'You gave up?'

'In this town, you kind of have to quit.'

'Yeah, I can see that.' I swallow the rest of my vodka. Nelson orders me another one before I get a chance to decline. It's a double, same as before. I nod my thanks.

'So what do you do for a living, Callum? Apart from babysit.'

'Nothing much.'

He stares at the label. 'You must do something. Plane tickets don't just fall out of the sky.'

'The tickets were paid for. Part of the babysitting job. And I had some cash left over from my previous employment.' I can't help but hit that last word with a measure of disgust.

'And what was that?'

I sip the vodka and smile at him. 'I was a private investigator.'

Nelson looks vaguely impressed, as if I've lied to him but he's too polite to call me on it. 'I didn't know you had private investigators in Britain.'

'We don't,' I say. 'Not really. We try.'

'Well, I was about to say, you're in the right city for it.'

'I don't do it anymore. I wasn't much cop, tell the truth.'

Nelson swigs from his beer, smacks his lips. 'Not as glamorous as it's made out, so I hear. We got these shows, reality shows, I watched a couple. Mostly just sitting around in cars waiting for parole violators, cheating husbands. A lot of pissing in bottles. Marlowe's given up the ghost, Callum. He rolled back to his apartment and got drunk one too many times. They found him slumped over his chess set with a pawn in his mouth.'

I blink. 'Sorry?'

Nelson smiles with one side of his face. 'I better ease off on the beer, huh?'

'You feeling it?'

'No, I'm just bloated.' He orders a Jim Beam over ice. 'I'm hungry. You hungry?'

'I could eat.'

'You want to get a hot dog?'

'They do food here?'

'Yeah, but it stinks. I know a place. How about we finish up the drinks, take a hike over there? You can smoke on the way if you want. And I'll tell you, Callum, this jazz band's annoying the hell out of me.'

'Man after my own heart.' As I reach for my vodka, my back gyps me hard. I suck my teeth.

'You okay?'

'I've got a bad back.' I get the bartender's attention. 'Here, mate, is it alright if I take prescription pills in here or are you going to point to another sign?'

The bartender gives me a full-on Colgate grin. 'No rules against pills, sir.'

'Good.'

I should've guessed. I'm sitting in the Valley of the Dolls.

TEN

These pills. Dihydrocodeine. Ibuprofen. Prozac. A couple of others to take the edge off, names I can't spell, can't pronounce without taking a concentrated look at the little brown bottle. And every time I needed a repeat script, I had to see my doctor. Which wouldn't bother me, but my GP was a bastard.

The first prescription I had, I needed more than air. Dr Dick scrawled it out for me up in Newcastle after a high-speed run-in with a Fiat. Dick was a tall slab of Milk Tray hunk, a friend of a friend, looked like he belonged on the front cover of a Mills and Boon. Watching him, I thought he was more than just a friend, but I wasn't about to turn down medication because I was jealous. I was positive I was paralysed from the waist down. Something like that happens, you don't care if they start fucking in front of you and you certainly don't give a shit where the pills come from.

But my back was still killing me when I came back to Manchester. And without Dr Dick at my beck and call, I had to trust my friendly neighbourhood doctor. The whole situation was sapping my will to live. Even more than being stuck in the waiting room, thumbing through an ancient copy of *Hello!*

'Mr Innes?'

I looked up. My name was scrolling across the board, started flashing. Very posh. The receptionist had a face on, like what the fuck did I think I was doing *reading* when I should've been watching the board? Maybe because I wasn't that desperate? I didn't think I was, anyway. I'd been trying to ignore the dull ache, throwing myself into a world of celebrities the country'd long stopped caring about.

'Sorry,' I said. I got up, dropped the magazine on my seat and headed down the corridor to where Dr Choudrey was waiting for me. I knocked on his door and stepped inside.

Choudrey didn't look up. 'How are you feeling, Mr Innes?'

A lot worse for entering his office. The place was a dead air zone, the windows permanently shut. Choudrey was adamant that any sickness would be confined to those four walls.

'Not so good,' I said.

Dr Choudrey was a lump of greyish fat in a bad suit, the shoulders dusted with dandruff. Or it could well have been ash – Choudrey had the look and hacking cough of a diehard smoker. A perfect advertisement for Nicorette. And to be fair to the man, he was the only doctor who hadn't collared me about my smoking. No, he had far more to nag me about.

'Your back still playing you up?' he said.

'It's still murdering me slowly, yeah.'

Choudrey smiled at the notes in front of him. Another one who'd rather look at paper than me. 'I don't think it's going to *kill* you, Mr Innes.'

'Well, you're not living with it, Doctor.'

'Right enough. I've been looking through your notes.'

'Anything interesting?'

'Mm.' Which I took for a yes. Choudrey removed his glasses, looked at me directly. Obviously grown a pair of balls. That was nice to see. 'I think we'll ease off on your prescription.'

I didn't say anything for a moment. Let it sink in. He looked like he was waiting for a reply. So I said, 'Right.'

'I don't think the codeine's working as well as it should.'

'It's working fine.'

He shook his head. 'I'm not convinced medication's the answer here.'

'I think I'd disagree.'

'I knew you would.' Choudrey shifted position in his chair. 'You've been on the painkillers for a while, Mr Innes. And yet you still have pain.'

'You don't know the half of it.'

'So the medication is not solving the problem.'

'It's solving most of the pain.'

Choudrey sniffed. 'It's temporary relief, I'm afraid. Medication isn't a long-term fix. It's not a long-term fix I'm comfortable with anyway . . .'

Who cared about his comfort? His comfort wasn't the fucking issue here. I tried to keep my hands from balling. At the back of my head, scenes played out in a courtroom, Choudrey being struck off for gross malpractice.

'I think what we'll do is, we'll see if we can get you into physiotherapy.'

'Who's this we? You got a mouse in your pocket?'

Choudrey's grin became wide and yellow. 'I must remember that one.'

'It's yours.' I put my hands in my lap. 'You're cutting my medication.'

'Yes,' he said. Just like that. The smile lost its way on his face, ended up flipping to a concentrated frown. 'The dosage you're on at the moment, it's not doing you any good—'

'It feels like it's doing me plenty of good.'

'In fact, Mr Innes, the current dosage may well be exacerbating your situation.'

'Exacer-what?'

'It may be doing you harm. So what I propose is we cut back on the codeine, replace it with cocodamol, keep the ibuprofen, and book you in to see the physio.'

'What's cocodamol?' I said.

'It's a painkiller.' Choudrey was nodding to himself.

'Right. Okay.'

He started writing a prescription, then stopped mid-scrawl. 'Actually, you might be best just buying the cocodamol over the counter, save yourself a few pounds.'

'Hang on, this is over-the-counter stuff?'

Choudrey shrugged. 'It'll cost less than the prescription. I'm doing you a favour.'

'You're prescribing me fuckin' headache tablets and that's a favour?' I paused, tried to control my voice. It had almost crept to a yell there. 'Look, if the dosage isn't working, then you up the dosage.'

'You don't understand,' said Choudrey.

'You're right, Doctor, I don't understand. I can't sleep at nights. I need pills to get me asleep, *keep* me asleep, else I wake up in the middle of the night screaming.'

'I'm sure it's not that bad.'

'Your bedside manner's pish, by the way. And you're not living with it.'

'If it's so bad,' he said, 'then physiotherapy's the only way to make it better. Really. It's the only way forward.'

'Tell you what, you just write me a repeat script and I'll get out of your hair.'

Choudrey leaned back in his chair, closed his hands together and stared at me.

'What?' I said.

'Mr Innes, I want to make this perfectly clear to you: I'm not going to write you a repeat prescription.'

'Why not?'

He waved the question off, leaned forward again. 'I'll book you in for a session at the hospital. If you honestly find that the physiotherapy isn't working, then we'll talk about some weaker medication for you.'

I shook my head. 'That's not going to be possible.'

'And why's that?'

'I'm going away.'

'Excuse me?'

'I'm going to the States. It's a business trip.'

'I wouldn't recommend you fly.'

'Well, I'm not about to fuckin' swim it, am I? I don't have a choice.' I was about to steam on, tell him exactly why I didn't have a choice, but he'd already figured me for a twat, so I caught myself. Took a deep breath. 'Look, Doctor, I appreciate the thought, but right now all I need is a repeat. When I get back from the States, I'll come and see you, you can book me in for the physio, drop the script down to fuckin' aspirins or whatever and we'll see how it goes. Does that sound fair?'

Dr Choudrey nodded, stuck out his bottom lip. He wrote the prescription. Then he pulled a notepad across his desk and wrote something. Tore off the sheet and handed it to me along with my script. The note had a phone number on it. A name underneath: Rebecca Mooney.

I held the note up. 'What's this?'

Choudrey cleared his throat. From the sound of it, there was plenty to clear. He swallowed, and then when he spoke, it was with a voice that dripped with practised sympathy. 'I'm lowering your dosage, Callum. I don't know who prescribed them for you in the first place, but I think they were wrong to do so. In a very real way, the dosage you've been on has been doing you a great deal of physical harm. Now I understand you're in pain, and I'm afraid you'll remain in some pain after the dosage is cut, but that will be purely psychological. That's why I'm going to keep you on the antidepressants for the time being. But I have to lower the painkillers, Callum. You can make up the difference with coco-damol.'

'What's the phone number in aid of?'

'If you have any problems, you need someone to talk to about it and you don't want to talk to me, I want you to phone Rebecca.'

'And what exactly does this Rebecca do?'

'She works in an Outreach programme.'

I didn't say anything. I stared at Choudrey for a long time. His eyes dropped from me. Looked like he hadn't just figured me for a twat. He'd thrown in junkie, too. I looked at the note, folded it in half. 'You've got the wrong Innes, pal. It's my brother who's in the Outreach programme. And he's doing great, thanks for asking.' I shook my head, tapped the note. 'All I wanted was a repeat script so's I could get on a plane without being in agony. Not like I was asking you to fix me a bogus for methadone, was it?'

'I understand that. All I'm saying, if you need someone—'

'I got plenty of people to talk to, Doctor. And those people aren't so quick to call me a fuckin' addict.'

I got out of my seat, looking at the prescription. My gut knotted. This was never going to be enough. It might have been a fine excuse for not going, but I dreaded having to explain myself to Paulo. Knowing the big man, he would've made me ring that bloody number too.

Dr Choudrey followed me out of his office. As I headed for reception, I heard a nurse telling him they'd had the results back. Could've been the 3:30 at Kempton, but I didn't give a toss. I stopped in my tracks. Listened to them walk away.

'Shit,' I said.

The receptionist looked up, obviously pissed off at my choice of words.

'I left my watch in there,' I said. 'Mind if I go back and get it?'

'You shouldn't really—'

'It's okay. I won't be a second. I'll just nip in and get it, then I'll be gone.'

'Be quick,' she said.

'Not a problem.'

I ducked back into Choudrey's office, snatched his prescription pad from the desk and froze.

This wasn't right.

But fuck him. The sweat had already started, which meant the pain wasn't far behind. And Choudrey didn't know the first fucking thing about relief. Thinking more about his budget.

I tore off a sheet, stuffed it into my jacket pocket.

Choudrey emerged with the nurse as I strolled back to reception. When he saw me, he frowned, glanced at his office door. I'd closed it before I left. Nothing out of the ordinary.

'Mr Innes,' he said.

'I was looking for you,' I said. Sweat was already bubbling from my forehead. 'I just wanted to tell you, I've been thinking. And you know what? You're right.' I gestured towards the office. 'I'm sorry about how I acted in there. My mam brought me up better than that. I should trust your decision. Just, you've got to understand, it was a bit of a shock.'

He nodded, but he wasn't convinced. 'You have Rebecca's number.'

I patted the pocket with the stolen script. 'Right here. I'll give her a call when I get back. Sometimes you need someone who doesn't know you, eh?'

'Going somewhere nice?' said the nurse.

'America.'

'Ooh, where?'

'Los Angeles.'

'Well, say hello to George Clooney for me,' she said.

'Yeah, course I will.'

I left them to it. The nurse with her Hollywood wet dreams of chocolate-box geriatrics, Choudrey glaring at me. He knew something was up. No way could my change of heart be that fucking sudden. When I got back, I'd have to find myself another GP.

At the chemists, Barbara didn't bat an eyelid. And why should she? It was a repeat and I'd had Choudrey's signature to practise on the way over. I made small talk with her, kept her smiling, and I got my usual.

As I stepped out onto the street, this wild-eyed lad accosted me. Obviously been waiting outside, thought I was an easy target.

'Here y'are, mate,' he said. 'I'll buy it off you.'

'No jellies here, mate.'

'Nah, I know. You got pills.'

'Yeah. Sudafed. I got a cold.'

'Fuck off, that's never over the fuckin' counter, that.'

'Doesn't matter anyway, does it? I'm not selling.'

I started walking. He followed.

'Fuck off,' he said. 'Course y'are, mate. Fifty pence a pop, right?'

'You what?'

'Fifty fuckin' pence. That's what. Fifty a pop.'

'Nah.'

'That's the going. Y'ain't making us go higher, man. That's the going.'

I stopped, looked at him. 'That right?'

'Yeah.'

'You know these things. You're up on the going rate.'

'Yeah. Can't put nowt past us, mate.'

'Then you'll know a proper fuckin' dealer. So fuck off and find one. *Mate.*'

I got in my Micra, made sure the door was locked as I got settled. The lad moved back, a foul expression on his face. Choudrey might have been right. I might have been a junkie.

But I wasn't that bad.

ELEVEN

'D'you think I could get one of those?'

'I thought you gave up,' I say.

Nelson nods, looking at my pack of cigarettes. 'I did. But alcohol makes me crave 'em.'

I give him a Marlboro, light one for myself. Takes a few clicks of the Bic to get a flame, my hands are that numb with the drink. Nelson stands there sucking on the filter until I hand him my lighter.

'Pink suits you,' he says.

I smile. 'Where's this hot dog place?'

'Walking distance.' Nelson sucks on the Marlboro, holds smoke in his lungs until his eyes begin to tear, then blows it out in a long stream. 'Jesus, it's a nice night for it.'

Above us, a clear sky. 'I suppose so.'

'You can see the stars,' says Nelson as we start walking. 'Rare for this place. My father told me there was this time, him and my uncle, they went up to the Hollywood Freeway. They were just starting to build it back then. And my uncle and my dad, they'd go up there and look at the stars. Sometimes he said you could watch the planes flying out from California to the Pacific. Now you go up there and it's all smog and halogen.'

I grunt in agreement. At least I hope it sounds like agreement.

'That's why I don't drive unless I have to. I get behind the wheel, I think about those kids up on the Freeway.'

'You didn't make the place smoggy.'

'No,' says Nelson, cigarette in his mouth. 'But I sure as hell contributed to it.'

'These the only stars we're likely to see?'

'I hope so. You wouldn't like the other kind, Callum. They're all fucking fake.'

'I don't know.' I point at the pavement. 'They look real enough.'

'Keep following them, then.'

I do. It means I don't see the place we're going until we're almost there. When I hit Errol Flynn and Debbie Reynolds, Nelson stops me.

'Here we are.'

Skooby's boasts the best hot dogs in Hollywood, the best fries in Los Angeles and the best lemonade in California. Part restaurant, part outside diner, the place looks as strangely American as anything I've seen. Doesn't mean that the food's going to be great, but at least I'm taking in the city's culture.

'You want to try a Big German?'

According to a sign on the outside of the restaurant, The Big German is The Dog Of The Month, some gargantuan-looking thing heaped with sauerkraut. It already looks partly digested, and it's affecting my appetite.

'Nah,' I say. 'Sauerkraut gives me wind.'

We take seats at the counter. Nelson's quick to order: a Skooby's Original, bucket of fries and an Arnold Palmer. I don't know any different, so I order the same. And with jetlag creeping in, a coffee too.

'I thought you guys drank tea.'

'We do,' I say. 'All the time. But when in Rome . . .'

'I appreciate it.' He turns on his seat, points up the street at a church with a Spanish sign outside. 'You see that? Used to be a movie theatre.'

'Really?'

'Yeah. You know what movies they showed there?'

'Something about God.'

'Well, one of them was *Deep Throat*.'

'That so?'

'I'm telling you, Callum. This whole place used to be a meat market. You couldn't move for porno and hookers down here.' He shakes his head as our food arrives. Then he takes a large bite out of his hot dog, manages to get most of it on the counter. 'That's a damn good dog.'

'You come here a lot?'

'Sometimes. Enough. Not too much. It's good, huh?'

'It's quiet.'

'I don't cook so much. My wife used to.' He takes another bite, chews. 'We're not together.'

'Sorry to hear that.'

'Don't be,' he says. 'Really, don't be. Not one of those tragic tales.'

I nod, bite into the hot dog and try not to look like a complete gimp by getting it all over myself. I fail miserably. I grab a handful of napkins and start dabbing at myself.

'Don't bother. Wait until the end or you'll spend more time cleaning than eating.'

I drop the napkins, eat some more, then set the hot dog down. Big gouts of mustard spot the counter. 'I never asked you before, what's your line of work?'

'You really interested?'

'I'm asking.'

Nelson wipes his face, takes another bite. Chews and smiles at the same time. 'I used to fight.'

'No kidding. Fight, like what? Boxing or brawling?'

'Some said both.' Digs something out of his tooth with one finger. 'I turned pro for a while.'

'Don't get me wrong, but you don't look much like a boxer.'

Nelson pushes his glasses up onto the bridge of his nose and regards me. 'You don't look much like a private investigator.'

'I'm not.'

'And I'm not a fighter. Not anymore. Made some money, nothing fantastic. I do some coaching now and then. Scout on a freelance basis. I like to stay in the circuit.'

I grab a handful of fries. They're bloody good. I don't know if they're the best in Los Angeles, but they're still bloody good. 'You going to this smoker?'

Nelson smiles, and I wonder what's so funny. 'The Alvarez thing?'

'Yeah.'

'I'll probably drop in. Why?'

'That's why I'm over here,' I say. 'Babysitting a kid who's entering.'

'He British?'

'Yup.'

'I knew it was open, but I didn't think it was that open. He on a scholarship or something?'

'I doubt it. He got a letter.'

'Right.' Nelson eats the rest of his hot dog, drops the wedge of his bun on a napkin and wipes his hands. 'You're sure he's in?'

'I don't know how it's been worked out, mate. But he's definitely in. Bloke I know pulled a few strings for him. Thinks he's got a good chance of turning pro.'

'That right?' Nelson stares at something I can't see. 'Well, I hope he does well. It's a good way to get spotted, fighting in the amateur tournaments. They're not supposed to recruit there, but if a kid's got good hands, he can be taken on. What do you think about him?'

I shrug. 'Last time I saw him fight, it was a while ago.'

'And?'

'And he used his head.'

'I don't get you.'

'Take it literally, Nelson.'

'Shit.' Nelson sips his Arnold Palmer. 'What's he like now?'

'He's ambitious, seems to have his head together. He wants to turn pro. He's got drive. Doesn't stop him being a huge pain in the arse, though.'

'Comes with the drive, Callum. I was a pain in the ass when I fought. You want something that much, you think you can do it, that's all that matters. People, they're a waste of breath. Can't talk to people, because they're never gonna see the world like you see it. You get so wrapped up in yourself and your goals you can't see beyond the ring.'

'Right.' I finish my hot dog, wash it down with a drink of coffee. 'That's the way this lad operates. He's away with the fuckin' fairies.'

'And you think he might be okay?'

'I trust my mate's judgement on this. He's a cheapskate, wouldn't spend the cash if he didn't think the lad had a chance.'

'I'd have to see him in action.'

'Well, give me your number. Soon as he's got a fight lined up, I'll give you a bell.'

'Okay, great.'

Nelson writes his number on a napkin, hands it to me. I tuck the napkin in my pocket.

'That's my cell.' Nelson pauses and looks at me. 'You know something, Callum? I'm glad I met you.'

I nod. 'Might as well call me Cal, Nelson. Everyone else does.'

TWELVE

My throat's burning when I wake up and so's Los Angeles.

I pull myself out of bed, my vision blurred and painful, wondering what the fuck all the commotion's about. Then I realise I must've drifted off with the television on. I look across at the bottle on the desk: there's a dent in the vodka the size of my fist. That would explain the throat, the headache, and the hollow feeling in the pit of my stomach.

On the TV, a guy with a face that looks like he's permanently caught in a wind tunnel yells into a microphone. Under his voice, there's the steady beat of helicopter blades. They thrum in time with my head-throb. Now they're showing shaking pictures of what looks like a forest fire.

'Sources say that the brush fire started sometime early this morning in the Verdugo mountains, Bob. The fire department deployed fire bombers a couple of hours ago, but the inferno does not seem to have abated. This is the worst we've seen in a few years.'

I move to the bathroom to guzzle some cold water straight from the tap. As I'm bending over, my back spikes, so I drop a couple of codeine into my mouth, swallow them down.

'It looks like the Santa Anas are going to be bringing all that smoke and ash south right over the city.'

'Should citizens be worried, Dave?' says another voice.

'I've been assured that the fire will *not* spread, Bob. It's—'

I click off the television as I come back into the bedroom. Wander over to the window and if there's hell on earth out there, I can't see it because of the Hollywood Hills. I return to the bathroom and light a cigarette, blow smoke at the fan. Christ, what with the riots, the gangs, the earthquakes, the phoney fucking religious cults and brush fires, it makes me wonder why people actually choose to live here. But then there's Hollywood, I suppose. Enough promises there to keep people dreaming, even though nobody was ever really discovered at Schwab's drug store.

I told Paulo all this last night. Must've been about nine in the morning over in Manchester, and for that time of the morning the conversation went on longer than I would've expected. I was pissed, told Paulo that a couple of times. Liam was fine, but he was a shitty traveller – not like me, I was great – and then I went into what Nelson told me. Must've repeated myself before Paulo told me to sleep it off.

We're supposed to go to the gym this morning, get Liam registered and weighed in. No doubt the lad'll be battering my door down in a minute. Maybe I'll get a chance to ask him what he meant yesterday, but then a part of me reckons it's probably best I let it lie. It's Liam's time right now. He thinks he's got the rest of his life sorted, that's great. I'm not about to step on that. Fuck it, I even scored him a coach if he shows promise in the ring. Nelson seemed to know his stuff. And there's nobody better than an ex-boxer to show the new kid the ropes, so to speak.

I flick ash into the toilet bowl, sit back.

I should check if they've got a smoking room sorted for me yet. In the meantime, this'll have to do. Lock myself in the bathroom where there's no fabric to trap the smell of smoke and sneak a puff like I'm a fucking teenager.

Check my watch and bang on cue, there's a knock at the door.

I douse the end of the Marlboro in toilet water with a hiss, wrap the filter in bog roll and flush the lot. Then wave my hands in the air to dispel some of the smoke, hoping the fan'll take care of the rest.

By the time I get to the door, Liam's furious. There's a vein sticking out in his neck.

'Fuck's sake, Cal,' he says. 'We're supposed to be there in like half an hour.'

'It's okay.'

'You're not even *dressed*.'

'Stop your fuckin' pecking, Liam. Don't worry about it.'

'We're going to be late.'

I pull on some jeans, grab my jacket. 'See? Dressed. C'mon, let's go. I've got some news that might stick a smile on that puss of yours.'

Liam sniffs the air, narrows his eyes. 'You been smoking in here?'

'Yeah, Liam. Don't tell on me, eh?'

Outside it's pure lizard weather, a dry heat that scorches the inside of your mouth if you breathe too hard. The radio says 105 degrees, but that's Fahrenheit so I haven't the foggiest what it translates to apart from fucking hot. So I've got the air conditioning ramped right up which, along with the radio, has kicked the Metro in the bollocks. Lucky if I can get the heap past fifty. But air conditioning is a necessity with the weather. I wonder if it's got anything to do with the brush fire, then check out of the window for falling ash.

'What's this news then?' says Liam.

'I got talking to a bloke last night.'

Liam squints at me. 'If you ended up fucking him, I don't want to hear it.'

'You think I'm gay?'

'I don't care.'

''Cause I work with Paulo, that means I'm his boyfriend?'

'I didn't say that.'

'It's what you were thinking, you wee bastard.'

'You're close, is all I'm saying. Doesn't matter to me which hole you stick it in. Behind closed doors and all that. Just keep it away from me.'

'Liam, you're a fuckin' idiot. Shut your yap and listen to me. I got talking to this bloke last night, turns out he's an ex-fighter, does some scouting on the side.'

Liam gazes out of the window. 'And?'

'And he wants to see you fight.'

'It's open to the public, Cal. You can bring your bloke.'

'With a view to coaching you,' I say.

'He got any credentials, this bloke?'

'I don't know.'

'Then he's a fuckin' leech.' He turns in his seat. 'And what's this shite playing?'

'It's Johnny Cash, and didn't I already tell you you were a fuckin' idiot?'

'Sounds like he needs to blow his nose and cheer up. Look, Cal, I appreciate you talking to total strangers and trying to help me out an' that, but you can stop it now, alright? I need to concentrate on the comp. Paulo already briefed us on what it'd be like out here, said I needed to keep my brain on the bouts, nothing else.'

'He just meant stay off the booze, Liam.'

'Nah, he meant anything. Booze, birds, strange blokes you decide to pick up in bars . . .'

'What'd I tell you about that?' I wave my hand. 'Fuck it, forget it. I was just trying to help out.'

'And I said thanks, but no thanks. You're supposed to be taking a break, right?'

'Yeah.'

'So take a break, man. Let me take care of my stuff. You don't need to come to the bouts, you just need to drop us off. You're not my chaperone, you're my driver. How's that?'

I should've brushed my teeth. Got a sticky feeling in my mouth. 'Fine. That's cool. I'll be your driver.'

Little prick.

And we sit in silence until we get to Shapiro's Boxing Center. Which just looks like a posh way of saying slum-looking gym. I find a parking space, Liam pulls his bag from the back seat, and we go inside.

The gym is chocka with kids, all different ages and all of them registering. At the far end of the gym, I can make out a huge set of scales. On them is a black lad, his coach beside him, watching the weight like a hawk. Then the black lad steps off the scales, a look of relief on his face. On my right, a small, round Latino guy sits on a stool that shakes whenever he shifts position. He's behind a table, looking at a typewritten list. His mouth moves when he reads. Looks up at Liam and says, 'What's your name?'

'Liam Wooley,' says Liam.

'Which gym?'

Liam looks at me; I shrug.

'He's here to register,' I say. 'He's flown all the way from Manchester and boy, are his arms tired.'

'England?'

'Yeah.' I pull out the letter. 'We're supposed to see Phil Shapiro.'

'Phil?' says the fat guy. 'Lemme have a look at that.'

I hand him the letter. The fat guy's lips go into overdrive as he reads. When he's finished, he folds the letter in two.

'Lemme check this out,' he says.

'Go for it.'

The fat guy gets off the stool with a grunt and he's away, pushing through the crowd of lads. I watch him head towards an office at the back of the gym, windows in a partition wall looking out on the registration.

'Y'alright?' I say to Liam.

He glances at me, then surveys the crowd. His eyes are clear, but his jaw is set. 'Yeah, I'm good.'

The fat guy emerges from the office with another bloke. I'm guessing this is Phil Shapiro. Bloke's built like a brick shithouse. As he gets closer, I can make out his face, but his features are still blurred. Looks like something made mincemeat out of him at one point and a plastic surgeon had the job of his life putting the guy's boat back together. Shapiro wears a wifebeater, his gut straining at the fabric. A shamrock tattoo on his left arm, Chinese writing on his shoulder. Yeah, he's a hard bastard and international with it. I'd shit myself if it wasn't for the Chihuahua he's carrying.

'You Liam?' he says. Shapiro's voice is too soft for his face.

Liam nods.

Shapiro closes one eye and cocks his head. 'You're the warrior?'

'Suppose so,' says Liam.

'I don't see it.' Shapiro has a lisp. It's slight, but it's there. I get the feeling he wasn't born with it, either. 'Paulo speaks highly of you. Says you've got the talent to turn pro if you want to.'

'I hope so, sir.'

Sir? The fuck did that come from?

Shapiro nods at me. 'Who's your friend?'

Liam's about to say something when I interrupt. 'I'm his driver.'

'You ever fight?'

'I've fought, yeah.'

'Ever win?'

'Not once.'

'I didn't think so. Okay, Liam, let's get you weighed in.' Shapiro jerks his head towards the end of the gym and Liam follows, bag in hand. For a moment there, I'd put the lad's age ten years younger. A kid in awe, and more than a little frightened. I watch Liam go, scan the rest of the room. A gang of lads takes up one corner of the gym, all about Liam's age and watching the newcomer intently. One lad in particular. He's tall, blond, well-groomed. He'd probably be handsome if it wasn't for that foul look on his face.

I gesture at the fat guy, then at the kid. 'Who's the Aryan?'

The fat guy glances behind him. He turns round and scratches his balding head as he looks at the sheet in front of him. 'Josh Callahan. You think your kid's hot shit, Callahan's the real McCoy.'

'Yeah?'

'Absolutely.'

'Because he looks like a ponce with a pet lip to me. Look, you see Liam after he weighs in and gets all the shit out the way, can you tell him his driver's outside?'

'Sure.'

I step out into the sun, blink against the light. I look around for some shade to sneak into. Reach into my pocket for my cigarettes and spark one up, drawing hard to make up for the one I had to flush. That first drag makes my chest tight, so I force myself to cough up whatever's clogged my lungs. I spit something grey at the pavement, stick the Marlboro back in my mouth.

Something about this Josh Callahan makes my knee jerk. He has a rich, pampered look to him I've seen on countless American TV programmes, didn't think actually existed. One of those party hearty lads who fuck other people's lives and buy their way out of trouble. Maybe that's why I wanted to go over there and slap him. Or maybe it's because he reminds me of a younger Liam, all posture and piss and vinegar. Or could be it's just last night's drink coming back thick and fast, hangover following like a six-berth caravan.

Whatever it is, it's not going to stop me enjoying this cigarette.

I blow smoke into the sunshine, thinking Los Angeles is a real shithole when you're away from the city centre. And I thought Manchester was bad. I look down at my shirt, notice a big yellow stain near my belt. Thinking, well, at least I don't look like a tourist.

And that's when the shouting starts.

THIRTEEN

As soon as I push into the gym, I'm deafened by the heavy bloodletting threats flying back and forth. Mostly American voices, some of them angry, some trying to calm the situation, but one voice rings out loud and clear: Liam.

'You wanna fuckin' start something, posh lad, you come ahead.'

Liam's held back by a couple of lads, Josh out in the open. If anything, I think it should be the other way round, but Liam's cheeks are scarlet and now I'm like everyone else in here. Not sure what this Brit lad's going to do. The old Liam's back, and so's his rage.

What the fuck happened? He was supposed to be weighing in. I stride across to Liam as Shapiro comes bombing out of his office. Shapiro's presence pulls everyone's emotions down a notch.

'What's going on?' he says.

Josh lets his mouth go. 'What's he doing weighing in, Phil? There's guys tailed back in here and this kid goes first? He's not from around here, he's not one of us—'

'That's none of your business, Josh.'

'Course it's my business.'

'Go fuck yourself,' says Liam.

'You a tough guy, man? You wanna see a real tough guy, you cocksucker?' Josh makes a move, hands tense, but Shapiro's quick to step in front of him. He sees me and raises his hand: *don't get involved, driver, or I'll take you down too.* No Chihuahua in sight, but I can hear it yapping in the office. Shapiro moves his raised hand round to Josh, extends one finger. The lad backs right off. So do the lads holding onto Liam.

'Liam, bring your driver into the office,' says Shapiro. 'I want a word with the pair of you.'

Liam has lost his rage somewhere. Like it was a finger snap and back to normal. I move to him, put a hand on his back, but he shrugs me off. We traipse through to the back office. I glance at Josh, but the fat guy moves in front of him before I get a decent look.

In the office, the Chihuahua is sitting on the desk, its tongue hanging out.

'You want to explain that to me?' says Shapiro.

Liam doesn't say anything. Neither do I; I can't explain it. Christ knows how it happened so quickly. The best explanation I can come up with is that Josh Callahan's a fuckin' mentalist.

'I thought this kid was supposed to be focused,' says Shapiro. 'This is what Paulo told me. "The lad's ready," he said.'

'He is ready,' I say.

'You sure?' Shapiro closes the door behind us.

'Paulo wouldn't lie to you. He paid to get us over here, he's not going to send us if Liam's not focused.'

Shapiro walks to his desk, scoops up the dog. He brings the Chihuahua to his face, then holds it like a baby in one arm. 'You saw him out there. Didn't look very focused to me. You've got a way with first impressions, Liam.'

'It's that Callahan lad you want to watch out for, Mr Shapiro,' I say.

'You telling me how to run my business?'

'I'm telling you that kid's all kinds of fucked up. Soon as we get in here, he's giving Liam the fuckin' deadeye. You think Liam's going to start something in the first five minutes? Nah, he was provoked. That Callahan kid's looking for a smack.'

Shapiro leans against his desk. The dog is shaking, panting. 'What happened, Liam?'

Liam shakes his head. 'Nowt.'

'Excuse me?'

'It was nothing.'

'It was something, Liam.'

'He was calling us is all. He's all mouth. We'll sort it out in the ring.'

'If you get into the ring,' says Shapiro.

'You can't keep him out,' I say.

'Did I say that?'

'We come all this way and you're knocking him down before he gets a chance to prove himself?'

'I didn't say that. But I'm not running a fight club, either. The boys who come to my gym, they're expected to act like professionals—'

'Then tell it to Josh—'

'They're expected to follow rules. We went through those rules just now, didn't we, Liam? So you stick to those rules. Josh starts coming on at you like he did – *if* he did – then you back off, you let it alone. You keep the fights in the ring.'

'That's what he just said.'

'Did I ask you anything?' says Shapiro. 'I don't recall asking you anything. I'm talking to Liam.'

I look at Liam; he's shaking. Just a little, but if I notice it, so does Shapiro.

'You keep the fights in the ring, Liam. Because if you take it outside, you'll be outnumbered.'

Liam nods.

'Okay, then we're done here.'

'Actually,' I say, 'you want to wait in the car, Liam? I think I need a chat with Mr Shapiro.'

Liam looks at me like: *don't.*

'It'll be okay. Just wait for me in the car.'

He grabs his bag from the floor and pushes open the office door, heads out across the gym. I stand in the doorway, watch him leave, looking for Josh. The little bastard's nowhere to be seen. I hope to God he's not waiting outside for Liam. I give it a few seconds after Liam leaves, listening out. Then I close the door. Shapiro hasn't moved from the desk.

'You're too young to be his father,' he says.

'I'm a concerned acquaintance. What's the deal with Josh Callahan?'

'There's no deal.'

'He's a prick.'

'He has issues.'

'That what you're calling them now? Issues? Cause where I come from, a prick's a prick. He an ex-offender?'

'No. Josh wants to learn the sport. He wants to learn a few moves for his self-defence.'

'Moves are going to do them much good around here, are they? Christ, most of the kids are carrying guns, aren't they?'

Shapiro bristles. He puts the dog on the floor. The Chihuahua scurries over to a water bowl in the corner of the office, makes snorting noises as it drinks. Shapiro straightens up, says, 'You watch too many bad gangster movies, Mr . . . ?'

'Innes.'

'Mr Innes. These kids aren't all punks. They're not all fighting their way out of the ghetto. They're decent kids and it's a sport to them. But I wanted to help Paulo out. He had some trouble with the law, didn't he?'

'Paulo or Liam?'

'Either. Or.'

'Both. And they both did their time.'

'And it's managed to spread around here. I let the boys know there was going to be a new face. Josh is probably just jumpy. He's been the top dog for so long, he's just growling a little bit.'

'He's a rich kid,' I say.

Shapiro nods. 'His parents have money. A lot of parents do. There's a lot of money in this city. Why, you got something against rich people, Mr Innes?'

'I don't have anything against rich people. Just makes me wonder why Josh is interested in boxing.'

'Because boxing's a working-class sport, is that what you're saying? You think he should be a fencer or something?'

'No. I don't know. Maybe.'

'This isn't a *game* to these boys, Mr Innes.' Shapiro folds his arms. 'I make 'em do fifty laps of the gym right from the get-go or they can get gone. Then there's the push-ups, the leg-lifts, the jump-rope. And then there's six weeks of cardiovascular conditioning. You see, Mr Innes, the boys who come in here thinking it's a game, they leave after the first week, because I'm not playing. As it turns out, you're asking why boxing, Josh's dad has a keen interest and that interest has been passed to his son. Just because his parents are rich, it doesn't mean he's a spoiled brat. Happens that he doesn't do too well at school, doesn't make friends easily—'

'What a fuckin' surprise—'

'—so he needs a something else, a little discipline in his life. This place gives him that.'

'You going to have a word with him?' I say.

'Yes,' he says. 'I'll have a word with him.'

'And Liam's still alright to fight.'

'If he keeps his nose clean. You met Reuben before? He'll oversee Liam's training. He'll also be his second in the ring.'

'That fat guy? He any good?'

'He's a good cut man, knows his stuff.'

'Good.' I move to the door. As I do, someone knocks. 'I don't want this to fuck up his chances.'

'It won't as long as he doesn't let it,' says Shapiro.

I open the door and there's Josh, standing proud with his chin up and out. I rein in the urge to elbow the wee fucker in the throat as I push past him. It wouldn't do any good.

And besides, I think, if anyone's going to screw this up, it better not be me.

FOURTEEN

We needed to talk, me and Liam, so I made him break bread with me. I got us a table at a restaurant about a block from the hotel, thought we'd have some bonding time. I've got a burger and chips on the go, just so I can check it off the American Food I Need To Eat list. Liam hasn't eaten his chicken salad thing, seems content enough just moving it about the bowl. I take a bite out of my burger and feel relish drop out the sides. I hear it splatter against the plate. About the only thing I have heard since we got here, apart from our order and the buzz of a restaurant at low ebb.

I wipe my mouth with a napkin, ball up the paper and drop it by the side of my plate. 'So, you going to tell me what happened?'

Liam shakes his head. 'Nowt happened.'

'He call you names or something? Make fun of your hair? If it was me, I'd make fun of your hair.'

He looks up at me, a sneer in his smile. 'Oh, you're fuckin' hysterical, you.'

'I try. So what was it?'

'I told you, nowt. He was just being an arsehole.'

'You said I was an arsehole, you didn't try to leather me.'

Liam's eyes narrow. 'I'm biding my time.'

'I bet you are. Going to kick me in the bollocks when I'm sleeping, that it?'

'Something like that, yeah.'

I pick up the burger again, take another bite, set it down. Pick up a chip and wave it at Liam as I speak. 'You're going to have start trusting me, y'know.'

'No, I don't.'

'We're in this thing together—'

'No, we're not.' Liam pushes his salad around. 'Not in this together, Cal. It's me. I'm in it.'

'I forgot. It's all about you, isn't it?'

'Yeah. You got nowt to do but get drunk.'

I sniff. 'When's your first fight?'

'Bout. It's called a bout.' Liam's mouth is tight.

'Alright then, smart arse. When's your first *bout*?'

He takes a deep breath as if it's something he's already explained to me countless times. 'Tomorrow.'

'Afternoon?'

'Morning.' And you better be up.' He lays down his fork. 'I don't want to be late for this, okay? I need to be there like two hours beforehand, at least. I need to get weighed in.'

'You already got weighed in,' I say.

'You don't know the first fuckin' thing about this, do you?'

'Can't learn if you won't talk, Liam.'

'Why'd Paulo tell you to come with us?' He sits back in his chair. 'Honestly. Why'd he tell you to come? What, he thought you'd be able to help us out when it came to the comp?'

'I don't know.'

'Cause that's not likely to happen, is it? Look at you, you never done a tournament in your life. Fuck's sake, you ever even been in a gym?'

'Paulo's.'

'Not counting Paulo's.'

'A couple of times.'

'Where?'

'Strangeways.'

'Uh-huh,' he says.

'I went in there twice, then I didn't bother,' I say. My appetite's fading fast. Too much rich food. 'Think they've got enough rules in that place, they've got even more in the gym. Trouble is, you don't know what they are until you've broken them. Took me two visits and a fuckin' beating to call it a day.'

'Gonna give us a sob story, Cal?'

I stare at Liam. Sitting back in his seat like the cocky wee fucker he is. I want to get out of my seat and plant my foot in his chest, but I stay put. Can't fault the stupidity of youth, even though if he's putting it on like he's older, he should get a kicking like he's older.

'Forget it,' I say. I catch our waitress' attention. She comes over, all smiles, and I ask for the bill.

As soon as she leaves, Liam says, 'You not eating that?'

'You want it?'

'No fuckin' way. You know how long that's going to be in your stomach?'

'A long time, I hope. I want my money's worth.'

The waitress returns as Liam leans across the table. 'Every time you get wind after you mix your starch and protein like that, that's because you're digesting the two at different rates. That wind coming up, that's because you've got rotting meat in your gut.'

I don't pretend to look interested. Fish out cash from my wallet and leave a decent tip. The waitress walks away. Then I force out a belch.

'Rotting meat,' says Liam.

'Fuck yourself,' I say.

Nelson swallows the last of his beer, but waves at the bartender to keep them coming. I'm guessing he's a regular here, because a tab is on the go. I haven't tried to talk him out of it yet. I'll settle at the end of the night.

'You tried talking to the boy?' he says as the bartender plonks down another bottle.

'Yeah, I've tried talking to him. It doesn't work.' I suck my teeth, peel the label from my Budweiser. 'And the lad's got a point, Nelson. I don't know why Paulo wanted me to come over here with him. I said I'm not good with the lads, got nothing in common with them. What am I going to talk to him about, eh? How was stir, Liam? Yeah, pretty shitty, wasn't it? How was the food?'

Nelson pauses with his bottle, then he takes a drink, swallows. 'You were in prison?'

I nod. 'Dim and distant, mate. Ancient history.' My head's started to feel heavy. When the drinks are free, you lose track. 'He's got a *bout* tomorrow morning.'

The world grows furry at the edges. It's no wonder. I've been sitting in this bar pretty much since I left the restaurant. Saw Liam go up to his room, no doubt to sit on his bed and read that fucking notebook that doesn't leave his sight.

Dear Diary, today some rich lad said horrible things to me . . .

What's worse is I haven't been able to get Liam's shit about my digestion out of my mind. The burger's taking an age to break down, giving me a dull ache in the pit of my stomach. Probably doesn't help that I've been drowning the rotting meat with vodka and beer. I should get an early night, but I'm too pissed off to care that much.

'Here,' I say. 'You want to swing by tomorrow morning and see if he's worth taking on?'

'Sure. Where is it?'

'Shapiro's place.'

Nelson pauses again. Thinks I haven't noticed it.

'What?' I say.

'Phil Shapiro? Big guy, face like it's been through a meat grinder?'

'You know him then.'

'I knew him.' Nelson swallows some beer. 'I didn't know he was still on the circuit.'

I frown. My thinking's not straight, but there's a part of me that reckons Nelson should know where the comp's being held if he's so connected. I put it down to crossed wires and alcohol. But the gym thing . . .

'He's got his own gym, Nelson,' I say. 'His name's above the door. I'd say that was on the circuit.'

'Yeah, I know,' he says. 'I just didn't know he still ran it.' Nelson puts down his bottle and looks at what's left of the label. 'I'm not sure about this, Cal . . .'

'What's up?'

'I may be wrong, y'know? I knew Phil a *long* time ago. He may have changed since I last saw him. That's possible. I wouldn't count on it, but it's possible.'

'How d'you mean, changed? From what to what?'

Nelson smiles, but it doesn't look comfortable. His eyes light up full beam when he turns to me. 'He was a fighter. You must've guessed that, looking at him. But he was a real good fighter, had a record that put mine in the damn doghouse.'

'Good?'

'That face, I don't know what happened to that face. He's always been like that. But whatever caused that face made him a strong sonofabitch, I'll tell you that. He went down *twice*.' Nelson holds up two fingers in a peace sign. 'Twice. That's all. In God knows how many fights. And he was mismatched in those two. Real badly mismatched, someone should've done something about it. The last two fights he had, he went down because of that mismatch. And that was it; he didn't want to get knocked down again. But, Christ, he was mid-forties then, y'know? It was probably time to quit.'

'Why do I get the feeling this is going to get dark, Nelson?' I try to match his smile, but I fail.

'Aw, hell, I don't know, Cal.' Nelson gestures to the bartender, orders us both a couple more drinks, this time the hard stuff. 'Just rumours is all I heard. And you bite on them, you're biting on thin air.'

'Yeah, but you're concerned. C'mon, man, you know this place better than I do. I don't know the first thing about boxing, do I? And I know fuck-all about LA. So chuck me a line here. If I'm putting Liam into something unsavoury, I want to know about it.'

Nelson shakes his head, finishes his beer. 'I'm not going any further. For your own sake, okay? Phil Shapiro's got all the heart in the world, just made a few mistakes, and for all I know he's a changed man. All I got to offer is rumour and speculation, and I been drinking far too heavy to make any sense of it. Just forget I said anything and let's change the subject, okay?'

'Okay,' I say with a shrug. Drink some more beer to stifle the questions flying around my brain. 'Read any good books lately?'

Nelson laughs, a real bark of relief. 'I've been catching up on my Louis L'Amour.'

'Who?'

'He wrote westerns.'

'Sounds like he should be writing porn.'

'You don't know him.'

'I don't read westerns. Sorry, mate.'

'You should,' he says. 'Build up your moral fibre.'

'I bet.' I sip my Absolut.

'I'm serious, Cal.' Nelson adjusts his seat. 'You know what I miss?'

'What do you miss, Nelson?'

'I miss heroes.' He nods to himself. 'I miss real heroes. Used to be, you knew who the heroes were just by looking at them. Good guy in the white hat, bad guy in the black hat. You knew where you stood. Good guy rides into town, gets caught up in some strife with the townsfolk – there's a bad guy about – good guy goes and finds the bad guy – *blam, blam* – bye-bye black hat. The hero's a dead shot, the women are righteous, tough and pretty, the black hat's a snarling murdering rapist or rustler or something. Anyway, after the shoot-out, peace is restored, the townsfolk are all over our guy in the white hat, and the hero rides off into the sunset.'

'Like *Shane*.'

'Yeah, except alive.'

I stare at him. 'You what?'

'You saw the movie. Shane's dying at the end.'

'You're kidding.'

'No.'

'Fuck.'

'But he's still a hero. He's a *pussy* hero, but he's still a hero.' Nelson swallows some of his Jim Beam – the ice clinks in the glass. 'Now you can't rely on anyone. Can't tell the good guys and the bad guys apart – everyone's wearing grey, talking like they're Jesus.'

'I think we should slow down.'

'I want my fucking heroes back, Cal.' He prods the bar top. 'Used to be, you could rely on people. You could at *least* rely on the authorities. Over here, we can't even trust the fucking cops anymore.'

'Same in Britain, Nelson.'

'They didn't catch it on videotape, though, did they?'

'The guy in the Underground, they did.'

'We got fucking Rodney King, we got that – did you hear about this? – that guy in Washington? Cops shot him forty-one times, guy wasn't even carrying.'

'I didn't hear about that.' I don't say any more. Looking at Nelson now, he's got the raving drunk face on and that early night my body wants me to take is looking sweeter by the second.

'We're all so fucking *scared*.' He pushes his glasses up to his eyes and looks at me. 'But we react to it like, "Ah, fuck you and your family . . ." It's sickening, Cal. It sickens me. Government's scared, cops are scared, civilians are scared . . .'

Yeah, and now I'm getting scared.

'We should start over,' says Nelson. 'Sometimes I think that'd be the best thing. Sometimes I wish for something big to happen, something to shake the shit out of this city.'

'I watched the news, Nelson. You've got plenty of stuff happening over here. More natural disasters than you know what to do with. You just had—'

'Natural?' Nelson looks like he's caught a whiff of something foul. 'Most of these disasters, the ones in California, they're not *natural*. Yeah, brush fires, they used to be natural. It's nature's way of purging the vegetation. But recently? No, those fires are started by cigarettes or construction firms levelling the fucking land. Spark catches there, those nice, new and cheap-material condos are burning like kindling. And if the fire doesn't get 'em, the land-scaped surroundings will. Because when the rains come, the dirt's got no roots to keep it together. You got landslides and floods, Cal. So we do it to ourselves. And then you get the real ones. You got Katrina and here you're waiting on the Big One. That's something to wait on, Cal. Because that's what I want. Something big to clean the shit off the land, give us something to be really scared about. We need that relief when it does happen, like "Fuck, okay, it happened, some of us made it, some of us didn't, now we can re-evaluate our lives and move on". And we need to be *forced* to pull together. Look at New York—'

'Nelson . . .'

He raises his head, takes a deep breath. Lets it out and smiles wide. The clouds pass. 'I went off, didn't I? Jesus, I'm sorry, man. Guess I'm just sick of being scared.'

'Sounds like it.'

'And I let the beer do the talking.' He finishes his Jim Beam, looks at the bartender. 'What do I owe you?'

'I'll get it,' I say.

'No, I got the tab, I'll pay the tab. Offer me any cash and I'll knock you down.'

He's too serious for me to argue.

Once he's paid the tab, Nelson swivels round on his stool. His feet take a few seconds to find the floor and stay flat. 'Yeah, that's me. Look, you give me a call on the cell first thing tomorrow morning, make sure I'm up. I'll swing by, check out the kid if you still want me to.'

'That'd be great.'

He steadies himself against the bar, gets in close. 'I'm sorry, Cal. I don't mean to keep on.'

'No problem.'

'Just drunk talk, y'know.'

'I know. Get yourself some sleep, Nelson.'

'I will.'

Nelson sways as he walks to the door. Once he's gone, the bartender appears. 'Another?'

I shake my head. 'Nah, y'alright. I've got an early start in the morning.'

A full day too. Nelson's got me worried about all sorts of shite. And Phil Shapiro's right at the top of the heap.

FIFTEEN

Shapiro's not about. Or if he is, I can't see him. He's supposed to be running this thing, the least he can do is show his mangled face. Because the place is just starting to warm up, ready for Liam's first big fight.

Sorry, *bout*.

It's early in the morning and I'm still half-cut. The stink in here reminds me of Paulo's, a smell that seeps into the walls, becomes part of the building. In Paulo's club, I think the sweat's about the only thing keeping the place upright. They ever clean it, the roof'll come down.

I called Nelson's mobile from the hotel, but I had to leave a message. The guy's probably in the middle of a killer hangover by now. I just hope he manages to get himself over here, because Liam's psyched. The lad hasn't said anything to me, he's that concentrated. When we came into the gym, Liam was straight across the floor and getting changed. If it'd been me, I'd have kept my eyes peeled for Jumpin' Josh Callahan, or whatever the fuck his ring name is. A kid like that, he's got to have a ring name. But if Jumpin' Josh is due in, he's taking his sweet time about it. Maybe Shapiro's told him to stay home this morning, give Liam some breathing space.

I hope that's the score, anyway.

Liam warms up, stretches. He saunters over to a speed bag and gives it a few hard punches, then settles into the *duggida-duggida-duggida* rhythm of an old pro. His feet move slightly, the weight shifting with each change of hand. He'll keep the bag flying for a few minutes, then stop, take a step to the right, and continue. As he comes round, he glances at me, but that's all it is: a glance. His eyes flit and then back, the speed building, a harder beat.

Paulo was right about the kid's discipline. What he didn't mention was that there's a borderline psycho lurking just beneath the surface, waiting to pop out and knock some heads. Remembering the way Liam used to be, that's not much of a stretch. He had what his social worker would call 'anger management issues'. They always called it that, said I'd had some myself. But in Liam's case, it meant he was a fucking bampot and shouldn't be allowed anywhere near a ring. I'd seen the lad spar a few times. He swung so wild, it looked like his fist was about to come flying off the end of his arm. And his forehead made a nasty appearance when the spar didn't go his way.

Some gangly ginger kid with a bloody face, black eyes swelling and a broken nose. Trying not to cry, but the tears coming anyway. Paulo stepping into the ring, one hand clamped tight on Liam's shoulder.

Saying, 'You keep this shit up, you're going back.'

'Yeah—'

'I mean it, Liam. You want to act like a prick, you act the prick with me, see how far it gets you.'

Liam spluttering, 'Big fuckin—'

And Paulo's voice, always low and calm. 'Try that headbutt shite on me, son. We'll step in the ring and you try the headbutt shite, we'll see who comes out on top. Cause I will fuck you up all over and knock you on your arse while I'm doing it. I'll do it in front of everyone and they'll think you're a proper poof for taking it. And you know what else? You'll be gone, out of it. I'll file a report with your social worker. She's got enough on her books that want to make a difference to their lives. You honestly think she cares that much? You'll be out in the cold and you'll screw it up again because of that head of yours and you'll end up in prison.'

'You—'

'Proper big prison for proper big pricks. You'll be in the 'Ways, son.' The grip on Liam's shoulder loosened. 'Here, look, I'm not kidding you about. You know me, I don't have a sense of humour – I'm talking to you, look at me when I'm talking to you. You keep this up, you'll go to prison and you'll end up a fuck-puppet like your father.'

Liam didn't expect that. It was a low blow, but Paulo wasn't above the odd foul to get his point across.

'You want to be like your dad?' he said.

Liam didn't say anything. He was still processing. Working his mouth, chewing on his gum shield. Probably had a bunch of one-liners to throw at Paulo, but he didn't have the balls to deliver them in anything other than a mumble.

'You want to be like your old man, Liam?'

'Nah.'

'I can't hear you.'

'*No.*'

'Then buck your ideas up.' Paulo slapped Liam on the back.

Liam spat out his gum shield, worked his mouth some more. He wiped his nose with one glove, looked around. The ginger kid had his head back, blood drying on his lip. Liam didn't look at him.

There'd been part of Liam Wooley that didn't give a shit about boxing. That part died quick enough once Liam picked up a few moves. The way Paulo told it, you could see the lad change in front of your eyes. He became a boxer who thought he was Amir Khan or Kevin Mitchell, a lad with speed, fire and a big punch. And while it was true that Liam had the ability to put other lads to the canvas quickly, he was an animal with it. His early amateur fights were won by stoppage, but that didn't make him a credible fighter.

I once asked Paulo if teaching these kids boxing was a good idea. Fuck it, it seemed like a pertinent question at the time. Because if these lads were violent criminals – and there wasn't one of them in there that hadn't been remanded for something that didn't involve blood on their hands – then what was Paulo doing teaching them new moves? They'd take those new moves onto the street and be more efficient violent criminals.

'You think this is about beating the shit out of someone, Cal?' he said.

'Looks like it.'

'I'm not teaching them that. I'm teaching them discipline. The beating the shit out of someone, that's just a way to get their minds focused. Most of them, they'll knock seven shades out of each other, but they'll do it in a safe environment. And in the meantime, they'll get some respect for themselves. Get themselves a routine. That's all they need, y'know . . .'

It was Shapiro's way of thinking too, I could tell. Get the lads so tired, the last thing they have the energy for is causing trouble. I just wish it'd worked on Josh. Having that boy about, it's making me tense. Because if there's any way Liam's going to lose that discipline he's worked hard at, it'll be down to Jumpin' Josh.

Talent's one thing. There's no doubt, the way Liam's working that speed bag, that he's light on his feet, knows where his centre of gravity is at all times. He's a quick jabber, too. Unfazed by the other lads in the gym, tuned the buzz of conversation and other sounds out of his head, concentrating on his one goal. Liam's talented, but talent's not the least of it.

Something Paulo told the lads: 'You can be talented all you want. Talent's key. You don't have talent, you'll struggle. But you can be the most talented, spit-in-yer-eye destroyer of men you can think of. If you don't put in the graft, you don't put in the time and the effort, one night you're going to get your head caved in by someone who *has* put in the work and someone who's a damn sight less fuckin' *talented* than you. Put it this way, you don't want to cruise on talent, end up in Las Vegas staring down some hardened Latino lad who's going to make sure you're shitting in a bag by the time the first bell goes.'

The lads laughed at that, but it was nervous laughter. I didn't crack a smile. Most of the lads there didn't have what it took to be amateur, let alone pro. They'd never get to Vegas. But that wasn't the point. Don't get ahead of yourself, Paulo was saying. Don't go walking down the road thinking you can kill someone just by looking at them funny. The one thing you'll learn in this life is that there's always someone faster, stronger and harder than you are. Even if you never meet that person, you have to accept that as a fact. You live with that knowledge, and that's what makes you a man.

I'd learned that, but if I was a man, I didn't know it.

Looking at Liam now, though, I hope he picked up on what Paulo was talking about. He's light years from the kid he used to be. That's a good thing. But knowing that this is something like his final chance . . . well. I almost feel sorry for the lad.

And then I remember what a prick he can be.

'Wooley!'

It's the fat guy, Reuben. He's waddling over to Liam. I move towards them both. Reuben notices me, frowns.

'You fighting?' he says.

'No.'

'Then step back.'

I grab Liam's bag. 'Just thought I'd keep a hold of this.'

'You don't think it's safe here, man?'

'I'll keep a hold of it,' I say.

'Let him,' says Liam. 'He's got to do something to make himself feel important.'

I let that slide. 'You have a good one, Liam.'

He nods.

And I move to the back of the gym, sit on a bench and wait for the bout to begin.

PART 2

A Bible and A Gun

SIXTEEN

The way the tournament works, the boxers don't get much time to wind down. That's the way Paulo told it to me. Liam wins this one, he'll have another tomorrow. And he wins that, there's another looming. On until the finals.

It wears me out just thinking about it.

Somewhere between the warm-up and the bout, a crowd manages to develop. I hardly notice it at first. Too busy watching Liam's every move, thinking that it'll kill the kid if he breaks now, worrying in spite of myself. I shouldn't care, the way he's been playing the fucking diva, but I do. If only for Paulo's sake.

Now Liam's ready to step into the ring with a stringy Latino kid who bounces on the balls of his feet, shaking his head like a gelding. Liam is breathing hard through his nose, chewing on his gum shield, but that's about it. Looks like the only nerves in him are from anticipation of a solid win.

I'm still on the bench, Liam's bag open by my feet. I can see that notebook laying on top of his kit and I'm tempted to reach down and have a skim through, find out what's so bloody fascinating about it. But then, say Liam sees me nosing. He'll go apeshit, lose his focus. I zip the bag. Look up as Shapiro appears from his office, dog in hand. The Chihuahua doesn't seem bothered by all the people in here, its head lolling, tongue out. And there are a lot of people in here. Got the elderly guys sitting ringside who I'm guessing are the judges. Other fighters shaking out their nerves for later bouts. A crowd of spectators, but I can't see Nelson anywhere. A couple of blokes wearing suits in this heat, they must be scouts. That, or they're mental.

Shapiro looks my way; I nod at him. He doesn't acknowledge me, looks back to the fighters. The ref is in place, Liam and the Latino in their separate corners. The ref announces them both, Liam's opponent as Lorenzo Puentes. It's a boxer's name, but that's as far as this kid's ever going to get. The boxers come to the middle, knock gloves.

And there's the bell.

Liam and Puentes come out slow and circle each other. Not much going on, the two of them sizing each other up. Liam keeps his head low, his hands up.

I stand to get a better view as a guy in a sports jacket walks in front of me. He's got a bottle of water in one hand. For a second, I think it's Nelson, but that quickly disappears. This guy is taller, blonde hair turning to grey. Powerfully built and well-dressed, this guy has to be a scout.

'You know the Latino kid?' I say.

He takes a gulp of water, says, 'Lorenzo Puentes. And he's Mexican.'

Like that makes a lick of difference to me. Unless Mexicans are known for being a race of killers. So I ask, 'He any good?'

'Yeah, he's good.' He gestures towards the ring. 'Be even better if he could keep his damn feet on the ground.'

I look across at the fight. Puentes has stopped with the circling, losing patience. Busy now dancing around the ring, throwing moves. Showboating. Liam's still hunched up, biding his time. Or it looks like he's biding his time. He could just be petrified.

In the middle of the dance, Puentes lunges. He backs up quick as Liam bobs out of the way and counters with a swift, darting jab. Then Liam ducks in, taps Puentes in the ribs. Shifts fast as Puentes covers, knocks another jab with his glove, then Liam hooks a left across his opponent's nose. Puentes weathers it, but keeps his distance. Just at a glance, it's easy to see the Mexican has a bigger reach and he's now looking forward to using it. They part, Puentes breathing heavily. Liam doesn't look like he's broken a sweat.

'That's the thing with these bouts,' says the water guy. 'No stamina.'

Liam pushes forward to Puentes, the Mexican trying to get some boxing room. Puentes throws a right hand lead and Liam's under it, lays a one-two that devastates Puentes. The Mexican kid drops back three staggered steps – *tha-thump-thump* – as Liam digs in. A wild punch under the ribs and Liam's gloves come up. Puentes' face is twisted behind his gloves, his body twisting too, dropping to one side as Liam forces him into the ropes.

'Jesus,' says the water guy.

The ref lets the infighting go for a few seconds, both fighters scoring weak punches. Puentes wraps his arms around Liam.

And then it's 'Break! Break!' from the ref.

Puentes pushes Liam in the shoulders. Liam backs up a few considered steps. He knocks his gloves together, lets his left drop to one side. Puentes finds his feet, but he's stopped dancing. That was a lesson learned. If this kid had been told the bout would be a piece of piss, he's found out different now. Because Puentes can dance all he wants but it won't last long. Liam's cutting the ring, backing the Mexican into the ropes.

It takes a second for Puentes to switch tactics. He paws at his singlet, chews on his gum shield and slows down. His head bobs, like he knows the moves, he's been here before and he wants Liam to know it. But he's not ready to throw anything at the moment. Puentes looks a lot heavier now, his feet more assured.

Circling again.

I expected more, having seen the lads sparring at Paulo's, but then this bout isn't about knocking the other guy down. This is about scoring points, landing blows clean and square. It's boxing, not fighting. That's what I was told.

And then Liam proves me wrong. Vicious and shoddy, a jab to Puentes' headgear, throwing him off-balance. Liam steams in, gets a couple of half-hearted jabs to the body for his troubles. Liam twists out of the way, planting an angry punch against the side of the Mexican's neck.

The bell rings and they break.

Puentes hangs his head, shaking. Liam retreats to his corner, slumps to his stool and Reuben gets busy with the water. From what I can see, apart from a few red marks on his torso, Liam's clean.

'Longest two minutes of that kid's life,' says the water guy.

'He doesn't know who he's dealing with.'

'Three more rounds to stand upright.'

'They'll give him an eight count,' I say.

'Not this kid. He's warming up.'

'Take all the time he wants warming up, mate. He'll be down before he hits his peak.'

The water guy looks at me. 'You know something I don't?'

'I've seen this lad fight before.'

'Wooley?'

'Yeah.'

'And?'

'And this Puentes kid's going to have his arse handed to him on a platter.'

The water guy smiles and looks back at the ring. 'You think so.'

'I know so.'

'Where you from?' he says. 'Britain?'

I watch Liam and Puentes pull themselves out of their respective corners as the bell goes again. 'Britain's not a country.'

'Sure it is.'

'Scotland's got its own parliament; Wales is on the way.'

'Right,' he says and swigs water. 'I guess it's like the difference between Latino and Mexican, isn't it?'

Liam and Puentes stalk each other. Puentes looks like he's soiled himself. His nose is red, might be bleeding.

'You got a fighter?' I say, getting into it now.

He nods. 'Kind of. My son's competing.'

'Really?'

Puentes throws a couple of weak punches, his face solid with determination. Liam takes them, rolls with them, doesn't fight back. Waits for a singular opportunity, just like Paulo taught him.

'Yeah, I think he's got a good chance,' says the water guy.

Liam shifts his weight, feints a right, scores with a left. Then a scalding right. Thick, wet slaps of the ten-ounce gloves. Then Liam drops his left, turns his body and keeps his right hand up.

'What's his name?' I say. 'I'll watch out for him.'

Puentes sees an opening on Liam's dropped left . . .

'Josh Callahan,' says the water guy.

. . . and lets loose with a cannonball right. It's a loud, nasty blow that cuts through the crowd's babbling, draws breath from spectators. Liam catches it right in the nose, a dirty exhalation as he stumbles, his guard all over the shop. Puentes fires forward, jackhammers uppercuts into Liam's ribcage. He's caught Liam without feet, wants to get as much pain in there as possible before the lad can shake off the blur. Liam doubles up, his elbows tucked into his midriff. Trying to ride it out but not knowing how. Puentes has lost the bounce, his energy battering Liam's gut. Liam backs into the ropes, plants his feet firm.

Puentes curls a left at Liam's head.

And there's that opportunity.

As the ref moves towards them, Liam responds to Puentes with a swift rib shot that hits like a stiletto blade. Makes the Mexican back the fuck up. Liam pulls himself out of the line of fire, bearing down on his opponent. He catches a gulp of air and slams a glove hard in Puentes' gut.

Breathing's key, I heard. Breathing's what keeps your game going. Tear the breath from your opponent and dig in.

'He your son?' says Callahan Senior.

'No.' Wishing he'd shut the fuck up.

'Brother?'

'What?'

Liam alternates head and gut, sets the Mexican lad up to batter him raw. Knowing he'll score more nasty with the gut and chest, ripping the oxygen from the kid's lungs. Puentes can't seem to pull himself away, can't defend himself. And they're not hugged, so there's no break. Puentes starts to curl like plastic in a flame.

'It's over,' says Callahan.

'He's just getting warmed up, you said.'

Josh's dad shakes his head. 'They're going to call it.'

Puentes' corner man is hanging over the ropes. The ref steps into the breach. Liam staggers away, head still going. He wants more. He wants to finish the fucking job.

But that's it. The fat lady sings long and loud. Reuben's shouting at Liam to get the fuck back to his corner. Puentes slumps onto his stool, Liam still standing there, glaring at him. His right glove is up, his left down again. Like, *I can take you with one fuckin' hand, come ahead, man.*

It's over. Liam seems to hear Reuben and the fight drains out of him. His right glove drops as he backs to his corner. Reuben's in his face now, doesn't look too happy even though his boy just won.

No, it was Paulo's boy that just won. My boy.

'Mismatch,' says Callahan.

'Yeah,' I say.

He swigs his water, screws the cap onto the bottle. 'It won't be a mismatch with Josh.'

Callahan strides away across the club. I watch him go. Josh is in the crowd. I didn't see him before, but he's staring at the ring. Looks nervous.

Good.

I grab Liam's bag and head over to congratulate him.

SEVENTEEN

'How'd it go then?'

The slight delay on the line is enough to grate, especially when I forget about it and end up having to repeat myself to Paulo. It didn't matter so much the other night when I was drunk. Courtesy goes out of the window then. But now Paulo sounds excited and far away, which is exactly what he is. And he's just as frustrated as I am when we speak over each other, that hiss on the line, an echo somewhere.

'I told you,' I say. 'He won. They called it.'

A pause, then: 'They called it?'

'Yeah, they had to.'

Another pause. 'He didn't go nuts, did he?'

'Nothing to worry on that score.'

I look across at Liam. He's sitting on the bed, his hands in his lap, staring at something out of the window. When he came out of the ring, he had a sweat on and a lot of snot in his nose. But no victory dance. The lad had always been cocky in the past, but once the bout was over, it was a complete U-turn of emotion. You'd have thought Liam lost. Me, I don't know what the fuck is up with him. I'd be doing cartwheels right now.

'How many rounds?' says Paulo.

'Two.'

'They called it after two?'

'They had to.'

The hiss on the line. Sounds like Paulo sniffs. 'I thought you said he didn't go nuts.'

'This other kid, he thought it'd be an easy bout, I'm telling you.

He didn't have his head on right, thought he could score for his pasa-fuckin'-doble. Liam took him apart.'

'He there?'

'Liam?'

'No, the other kid. Yes, Liam. He's there, I want to speak to him.'

'Okay.'

I hold the phone out to Liam, who shakes his head. I keep the receiver held out, give him a look. Fuck's up with this kid? He should be on that phone like a fly on shit, bragging about his first big win. But he's just sitting there, eyes wide and blue. Too calm, too slow for my liking. I start thinking he got hit one too many times in the head.

'Paulo wants to speak to you,' I say, loud enough for Paulo to hear.

Liam frowns, pulls himself from the bed and snatches the phone from my hand. Petulant little bastard. I move over to the window, feel an ache throb its way up my back. Check my watch: if it's time in Manchester, it's time here. I fumble out a couple of pills as Liam holds the phone to his ear.

'Y'alright, Paulo?' he says.

A pause as Paulo talks.

Then: 'Yeah. They called it.'

I dry-swallow the painkillers.

'Nah,' says Liam. 'I didn't.'

I wonder why I didn't see Nelson, wonder if he actually turned up at all. Yeah, I left him a message on his mobile, but that's no guarantee he made it to the gym. The way he was last night, it's entirely possible he's still nursing a killer hangover. I'm surprised I don't have one. A year ago, I'd be in the bathroom praying to a Lord I didn't believe in.

'Okay,' says Liam. 'I know, Paulo. No, I know.'

The more I think about it, the more I think we need someone else on our side here. Might just be that uneasy feeling of being in another country, but Nelson was picking at something last night. And that something was probably true, not some rumour. The hard and nasty truth is something most people don't want to spill. Rumours have their own method of transport, and it's normally fast. So if Shapiro isn't straight, then this comp is going to mean fuck-all when it comes down to it. And then there's Josh's dad. Taking an active interest as a parent is one thing, but Josh wasn't about until the fight was finished. No, that guy likes the sport.

'Okay, alright, fine,' says Liam. 'I'll see you later.'

Liam holds out the phone to me. His face is blazing red. I think it could be the first hit of sunburn. There's no respite in Los Angeles.

'Y'alright?' I say.

He nods, but his bottom lip moves a little.

'You should be proud of yourself, mate. You took the Puentes kid down.'

He looks at me, his eyes narrowing. 'Fuck do you know?'

'You what?'

'Fuckin' forget it.' He stalks out of the room, leaves me with the phone.

'What's up?' I say to Paulo. 'What'd you say to him? Lad's got a strop on.'

'Doesn't matter,' he says.

'Matters to me, man. I've got to spend time with him.'

'I just told him what he was there for, Cal.'

'And he's doing it.'

'A two-round stoppage? That's not boxing, Cal. That's fight-ing—'

'Puentes was taking the piss—'

'I want him to win because he's a good boxer, not because he's an animal. We worked it out, him and me.'

'C'mon, he's just had to spend all that time with me. Stands to reason he's got some frustration to work out, doesn't it?'

'Then he should be working it out in training, not in the ring.'

'You know what, you could be fuckin' proud of him. And how's *your* temper, by the way?'

A pause, Paulo thinking it over. 'I'm good.'

'You're good. You managed to calm down.'

'Mo's been about.'

'You called the police?'

'No.'

'Then call the police.'

'I'm not calling the police.'

I shift the phone to my other ear, sit down at the desk. I want a cigarette. Half think about taking the phone into the bathroom so I can light one, then decide against it. 'Call the police, Paulo. I mean it. If Mo's acting like a twat, let the coppers sort it out and get him locked up. He's got no protection now, man. He basically told me that. So get him locked up for the first time in his life, see how he likes it.'

'He told you that?'

'What?'

'When'd you speak to Mo?'

Fuck. *Fuck*. Hoping I could keep that under wraps, and look at it come spilling out.

'I talked to him,' I say.

'Before or after I caught him dealing?' says Paulo. 'Actually, no, don't answer that – it doesn't matter. What're you doing talking to Mo Tiernan?'

'I went to see him.'

'After,' he says.

'Yeah, after. I had a word with him.'

'What was the word?'

'I just told him to stay away from the club.' I *need* a cigarette now. 'Let him know what kind of situation he was in, y'know, with his dad and that. Reminded him that he didn't have a leg to stand on if he wanted to play funny buggers.'

'And you don't think the beating I doled out told him that already?'

'Paulo—'

'You don't think I can handle this by myself, Cal?'

I sigh. I have to choose my words carefully, can feel the rage on the other end of the phone. 'I know you can, mate.'

'Good.'

'I just don't think you'll handle it the way you want to.'

'The fuck does that mean?'

'It means I'm not the only one who's head's been in the shed recently, alright?'

'You let me handle this, Cal.'

'What else am I going to do? Not like I can hop a fuckin' bus and get home now, is it?'

'Yeah, that's a good thing.'

I bite a hangnail from my thumb. 'Just be careful, alright?'

'Yeah, right,' he says. 'I'll be careful. You just make sure Liam doesn't do anything bloody stupid. I want that lad to be winning on points, okay? He shouldn't be knocking heads. He can knock heads in Manchester all he likes, but it's a different game over there, especially at that level. He's supposed to have some control. That's what I told Phil.'

'He does have control, man. All I'm saying, he was probably a bit wound up.'

'Then unwind him.' Paulo breathes out heavily. 'I'm starting to think you were right, y'know. Maybe I should've gone over there with him.'

Because I can't handle it? I have to pause before I talk to him. 'I'm working on something,' I say.

'Yeah, the guy you met in a bar. Water's full of sharks, Cal.'

'This guy seems alright.' Wanting to add that Shapiro's the one he should be worried about. But there's no point in getting Paulo worked up over something he can't change. I've yet to feel my way with Shapiro, don't want to jump to any conclusions, even though it's not a long way to jump. 'But I'll be careful.'

'Okay then. Keep an eye on Liam, let me know what happens.'

'I will. And Paulo, look, if Mo turns up, just call the fuckin' police, eh?'

Paulo hangs up, leaving me with silence, then a purr.

Which I hope is a yes, Cal, of course I'll call the police, Cal.

EIGHTEEN

The place calls itself a ristorante, but it's about as Italian as an Aldi pizza. If the waitress who staggered up to our table is anything to go by, the staff are either genetically retarded or high as kites. I found myself checking for tracks on her arms, looking for her pupils. From the look she gave me, I put her down as retarded and bitter. It was safer that way.

But I still don't trust the food in here. If the waitress is the public face of the place, then I dread to think what the cook looks like. Probably a one-eyed, crack-addicted yeti.

Yeah, I'm in a bad mood. My blood's too thick for the kind of heat they have in this country. It's reptile climate and I'm all mammal. Been sweating since we touched down and it's not from lack of medication, either. Since I called Nelson, see if he wanted to meet up for lunch, I've been trying to ration out my prescription. Knowing full well I'll have an awful time of it once I get back to Manchester, but also knowing that if I don't keep necking the pills, I won't be able to move.

But I was good. I didn't neck anything. Rationing. I did well and I'm still walking. So I'm celebrating with a beer or two. Nelson's opposite me. He's scarfed down a pizza that looked like it had been used as a dartboard at one point in its long and miserable life, and now he's bent over a pot of tiramisu.

'Hangover cure to end all hangover cures,' he says, pointing at the brown mess with his spoon. 'You got sugar, coffee, eggs, cheese and the hair of the dog that bit me.'

'Literally in this place, Nelson.'

He looks around the restaurant and smiles. 'Ah, well, it used to be a great place. Owned by an Italian guy for a start. You'd think that was the prerequisite for an Italian restaurant, wouldn't you? Guy called Stella. Big guy, great sense of humour. Real Italian, like super-Italian, played opera and Dino, liked his sports. Great place.' He taps the bowl with his spoon. 'Great tiramisu, too. Used to be right up there with California Pizza Kitchen and Macaroni Grill.'

'Can't say I've tried them.' I sip my beer.

'I'll take you to the pizza place. There's a guy there, Oscar, he owes me a favour.'

'Okay.' I put the beer bottle on the table. 'So what'd you think about the fight?'

Nelson told me he was there. Turns out I was too busy talking to Josh's dad and watching Liam knock the shit out of Puentes to pay much attention to the rest of the crowd. But Nelson was there.

'I'm still hungover,' he says, mushing up his tiramisu. 'So my judgement may be off.'

'Judgement's judgement.'

Nelson sets the spoon to one side. 'I think he's got it in him. Definitely. He's pro material. But I was under the impression he was controlled. Didn't look that way to me.'

I shake my head. 'His first bout, Nelson. The lad's got a lot on his mind.'

'Then he needs to get it off his mind.' Nelson waves the thought away. 'Okay, no, he's got a lot on his mind. Throw in the flight, kid hasn't got time to adjust, you got jet lag, he's not going to be on top form. That's fine, I'll accept that. Way I see it, your boy Liam's got enough raw talent in him, he can go into a bout with the wrong strategy and he'll still probably win.'

I hold the bottle of beer to my forehead to curb sweat, then take a drink.

'I say that – he'll probably win – but he'll take more hits than he should. And I don't need to tell you, if he keeps doing that, his career'll be shorter than most.'

'He doesn't have a career,' I say.

'He will, given the right counselling.' Nelson goes back to his tiramisu.

'You up for it?'

He smiles, chews. 'I've got nothing better to do, Cal. And it sounds like you need all the help you can get.'

'You could say that.' Another swig from the beer. 'I can't talk to the lad, Nelson. I ask him what's wrong, he doesn't answer me or he tells me to go fuck myself. I feel like a parent and I didn't even get the fun of conception. This trip was supposed to be a holiday for me, y'know?'

'You look like you still need one.'

'I do, mate. But I don't know what I'm going to do.' I lean back in my seat. 'You want to talk to him?'

'I don't know, Cal . . .'

'He's more likely to listen to you than he is me. You've been in the game, you're carrying the experience. He might listen to that.'

Nelson looks at me for a long time, says, 'You don't want him to screw this up.'

'Course I don't. I got things I need to sort out. I don't want to be worried about him, do I?'

'Of course you don't.'

'I help this lad, give him a break and it works out, it'll be great for all of us. We go back to Manchester local heroes and we get the ticker-tape parade, pictures in the rag, the whole lot. And we might not get on, him and me, but that doesn't mean I need to piss on his chips and tell him it's vinegar, know what I mean?' I stare at the bottle in my hand. 'I don't know, Nelson. I just don't see this working out well without you.'

Nelson pushes his tiramisu to one side, puts his elbows on the table. 'It'll be fine. And I think you care a lot more about that kid than you let on.'

'Right, Nelson.'

'Once all this is over with, I'm sure he'll pick up on that.'

'Yeah, well,' I say. 'He can send me a card or something.'

*

Back at the hotel, I take Nelson up to Liam's room, but the lad isn't there. If he is, he's not answering my knock. I step back from the door.

'He should be here,' I say.

'Look, if it's a bad time, we can arrange it for tomorrow.'

'Nah, he really should be here.'

Nelson follows me into my room and I tell him to make himself comfortable. He sits on the bed and looks around. 'Nice.'

I pick up the phone, call Liam's room. No answer. Then I call reception. 'This is Mr Innes. I don't suppose you've seen the lad I checked in with, have you? His name's Liam Wooley.'

'Mr Wooley left a message for you.'

'He left me a message,' I say to Nelson. He nods.

'Mr Innes? Mr Wooley said he's gone to train.'

'Train? Where?'

'Uh, he didn't say.'

'Okay, thanks.' I'm about to put the phone down when I say, 'Actually, sorry, no. I'm his driver. He's supposed to tell me if he needs to go somewhere.'

'Well, we called a cab for him.'

'Where was it going?'

'I don't know,' says the receptionist.

'It's okay,' I say. 'I think I know anyway. Thanks a lot.'

I hang up. Stand there, Nelson watching me.

'What?' he says.

'He's gone to the bloody gym. He's gone back to Shapiro's to train. You want to come along?'

Nelson checks his watch and pulls a pained face. 'Ah hell, I can't, Cal. I've got to be somewhere. Sorry.'

'Not a problem,' I say.

'Can we reschedule? Tomorrow morning?'

'Yeah, he's got another bout tomorrow night, I think. I'll have to check. But yeah, I'll do that, give you a ring on your mobile, maybe we can go out for breakfast or something.'

Nelson stands up, offers his hand. 'Deal.'

NINETEEN

By the time I get to Shapiro's place, the air has cooled off. I get out of the Metro, walk from the parking lot to the gym. Light a cigarette on the way, counting them off. This is the sixth Marlboro I've had today and it's, what, getting on for five o'clock? That's a good day for my health. Paulo would be proud.

I grind the cigarette into the concrete as I approach the gym. The lights are permanently burning here, but as I step inside it's apparent that there can't be more than half a dozen people about. It makes Liam easier to spot. He's working the heavy bag. As I head towards him, he glances at me and slows the workout. When I reach the bag, he moves away.

'That's it, keep it up, son,' I say. 'How long are you going to keep the spoilt kid act up, Liam?'

He doesn't answer me, takes a gulp of water and swills it around his mouth before he swallows. Cricks his neck, then eyes the bag like he's ready to knock a hole through it.

'I asked you a question.'

'I'm training,' he says.

'If you're training, where's Reuben?'

'He doesn't have to be here all the time. You go off, get drunk, whatever you have to do. I'm training.'

'You had a bout today. You don't need to train. You need to rest. Got another one tomorrow, you're going to be sparked out.'

'That's not the way it works, Cal. You knew the first thing about this, you'd know that.' Liam shifts his weight, plants two in the heavy bag, then another two. 'Fuck do you care, anyway?'

'I care because I'm supposed to be keeping an eye on you, son. And you fuck off at the first opportunity.'

'You weren't there.' Building up a rhythm now, hammering the bag so hard it would break a weaker lad's wrists. 'I don't need a babysitter, anyway.'

'And I don't need to wipe any arses, Liam. But the fact is, I had someone who wanted to meet you today and you weren't there. You want to keep tabs on your career, mate. You want to start using your brain instead of throwing a hissy fit because you don't like me.'

Liam loses the rhythm. Frustration creases his face. 'Fuck off. Just leave us alone.'

'I'm supposed to drive you about. Let me do it.'

He holds up his gloves. 'I'm trying to get some work done here, alright? You want to have this conversation, right, we'll have it some other time.'

'You should've called me.'

'I needed to train and—'

'You needed to work out some temper tantrum because Paulo gave you a rough ride,' I say. 'And it looks like you haven't worked it out yet.'

'Here, Paulo was right,' he says, wiping his nose on his glove.

I look at the floor for a second and fold my arms. 'Yeah, he's right. But Paulo's got his own shite on at the moment. He's always been a bit mental, you ask me. And you know that.'

'I know.'

'So what's the deal? You going to keep spitting at me or what? Cause if that's the case, then fine. I'll wipe the tears and try to live the rest of my life. But I still think you should meet this guy. I think it'd be helpful for you. The bloke used to be pro, coaches a little, definitely knows his stuff. It can't hurt for you to talk to him, at least. Make me out to be less of a Tagalong Timmy, eh?'

'Tagalong Timmy?' Liam's face cracks a little. Christ, almost a smile. Would you credit it.

'Is that a yes?'

'He'll be a bampot, Cal. Paulo told us about it.'

'Yeah, and if you think he's a bampot, then you tell me. I'll get rid of the guy, no harm done. I'm the one that talked to him in the first place. I'll just tell him you're not interested, make some excuse that makes me out to be the dickhead I am and that'll be it.'

'Nah, I don't think so,' says Liam.

'You're not even going to chance it, are you?'

'I'll stick to the original plan.'

'Fine,' I say. 'That's fine. But I'll be fucked if you're getting a cab back to the hotel. I'm parked up the street and I'll be waiting outside. You let me know when you're finished, alright?'

'I'll be a while.'

'You be as long as you want, son. I'll be outside.'

I turn on my heel, let him get on with his precious bloody training. And I almost light a cigarette before I'm out the door.

So I *was* having a healthy day. Six cigarettes, and try bumping it up another ten because there's nothing else to do apart from sit on the wall outside the gym and smoke. Takes me back to my school days.

Light starts to creep from the sky, leaving it dark blue turning to black. Cloud or smog or smoke knits a blanket over the stars and I get to thinking about what Nelson said. This place with its smog and halogen, where you could watch the planes head out across the ocean to fight some war you'd read about in the papers or heard on the radio. Days long gone. Now every part of LA looks like every other part of LA. The kind of shabby you see in an aging beauty queen who thought a pageant would change her life. Down the street there's a liquor store with bars on the window. I feel like getting up, rubbing the ache out of my lower back, taking a stroll down there and buying whatever brand of vodka I recognise. But that would mean deserting my post, and that can't happen. I know Liam'll be out the moment I'm gone. The way he's been, I wouldn't put it past him to walk rather than take a lift from me.

Lad's got a cob on about something. Same as Paulo, like everyone I know's gone mental. Not surprising, considering the tension. The idea of Mo Tiernan sniffing about the club back home doesn't exactly fill me with calm, I have to say. I thought Mo and I had gone through what we needed to go through. Back in the toilets, back in Newcastle, even before that when I headbutted him in front of a pub full of people because he was trying to put the fucking screws on my brother.

Mo's a nuisance. He's thickheaded. And like I said to Paulo, he's got no protection. I just hope the big man doesn't do anything stupid.

There's movement behind me. I turn, thinking it's going to be Liam, but Reuben steps out, light reflecting from his head. He's supposed to be helping Liam out with his training. I want to ask him what the fuck he's playing at, but I keep my mouth shut. What the hell, the way I see it going, Reuben's not going to be Liam's trainer much longer. Not if I can persuade Liam to sit down with Nelson.

'Y'alright?' I say with a nod.

Reuben pulls out a pack of cigarettes and lights one. The flame catches, illuminating his sagging features. 'I'm okay.'

'Phil doesn't let you smoke in there, eh?'

'No.'

'Same with my guy,' I say. 'I'm stuck in the back office with the window open. They're making martyrs out of us.'

'Huh.'

Silence. I take a drag from my cigarette, blow smoke. 'Hell of a fight today.'

'Today?' Reuben comes over and takes a seat on the wall. Not too close. 'Yeah, hell of a fight. Your boy's got some technique. Still rough, though.'

'You think?'

Reuben lets his left arm hang, points to it. 'He keeps his left at his waist. Bad habit to get into. The boy's on the offensive, that's his strength. He likes to get in there hard and fast, but that left, man. That'll get him into a whole lot of trouble.'

'I'm sure he'll be fine.' Thinking, I'll pass that on to Nelson, see what he makes of it.

'No, he needs to tighten his defence,' says Reuben. 'That low left, even pros shouldn't do it. It's a showboat move. He can't be giving away fifty percent of his defence like that. He *really* wants to keep his left down, he's gotta learn to roll his body or block with the right, else his opponent's gonna sneak in there like Puentes did.'

'He'll learn.'

'I got him working on it.' He shows me. 'Keep it up. Keep a tight guard, play peek-a-boo, you get me?'

'I taught him everything he knows,' I say.

Reuben drops his hands and smiles. 'Yeah, I'm sure you did.'

'Cal,' I say.

'Reuben,' he says, like I don't already know. 'Call me Rube and I'll cut your throat.'

'Good to meet you, Reuben. You work here long?'

'A while.'

'Enjoy your work?'

'Hell is this, an interview? You gonna offer me a job?'

'Just chit-chat, Reuben.' I drop my filter, grind it out. Light another. 'Small talk.'

'Sure.'

'You see a lot of these competitions?' I say.

'We do some here, yeah.'

'Shapiro have a hand in all of them?'

Reuben stares at me. 'You want to ask something, pal, you just come right out and ask it, okay?'

I smile, do my best innocent expression. 'Sorry, mate, I was just—'

'Making small talk, I know. Seems to me the talk ain't small enough, though.'

'Hey, I didn't mean anything.'

'You want to talk about bigger things.'

'There's nothing you can tell me about Phil Shapiro I don't already know.'

'That so.'

'Yup.' I blow some more smoke, watch it drift. 'I know he was a hell of a fighter in his day.'

'His day ain't over. And he ain't a guy who takes ball-busting well.'

'I noticed that.'

'That's good. Because all these questions, you're sounding like a cop. And you ain't a fuckin' cop, are you?'

'No, I'm not a cop.'

'Then quit it with the first degree. You sound like you're trying to dig dirt.'

'Is there dirt to dig then?'

Reuben takes a few puffs from his cigarette and drops it to the ground, half-smoked. 'Yeah, good to meet you too, Cal. Let's do this again sometime.'

He grunts as he gets off the wall, waddles back to the gym.

'Yeah, let's,' I say.

I grind out Reuben's still smoking cigarette.

TWENTY

Liam comes out of the gym with his bag slung over his shoulder. He looks relaxed, smug even. He should be, too – the bugger's kept me waiting three hours. Lucky for me I lost track of time. I get to my feet.

'You done?' I say.

Liam flinches. And now I know why he was looking smug. He thought I'd gone. 'Yeah, I'm finished.'

'Good.' I jerk my thumb up the street. 'Parked up a way. Hope you've got enough energy left for a walk.'

He nods. I don't offer to take his bag. He wants to keep me waiting, he can carry his own shit. As we walk, I keep my distance. Don't want to crowd him into another one of his moods. The street's deserted.

'You up for tomorrow then?' I say.

'Yeah.'

'You know the kid?'

'I seen him about.'

'What's he like?'

'Streak of piss.'

'That's the spirit. Hope you beat him to a pulp.'

'I can't do that, Cal. Straight and narrow.'

'Yeah, I forgot. Straight and narrow. Then beat him like that. You do that, you know who you're up against?'

'That arsehole from the other day,' he says.

'I didn't tell you, but I met his dad at your bout.'

'He was there?'

'Checking out the competition, must've been. I didn't see Josh turn up until you'd already pasted Puentes. And you know what? He looked worried as fuck. Watching you smack that kid around, he got a bit scared for his son's future well-being.'

Liam regards me, doesn't say anything. He keeps walking.

'And who's going to know his son but his father?'

'Uh-huh.'

When I look at him, Liam's staring at something in the distance. I follow his line of sight. Up by the car park, there's three lads and a girl standing round a couple of expensive-looking motors. After a moment's lapse in Liam's pace, he speeds up. I have to stride to keep up with him. Liam's face has dropped into that scally stone I've seen too many times.

As we draw nearer, it's obvious why he's putting on the attitude. Josh Callahan, standing around with his buddies. One of the lads is big, wide, looks like a quarterback. The other's weedy. The girl looks like she's had her fair share of frat-boy fingers. She's blonde, barely dressed, sitting on the bonnet of an Audi. In her fist is a pint of Wild Turkey. The quarterback takes the bottle from her as we approach. It's the American version of a bus shelter posse turned rich and proud.

And mouthy.

'Jesus Christ, if it isn't the Brit,' says Josh at the top of his lungs.

'How *are* you, old bean?' says the weedy lad, sticking his top teeth out in some drunken fucking parody. 'By Jove, sir—'

'Keep walking,' I say to Liam.

But the flame's already caught, made his cheeks rise red. He's burning.

'Liam, Liam, I hear you fucked up the Mexican, man.' Josh peels away from his mates. A swagger in his walk.

'*Dios mio*, Josh, motherfucker's a taco-banger,' says the weedy lad.

The quarterback takes a long pull on the Wild Turkey, almost chokes on his laughter. Yeah, the weedy lad's definitely the joker in the group.

'No, man, he didn't kiss him first. You didn't kiss him, did you, Liam?'

Liam stops in his tracks. I nudge him to move; he doesn't.

'I hear you fucked Puentes good, man.' Josh moves forward now he's got Liam's attention, his voice dropping a notch below a yell. He busts a few combos that look inebriated. 'I hear you slaughtered him in the old one-two-three – *wop, wop, wop . . .*'

'. . . or *spic, spic, spic,*' says the joker. That twat's getting on my last nerve. Doesn't help that the blonde girl's giggling. I get the feeling she'd giggle if someone set her on fire. Wouldn't mind giving it a try, either.

'That the way they teach you in England, man?' Josh screws his face up. 'They just tell you, "hit the bloke, mate"? That's no fuckin' technique.'

The joker flaps his hand for the bottle of whiskey. The quarterback takes another drink and passes it over.

Josh runs his tongue inside his bottom lip. 'You try that shit on me, I'm gonna be dancing you to your fuckin' death, man.' He feints a left. 'Down in one – *bang.*'

'He won't get past Charlie, man,' says the quarterback.

'Yeah, man, you got *Charlie.* Charlie's a wop gonna fuck you up. And if he doesn't, then you came over here for three fights and you'll be going home in a wheelchair.'

'How's about you stow the WWF shite, son?' I say.

'Liam, your boyfriend talks a lot of shit. You want to step in for the baby, my man?'

Liam pushes in front of me.

'C'mon,' he says.

Just that. Soft. Deliberate.

'Liam,' I say.

'Nah, Cal. The cunt's been wanting a slap since the moment I saw him. Now's his chance.'

The joker swigs whiskey and grips the bottle that little bit harder. This isn't going to end well. Everyone squaring up like it's *West Side fucking Story.* This is going to end with the pair of us in hospital and no medical insurance. This is going to end with me explaining to Paulo how his star pupil ended up with a bunch of expensive stitches in his head and chucked out of a competition when I had the opportunity to nip it in the bud.

Josh rolls his shoulders. The blonde girl giggles again, starts clapping. I want to snap her fingers off and stick them in Josh's eyes. Because the blonde rich lad has the same glazed expression of every violent drunk I've ever met.

'You want me to tell your father where you've been, Josh?' I say.

He doesn't look at me – too busy glaring at Liam – and says, 'You don't know my father.'

'Yeah, I do. I met him at Liam's bout. You take after him. He looks like a fuckin' lightweight, too.'

Josh snaps his attention to me. 'The fuck you know about my father, man? Look at you. My father wouldn't talk to you. You look like a fuckin' hobo.'

'Let me handle this,' says Liam.

'You lads need to calm down,' I say. 'Otherwise you're both out the comp, you know that.'

'He shouldn't be in the comp in the first place,' says Josh. 'We've already been through that.'

'Then you prove it in a couple of days.'

'I'll prove it now. I don't give a shit.'

More clapping from the girl.

'Why? So you can wake up tomorrow with your face on the pillow next to you? Don't be a prat, son.'

'*Prat*,' says the joker. 'Fuckin' asshole.'

I can't help myself. I grab the joker by the neck of his T-shirt, pull him round and push him hard up against the side of the Audi. Grind his face into the roof. The girl shrieks and jumps off the car – violence too up close and personal for her. I keep an eye on the quarterback in my peripheral. He's standing, arms heavy by his sides. I wish I had a knife or something I could show them, scare the bollocks off them.

'What'd you call me?' I pull on the weedy lad's hair, slam his head against the roof. He drops the Wild Turkey, bottle clinking and rolling onto the street.

'*Jesus*, man.' Blood is welling up in his bottom lip.

'You're a hard lad, are you?' I stare at the quarterback. 'You a hard lad, too?'

'Jesus fuckin' Christ, let go of me.'

'Let go of him,' says Josh.

'You're a hard lad, the man-child over there's a hard lad, Josh is a hard lad and Liam's a hard lad. And guess what? I'm a fuckin' hard lad, too. Except I don't have Phil Shapiro to worry about. So how about you and Josh calm it down and knock the shite on the head, alright? Else I'll put your fuckin' heads together.'

'Let him go,' says Josh. His voice shakes.

'You sobered up now, son?'

'Just let him go, okay?'

I raise my hands empty. Josh's mate stays leaning against the roof of the car, too scared to move. I turn to Josh. 'You want to sort this out, you do it like Shapiro said. You do it in the ring. You can't do that, you'll have me to deal with. And I might look like a streak of piss, but I'm a streak of piss you don't want in your life. Cause I'll buy a cricket bat and take it to your fuckin' knees.'

Josh bends over, picks up the Wild Turkey. He swills what's left in the bottom of the bottle. 'You don't want to fuck with me, mister.'

'Is that so, Richie Rich? You going to buy an army to wipe me out?'

'I'm telling you,' he says. 'I'm warning you.'

I smile, push past him. 'I been told and warned by people who could shit you without grunting. So get yourself home and sleep it off. You'll need all the energy you can get when my boy Liam kicks your fuckin' arse.'

Liam follows me to the car, leaving the Josh Posse behind. I slip behind the wheel as Liam gets in the passenger side. He has to slam the door three times before it stays closed.

'That bloody door,' I say. 'Remind me on, Liam. I need to talk to the rental place.'

I start the engine, pull out of the car park, wave at Josh as we pass. He's leaning against the Audi, his joker mate dabbing at his bottom lip with his fingers. Once we're on the road, I turn on the radio. A whispering, gravel-voiced DJ is playing 'white hot blues till the orange dawn', which is just fine with me. I turn it up. I try to ignore my shaking hands, the agony in my back. I shouldn't have been so fucking physical, but it was the only way. I couldn't touch Josh, not without a whole hurricane of shite heading my way. And that lippy fucker got what he deserved. So hopefully I proved my point and I wouldn't have to slip a disc proving it again.

John Lee Hooker comes on the radio and I have to turn it off. He reminds me of someone I don't want to think about.

'Cal.'

'Yeah.'

'Thanks.'

I look at Liam; he's staring out the side window.

'No problem,' I say. 'You might want to think about staying away from the gym until tomorrow night, though.'

He nods. 'I've been having trouble focussing.'

'I'm not surprised, mate.' I glance at the road. 'You want to reconsider on what we talked about?'

Liam sighs. It turns into a low laugh.

'I'm just saying, Liam. If you're having trouble focussing, maybe this coach is what you need.' I look across at him. 'You can't do this on your own. Nobody's expecting you to. And I'm no good to you, am I? So we need some help, and Nelson's the bloke who can maybe deliver that help. You want to stay on the straight, that's what he'll be there for – keep you focused. Then I get to have my holiday, you get to have your career and everybody's happy.'

Liam smiles with one side of his mouth. 'I don't know, Cal.'

'Just, for me, just talk to him, okay? We'll have breakfast. My shout.'

He doesn't say anything, stares out of the window. I think he's a dead loss. There's nothing I can do to change his mind.

Then he says, 'If he's nuts, I walk.'

TWENTY-ONE

I set an alarm call for six, drag myself into the bathroom to get ready for the day. A quick glance at the television, and there's no more brush fires, no riots. Everything is hunky dory in the City of Angels and the sun is burning high in the blue. I wonder why people don't pray for rain, but then it's probably only the likes of me that misses Manchester rain, the kind that makes you think you're drowning as you walk. All this sun isn't good for my mental health, though it seems to be working on the parade of tanned, coiffeured presenters on the television. I close the door to the bathroom, sit on the toilet, smoke a Marlboro to the filter, drop the butt in the bowl, flush and hop into the shower. Hawk up a nasty greyish-green lump and spit it straight into the plughole. Life is good.

I called Nelson as soon as Liam and I got back to the hotel. When he answered, he sounded like he was dug in for the night at a bar. He assured me he was at home, and I didn't question him. Tried not to get worried, thinking that Nelson was no longer a boxer because he was a full-time alkie. I had room to talk, of course. And Paulo used to be a souse, so it wasn't a slur on the man's character. I just would've preferred Nelson clean and sober when he talked to Liam.

Which he is. After I've knocked on Liam, we meet Nelson down in the lobby and if the bloke's been on a bender, he's scrubbed himself beyond sober. It all feels like clockwork. Liam takes one look at the ginger guy and something clicks with him. I don't know how he pictured Nelson – probably some cheroot-chewing guy like Reuben – but looking like a clean ex-boxer obviously hadn't figured in his imagination.

'Liam,' says Nelson, sticking out a paw. 'I'm Nelson Byrne. I saw your bout yesterday.'

'You were there,' says Liam.

'Yeah.' He smiles full wattage. 'Cal asked me to pop by. Hope you don't mind.'

'Nah, I don't mind.'

'You hungry? I'm buying. Know a great place we can start the day off slow and easy.'

That place turns out to be a Denny's. I've heard of them, but never been in one. It's about the closest a lad from Leith is ever likely to get to a full American diner experience. We grab a tidy booth in the corner of the restaurant. I bury my nose in the menu while Nelson orders coffee for him and me, a herbal tea and orange juice for Liam. I'm leafing through the specials – food photos shot like hazy pornography – and my appetite comes roaring back.

'Let me ask you something, Liam,' says Nelson. His eyes haven't left Liam since we settled, like he's trying to size the lad up. 'Where d'you see yourself in five years' time?'

'Manchester,' says Liam, leaning back in his seat. Giving Nelson the same look he's getting. Or at least trying to.

'You still going to be fighting?'

'Dunno. Depends on how the comp goes.'

'Forget the competition for a second—'

'Can I smoke in here?' I say.

'No,' says Nelson. 'Not this table.'

'Shit.'

'I want you to forget the competition, Liam.'

'It's why I'm over here.'

'Yeah, but put it out of your mind for the time being. The competition's a way to get in there, but if it doesn't happen, there are other options.'

'Paulo said there's scouts at these things.'

'Doesn't mean they're going to pick you.'

'If I win—'

'If you win, they could pick the runner-up. See him as someone they can mould better. See, the competition, it isn't the be-all and end-all. So if you don't kick pro while you're here, what're you going to be doing in five years' time?'

'I'll still fight.'

'That's good. That's the answer I was after. You want to go pro?'

'Course I want to go pro. Kind of question's that, man?'

'It's a damn good question. Why?'

'Because of the money. And I want to be the best, Mr Byrne.'

'Call me Nelson.'

The waitress brings our coffee and Liam's tea and orange. Nelson sits back in his seat and smiles at the waitress until she leaves. Liam sips his orange juice.

'Did he answer right?' I say.

'He answered fine, Cal. You answered fine, Liam. Especially that second part. Any kid says he's not interested in the cash, he's lying through his damn teeth. A lot more think that's the only way to make the big bucks. And they're deluded. They're the kind of kids, they turn pro and get their asses beaten and the rest of them fleeced. They don't see dollar one. It's really only the managers who make money.'

'You ever manage?' says Liam.

The waitress returns. 'Can I take your order?'

Nelson orders, then me. Liam opts for an egg-white omelette that flusters the waitress for a second.

When the waitress leaves, Liam plays it like he's in control. 'I asked you a question.'

'I know you did.' Nelson smiles. 'No, I never managed. I coached. Not a lot. But I coached and I did my time as a cut man.'

'I'm asking because you don't seem to have many credentials.'

The smile wavers on Nelson's face. 'I boxed for ten years, kid. I don't need any credentials.'

Ah Christ, Liam, don't fuck this up. 'He's asking—'

'Nelson knows what I'm asking,' says Liam. 'Look, I'm sorry, Nelson. I got to ask you, know what I mean? All I know is you met Cal in a bar. And what does that tell us apart from you like a drink?'

'No, that's fine.' The smile's gone. 'I appreciate that. Cal just asked me if I could lend a hand.'

'And I'm not saying that's not welcome,' says Liam. 'I'm really not. I just have to be sure you're going to lend a *helping* hand.'

'You're suspicious still. That's okay.'

'I'm not suspicious.' Liam laughs. 'But, y'know, I've got to wonder about the type of bloke who offers his services in bars.'

'Liam, don't be a twat.' He said he'd talk to Nelson; he didn't say he'd talk to him like that.

'I'm not being a twat, Cal. Nelson, you see my fuckin' point, don't you?'

There's a long pause as Nelson looks at Liam. He reaches forward for a pack of Sweet 'N' Lo, shakes it, then tears it open and adds the contents to his coffee. He sips from the cup, sets it down.

'You need to stop being such a fighter, Liam,' he says. 'Battling all the time, you'll have no energy for the big ones.'

Our food arrives. Massive plates piled high. I get stuck into my Denver Scramble thinking, fuck it, I'm not going to get involved. If this goes tits up, it's Liam's fault. No one to blame but himself. I'm helping the lad out, but he's acting like he's the one doing *me* a favour. Bollocks to that. Dig your own grave, son.

'My next bout's—'

'Tonight,' says Nelson. 'So this could be academic, this talk.'

'You think it is, you can leave.'

'If I thought it was, I wouldn't be here.' Nelson studies his food, picks up a piece of toast and sinks his teeth into it. As he chews, he says, 'But I think you'll win tonight. You got Charlie Polito tonight, don't you?'

'That's the name.'

'You don't know his style?'

Liam shakes his head, pokes at his omelette. It looks disgusting, but then that's what you get when you forsake the yolk.

'Well, I do,' says Nelson. He brushes the crumbs from his hands. 'I'm not going to pretend I know all the kids taking part, but I know

Charlie Polito. And if you're not prepared, you won't see much of the next bout.'

'I'll take him.'

'I'm sure you will. That's not what I said. You'll see the next bout, but Polito'll open up a whole new bruise pattern on you. You ripped the breath out of Puentes, that's great, but Polito will do the same to you. And you'll lose the next bout, you'll be hurting.'

'I need a place to train,' says Liam, as if he hadn't heard. He sips his tea and avoids Nelson's stare.

'I have a gym at my place.'

'You've got a gym?'

'Yeah. At home. It's all good equipment. I still work out.'

Liam looks at me, then pokes his omelette some more. 'I don't know, Nelson.'

'Well, I'll tell you something, Liam. I don't know either.'

The silence is thick. They sit there, staring at each other.

'These are good eggs,' I say.

Liam shoves a forkful of omelette into his mouth, starts chewing. Drops his gaze again.

'I don't know,' says Nelson. He's still leaning back in his seat. Apart from the bite out of the toast, he hasn't touched his food. He reaches forward for his coffee. 'Seems to me like I'm having a job interview, Cal. Haven't had one of those in a long time, and I didn't like the bullshit then, either.'

I blink at Nelson. There's anger in his eyes, a new kind I haven't seen before. And then I realise why: he thinks the same as me, that Liam's trying to fuck this up on purpose, that's he's being a stroppy bastard because he wants to be the one controlling the situation. A wee power struggle that Nelson's not about to lose.

'Liam, something you're going to understand one day is that when you're offered help – and you *need* help – you take it without question.' Nelson sips his coffee. 'I came here in good faith, thought I'd do my duty and help out a kid with all the talent but none of the technique.'

'I got the technique.'

'If you want to spend the rest of your life brawling for pennies outside a fucking bar, yeah. But if you want to be a sportsman, Liam, you want to be an *athlete*, you're going to have to learn a little about discipline.'

'I got discipline.'

'That bout with the Mexican kid says different. You let Puentes in with far too many free shots because your temper got the better of you. Don't get me wrong – temper's a solid thing to have and use. But don't let it use you. You learn to control that temper or you'll come up against someone who can.'

'I heard this before, Nelson,' says Liam. He takes another bite of his omelette, talks through his chews. 'Paulo told us that story before.'

'Nice to know I'm not the only one who knows what he's talking about.' Nelson reaches for the syrup and pours a long zigzag stream across his pancakes. 'Okay, you heard that story. I got another one for you. True story, too. Back when I fought, my manager, he was like my best buddy, okay? Great guy. Do anything for you. And he did. Trouble is, the great guys are a step away from the shitty guys.' He cuts the pancakes with the side of his fork. 'This sport, it's a business more than ever now. The rankings don't mean anything. Those rankings were fixed when I was in the circuit, no reason to believe they're any different now. Talent talks, but it's the money that keeps you running. You got promoters paying off boards so their fighters can square off against each other and keep the dollars rolling through the gate. Doesn't matter who knocks down who, the promoter's the only one that really wins.

'I didn't know that back then. I thought it was all on the level. I honestly thought I was getting these shots because I'd earned it. And it turned out my manager – that great guy – and the promoter, they'd been paying people off.'

He jams his fork into a hunk of pancake, pops it into his mouth.

'It didn't matter because I could take those motherfuckers down with a harsh look, y'know? Lot like you are now. But the thing is, I was mismatched to my *advantage*. I was a big fish in a small pond.

My promoter kept pushing me to put on weight because the bigger you were, the bigger you were. More bucks. Always more bucks. Nobody gives a shit about the light-middleweights, they want to see a couple of heavyweights clash like fucking Godzillas in Las Vegas.'

Nelson plucks a napkin from the table and wipes his mouth.

'The trouble was,' he says. 'I put on the weight and suddenly I was the same kind of guy I'd been fighting a year before. The mismatch tipped the other way. I was the lamb. I thought I was doing great, zipping up the ranks, and then I realised I was being positioned for a fantastic finale. I had Enrique Alvarez – yeah, *that* Enrique Alvarez – pound me into the canvas to preserve his precious winning streak. I'd been hyped, primed and slaughtered in six months.'

Liam stops chewing, puts his fork down. He reaches for his orange juice.

'So.' Nelson swallows his food, shrugs. 'You want to go down the same route I did, you be my guest. I'm telling you you'll be able to go pro with or without this competition and that's not an empty compliment. But I'll also tell you that without your head in the right place and a guy who knows the business from the inside, you'll end up in the cold by the time you're twenty.'

'You think so,' says Liam, but there's no real defiance in it. The fight's drained from him.

'I know so. I've been there. Now, you want to be a baby about this, you can. Go ahead, take your chances. You'll probably prove me wrong, do very well for yourself. All I'm saying now is if you want to stow the bullshit and take some well-meaning advice, then I'll have you trained to the next level.'

'I'll beat Polito.'

'Yeah, and you'll beat him on your own terms,' says Nelson.

Liam looks into his tea, sniffs.

'You don't want to go back to Shapiro's,' I say.

'I know.'

'So?'

'So,' says Liam, looking up. 'We'll give it a try.'

TWENTY-TWO

Nelson lives about two hours away from Los Angeles. We drive through the blazing sunshine with the air-conditioning ramped right up. Down through the Coachella Valley, Nelson telling us various points of interest along the way. There aren't many. As we leave the city behind, the scenery falls into dusty desolation.

'Out here, you have to be careful,' he says. 'Especially this time of year. This kind of heat'll put you down quicker than God.'

I drink bottled water, swallow codeine, try to rest my back. Spend most of the drive adjusting my seat. I can see Liam in the back seat, staring out of the window with wide eyes. This is the most space he's seen in his life. Come to think of it, it's the most space I've seen too. But I'm an adult about it.

Because, to be honest, all this wide open space does is scare the living shit out of me. Especially with all Nelson's talk about those 'stupid hitchhikers two years back, they thought they'd go through the Valley – man, talk about chargrilled . . .'

Nelson's car is a real monster, a people-carrier. I didn't think he was the type, what with all that smog talk he'd given me. But according to him, he got it cheap: 'Nobody buys people-carriers anymore. Used to be soccer moms, but they traded up to SUVs. The real rich ones went for the Hummers. I ask you, man, why the hell would you need a Hummer in the city unless it's under martial law?'

Not the first question that popped into my mind, it has to be said. I was wondering why they named a car after a specialist blowjob. Shows what I know.

When we finally pull up to a sprawling white house complete

with double garage and tree out front, I must pull a face. It's easy to see where Nelson's boxing money went.

Nelson catches my look, says, 'We don't build up in this country, Cal. It's cheaper to build out.'

'Obviously.'

And it's obviously cheaper to have a massive telly, too. We're shown into a living room and that monolithic television's the first thing I see. Must be all of seventy inches.

'Shit,' I say. 'That's a monster.'

Nelson smiles. 'I don't watch much anymore. Mostly just use it for tapes and DVDs. TIVO the fights. You want to flip it on, check what's showing, go for it.' He hands me a remote as big as my head. '*Mi casa es tu casa.*'

I squint at the remote. 'Maybe later.'

'Cool. You want to check out the gym, Liam?'

Liam nods and they head off. I'm left behind for a second before I dump the remote on the couch and tag along behind. I see Liam following Nelson down an enclosed staircase that must lead to the basement. The lad's like a bloody puppy. Amazing what a show of cash will do to a kid's frame of mind.

The basement is chilly. Light bulbs and pull cords hang from the ceiling. As Nelson walks around, he yanks light into the room, illuminating equipment like prizes on a game show. The kind of stuff Paulo would probably kill for. Dated, yeah, but certainly not obsolete, the equipment down here is used a lot, but it defies wear and tear.

'Better stuff than Shapiro,' says Nelson. 'And you got all the privacy you need. No distractions.'

Liam looks around the basement. It's obvious he's never seen this kind of equipment before in his life.

'What d'you think?' says Nelson.

Liam nods.

'Then you're in.'

'Yeah.'

'Good.'

Nelson grins. 'Okay then, let's get you started.'

As he details Liam's training, I make my silent excuses and leave the basement unnoticed. Best to let them get on with it; my work here is done. I head back upstairs, check out the kitchen. One of those gargantuan refrigerators you could lose yourself in. I open it up, see TV dinners and fresh fruit, a couple of six packs. The single man in charge of his diet. Back out into the hallway, and I realise I need a piss, all that bottled water thumping at my bladder now. I try a door; end up in Nelson's bedroom. It's neat, but I don't notice much else apart from the grey uniform shirt and black trousers that are laid out on the queen-sized bed. I don't cross the threshold. Something about snooping around another man's bedroom makes me uneasy. Call it a respect of boundaries. And that holster complete with gun lying by the uniform is enough to make me turn back, closing the door as quietly as I can.

The bathroom's across the hall, and the toilet looks like every other in this country: blocked. I have a moment of horror when the yellow-tinged water rises up with the flush, looks like it's going to overflow, then relief as the whole lot is sucked round the U-bend.

And then I'm back out in the living room after cocking my head to make sure Nelson and Liam are still in the basement. Liam sounds like he's slamming a heavy bag. All the different things he could be doing, the kid likes that the most. Building up his punch, heating it until it scalds.

I slump onto the couch, fish around for the remote and turn on the telly. Flick past a *Law and Order* marathon, surf through adverts for car insurance with the President from *24*, catch a bit of David Caruso trying his best not to peel in Miami. I reckon that was a sound piece of casting. Put a violently ginger guy in Florida heat and watch him struggle. Onto the news and the brush fire's history, therefore forgotten, the weather's hot-hot-hot with a high of 112° and a low of 74° (like that means anything to me) and the weatherman's still wearing a suit.

Nelson comes into the room as I'm watching a repeat of

Columbo, the one where Patrick McGoohan's a spy with a bag of disguises and murder on his mind.

'No time like the present,' says Nelson.

'Sorry?'

'Liam's still training. He went nuts for the set-up.'

'Good. That's great.'

'You okay. Can I get you a drink or something?'

I shake my head. 'Nah, I'm fine.'

Nelson looks at the television. 'How does he know this time?'

'I can't remember,' I say. 'I can never bloody remember. It's always something tiny.'

'They show the re-runs so you don't have to remember.'

'Actually, you know what? I'll have a beer if you've got one,' I say.

'Sure.'

I follow Nelson through to the kitchen. He hands me a Miller Lite from the fridge, takes one for himself. I wait for a bottle opener to appear. Realise I don't need one when Nelson twists off the cap on his bottle and takes a deep swig. The United States, always that one step ahead of Britain.

'How long's Liam staying?' I say.

'However long he wants.'

'You don't have anything else to do?'

Nelson looks at me as if I've just asked to kiss his cheek. 'No, Cal, I don't have anything else to do.'

'Okay.' I swallow some beer. It's cold piss. 'I just wondered, he's got his bout tonight. Wondered if you had to work or something or if you were coming along.'

'Work?'

'Yeah, like a job.'

A sheen comes over Nelson's eyes. 'I don't work a job, Cal. Haven't worked a job for years.' He sets his beer on the counter. 'I'll try to make it to the bout, but I can't promise anything. I think the guy at the gym is all Liam'll need when he's boxing. I'd prefer to take a back seat. Reuben's a good corner man. And I'll tell you the truth, Cal, me and Phil Shapiro don't get on. I'd rather not be seen hanging around his place.'

'Okay. Look, it looks like he's got a day off tomorrow. I've got stuff I need to do, so is it alright if you two go at it all day?'

'My pleasure. You gonna see the sights?'

'Something like that. I'm supposed to be on holiday, aren't I?'

'Of course you are. I forgot.' He pulls open a drawer, grabs a pen and a notepad and starts writing. 'You want to drop him off, that's cool. It's not that hard to get here, but I'll draw you a map too. Make it easier on you. Unless you want me to pick him up at the hotel?'

'Nah, I'll drop him off.'

'Okay, cool.' He hands me the map and directions, clicks the pen.

'Cheers,' I say. 'What's Liam doing down there?'

'Nothing too strenuous. We'll get him warmed up for tonight, but I don't want him tired, so it's all low impact stuff, keep the muscles working, the heart up. He's good.'

'I know.'

'I'll run him for another couple of hours, then I'll drop you both off, how's that?'

'Sounds good.'

'In the meantime, help yourself to the refrigerator. Anything you need. Like I said . . .'

'*Mi casa es tu casa.*'

'Exactly.'

When he leaves, the beer he was drinking still sits on the counter, one swallow gone. I take it with me into the living room and get back to *Columbo*.

I put the gnawing in my gut down to a Scottish temperament. When it's blue skies, we forecast three weeks of *dreich*. A pessimistic nation, which is why we've managed to take the hard times with a tight smile on our faces.

Liam is riding shotgun this time. I'm in the back seat, trying to stretch out, staring at the sky.

'You get many storms out here, Nelson?' I say.

'A couple. You should see them, Cal. They're really something.'

I bet they are. Sheet lightning sparking the sky, rolling thunder and a sick, creeping fear that you're out in the open and you're liable to be killed at any moment. We're not meant to be out in nature. That's why we invented houses, central heating, air conditioning, television. Keep us back in the womb. Safe.

That's the point of these people-carriers, too. More than being able to transport your screaming brood from school to football practice, it's like you're in your own wee capsule, shielded from the elements. I read that in times of political or economic strife, people in this country buy bigger, safer vehicles. They're scared, just like Nelson said. This thing I read suggested that, given time, people are going to be in the market for personal tanks.

With extra-large cup holders front and back, of course.

I try not to think about the uniform on Nelson's bed.

Or the gun.

Or that if he's not working a job-type job, then why was the kit laid out like that? Thinking that maybe, okay, it wasn't his room. But then it was clean. Knowing I'll need to take a pill soon and trying not to think about that, either.

Because I think too much, apparently. That's what Donna told me once and it's never left me. But then when I don't think – run on pure instinct and emotion – that's when people get hurt. Mostly me. It's a lose-lose situation.

Nelson drops us off at the hotel and Liam makes a beeline for his room. He hasn't talked to me since we left Palm Desert. Pissed off that he had to leave so soon, no doubt, and gearing up for the second bout.

Which we have to get to bloody soon.

TWENTY-THREE

If I didn't know better, I'd swear the kid fighting Josh Callahan was drunk. He stumbles, weaves like he's been topped with a bottle of vodka. Josh keeps it calm for a moment, striking hard when the opportunity arises. Which it does. A lot. But for some reason, the bout manages to get to the third round before it's stopped, Josh's opponent battered and bleeding.

Liam and I arrived in the middle of the thing, Liam watching for a few seconds, then scribbling in his notebook.

'What is that?' I said.

'What?'

I pointed to the book. 'That.'

'Nowt,' he says. 'Just notes.'

I tried to get a look at what he's written, but it just looked like scrawl. Liam pinched the book shut, pushed it into his bag.

They've announced Josh the winner. I look at the ring and the blonde twat has one glove in the air. His opponent is being helped through the ropes. He doesn't look disappointed, more resigned. A bit more showboating, and Josh is gone too. His father turns up and starts packing Josh's bag for him. Hands him the bag and points to the door. Josh throws on a tracksuit jacket and swaggers to the exit.

Mr Callahan stays where he is as they announce the next bout.

Whatever Nelson's done to Liam, it's worked. The first round is a slow burner. Charlie Polito is a mover, but he's deliberate with it. No bounce in his step unless it's called for to sweep out from under a jab. Liam strikes, then Polito. They trade blows, neither of them very hard. When Polito scores a hefty uppercut, I think that's Liam gone. He's bound to lose it, turn nasty.

But he doesn't. He recovers, shakes his head back, and carries on.

The next time Polito tries the uppercut, Liam's got it blocked and returned. No more hanging lefts – his gloves are up. When I glance at Reuben, he's smiling. Like, finally, the kid's learned something. And he has, I just doubt it was from Reuben.

No, this is Nelson's work.

Liam moves with confidence. He sees an opening, he takes it. But he doesn't hammer it. Patience is now his prime virtue. That, and a keen eye for a weak defence.

Second round and Polito's getting hazy. He starts throwing amateur punches, easily seen and avoided. His feet keep working, but working too much now. He's heard about Liam, he's expecting the explosion. When Liam moves, I can see Polito almost flinch. Liam knows it, too. But he's not about to start playing up. When the bell rings, Polito looks borderline exhausted. Liam's scored enough decent punches to mark the round his.

Third. Polito storming out. He's been fired up by his corner man. Obvious now that the next bout's with Josh Callahan, and Josh is a nasty fighter. Polito needs to counter this, needs to get out there and show this Wooley kid who's the fucking boss round here. But he can't find the power behind the punch. Seems like every jab, hook and uppercut, Liam's got a definitive answer for. Playing peek-a-boo with a tight cross guard, bobbing his head to draw the jabs out of Polito, then sinking a one-two to the torso. Polito shakes his head, backs a way off centre. Trying to re-evaluate, but running out of ideas. He looks to the ref, but the ref's no help, can't tell him how to penetrate that defence.

Liam pushes forward, always pushing forward. Not vicious, but calculated. Keeps his gloves high, knocks back Polito's serious blows with a deft swat. Keeps the pressure on, his offence as tight as his defence.

Two minutes fly by. And the next two see Polito lose his patience for good. He thunders at Liam, and Liam's got him caught dead cold. One solid glove through the headgear knocks Polito onto the canvas. Polito's quick back on his feet, but whatever he's been told has been knocked out of his head. He wanders about the ring as if he's not sure what the hell he's doing there. Liam keeps his cool, doesn't go for the easy win, lets Polito pull himself together.

It never happens. The bout ends with Polito back in his corner, staring at his lap.

I go to Liam's corner, Reuben grinning from ear to ear.

'You see that?' he says. 'You see that kid? I told you, all he needed to do was keep his left up, and he's got it made.'

'Well done, Reuben,' I say.

'Damn straight well done.'

Liam's announced as the winner. He doesn't play it up, accepts the win like it's a simple fact of life. But there's a smile on his face, a sparkle in his eyes that means he's well into what Nelson's been teaching him. He pulls off his headgear as he gets out of the ring, Reuben in his ear now, telling him what a great job he did.

'I don't know what got into you, kid, but you nailed it.'

Liam looks at his gloves, nods slowly. Looks up at me. I wink at him.

'You got Josh next,' says Reuben as we move away from the ring. 'You act with him like you acted tonight, you'll be fine. I know you got bad blood with him—'

'It won't be an issue,' says Liam.

'Better not be. You don't want to mess it up because of bad blood.'

'I won't.'

I usher Liam to a bench. Look across the club, and I see Callahan chewing something, watching us. He stops chewing when he sees me looking at him, then moves to the exit, rubbing at his nose as he walks.

'You got Josh's father scared shitless,' I say.

Liam looks around the club. 'He here?'

'Josh? He's gone.' I see Callahan leaving. 'That's his dad there.'

'You remember to keep that defence tight,' says Reuben. 'You remember that, you'll have nothing to worry about . . .'

'I know, Reuben,' says Liam. 'You got it told.'

Liam's gloves are off now. He stretches his fingers. Scratches at a spot above his eye. I look at the lad, and there's not a mark on him. I wonder how the hell he managed to do it. But then there's that defence that Reuben's still wittering on about.

'We should get going,' I say.

'Wait a second,' says Reuben.

And I see Phil Shapiro walking across to us. The Chihuahua is nestled in his arms and he's got what appears to be a grin on his face. As he approaches, Liam stands up. Shapiro holds out his hand and the pair of them shake.

'Good bout,' he says. 'You did well.'

'I was telling him, Phil, he's got to keep his gloves up.'

'And he did.' Shapiro raises one finger to Liam. 'Charlie Polito's one of the best boxers we've got in here. To be honest with you, I didn't think you'd handle him as well as you did.'

'Then you thought wrong,' I say.

Shapiro ignores me. 'You know it's Josh next.'

Liam nods. 'I'm fine, Mr Shapiro.'

'You sure?'

'Absolutely.'

'Because you look fine. You do look fine.' He smiles again. 'I can't believe this kid. One day he's fighting like the world's after him, the next he's like a seasoned pro. What happened, Liam?'

'I got some good advice.'

'You did, huh?' Shapiro nods. 'Wish Josh had been given the same advice.'

'He's sloppy,' I say. Probably because he was drunk last night, I want to add. But then that would open up a whole new can of worms. And there's no reason for the conversation to get nasty.

'I don't think Josh was on top form,' says Reuben. 'He was lucky.'

'You've got a day off tomorrow,' Shapiro says to Liam. 'Don't go nuts and we won't have any problems.'

'I'm going to train,' says Liam.

'Well, I'll look forward to seeing you.'

'Yeah,' says Reuben. 'We'll work on your feet. Couple of slips tonight. Nothing serious, but it's work needed.'

'Okay.'

I pick up Liam's bag. As we're leaving, I pat the lad on the back. 'Nice work, mate.'

'Thanks.'

The ride back to the hotel is silent apart from the radio, but it's not through any discomfort. Liam's content to look out of the window. When Johnny Cash starts singing, he doesn't say anything, so the lad must be happy. I park up, carry Liam's bag up to his room. He says goodnight and I wander down to my room.

Something red blinks in the darkness. I turn on the light and walk over to the phone. I have a message waiting for me, apparently. Pick up the receiver and mash the keypad until I get voicemail.

I listen. Smile. Then grab the vodka and a clean glass, pour myself a nice shot. Listen to the message again and punch in the number that's left.

This is going to be good. As the booze hits my stomach, there's a pleasant warm sensation. Could be I'm just feeling smug.

On the phone, the strange purring tone that means it's ringing. And when he picks up, I say, 'You rang, Mr Callahan?'

TWENTY-FOUR

Early morning sober, the sky a washed-out grey blanket. No longer in Los Angeles – this is Santa Monica. Nobody can say I'm not seeing the sights. But I'm getting pretty fucking tired of following directions, it has to be said. I lean against the railing, watch the surf kick at the beach. By now it's obvious that Callahan is a no-show.

'We need to talk,' he said last night.

'So talk.'

'I'd rather do it in person.'

'And I'd rather not do it at all.'

'Tomorrow morning. Early.'

And he gave me directions to this Santa Monica spot. It reminds me of an upmarket Portobello, but that could just be the white noise of the sea. The place has a mixture of faded coastal charm and new money. Probably hip and happening at one point, a little bit edgy, a little bit bohemian. Easy to imagine the arts and crafts crowd milling around. But like most bohemian places, Santa Monica swooned at the scent of hard currency. The piers are shopping malls, packed with boutiques that no doubt do good business and chain bookstores where the staff actually care about your choice of reading material. Juice bars and coffee shops. No real bars that I could see. Healthy living where the only comfortable sin is caffeine.

Yeah, I've driven around. Mostly because the directions Callahan gave me were pish. Down to my last three cigarettes and sick of waiting.

Nothing's open yet, but the cats are out to play. I spotted two, then four, their numbers rising until I began to think there was something I should know. Now it feels like I'm about to be mugged by the furry wee buggers; they're circling like it's *Assault on Precinct 13*. The cats must be stray, but I've never seen this many congregate. And I've never been much of a cat person, so the sight of them now is enough to give me the all-over shivers.

There's the sound of a car drawing close and I drop the Marlboro half-smoked. Squint in the early morning light at the vehicle, and if it's Callahan he's dropped more than a few notches in the automobile league. This is a beaten-up, unwashed rust bucket heading my way. I keep a close watch on it, though. Just in case. The last time I didn't watch a car, I ended up rolling over its roof.

The rust bucket pulls up about a hundred yards away. The cats stop whatever they're doing, tails in the air.

I watch a woman get out of the car with some difficulty. She's short, dumpy, looks like she's wearing all her clothes at once. The cats all trot towards her, some of the skinnier ones picking up their feet to a gallop, the only sound now the crash of waves and a cacophony of mewing. The woman makes weird noises at the onslaught of cats, some clucks, some clicks. Every now and then, she'll throw out something that sounds like a short, high-pitched trill. She reaches into the car, pulls out two large boxes and shakes them like oversized maracas. The cats go nuts, the mewing turned to screeching, look like they're about to attack. A couple curl around her tree stump legs, bashing their heads against her shins. One big black monster threatens to trip her up as the woman waddles her way to the grass verge. She's still making those clicking, purring noises. Like she's some insane Queen of the Strays, a crazy cat lady gone all the way feral.

I keep quiet. Still. Unsure if my presence is welcome. Thinking that one false move is all it'll take for this woman to slip into hardcore mentalism and sic her feline army on me.

She shakes the contents of the two boxes into the grass and the cats fall into a huddle of fur and tails. A pair of tabbies – one ginger, one grey – hiss and swipe at each other. A tortoiseshell tub of guts crawls and kicks its way over a mound of ratty fluff, who stops eating for a split-second to move aside. The rest of the cats shift and bump into each other. They're used to this. I watch the woman ruffle whatever cat is nudging her to get to the food. She sits on the grass among them. When I catch a look at her face, she's smiling. The eye of the storm.

Too weird. I get the chills. Reach into my pocket and light the second last cigarette in the pack.

'You're late,' I say.

'I said by the beach.'

'This is by the beach.'

'You can go further down.'

'And how am I supposed to know that? Do I look like I'm from around here?'

Okay, so Callahan's late, the last Marlboro is now a blackened filter by my feet and I went and forgot my fucking pills so my back's giving me hell. No need to forgive my mood when I've got valid reasons for it.

'Can you bitch and walk at the same time?' he says.

'I can certainly try.'

Callahan leads the way with large strides. Not the walk of a man who just got up. That very special breed of arsehole: the morning person. I hobble after him, my jacket pulled tight, feeling the cold of a two-hour wait at dawn. He glances at me.

'Your leg giving you pain?' he says.

'My back.'

'I'm similarly afflicted.'

'Oh, *are* you?' I say. 'You don't fuckin' look it.'

'Morning walks are the key, Mr Innes. Morning walks, a good diet and physical therapy.'

'Yeah, I know someone else who swears by it. What did you want to see me about?'

'One second.' Callahan drops a few steps to the beach. He moves out across the sand as if he's savouring every painless step. Then he turns, looks at me. 'This is why I live here.'

I stay where I am. Not keen on getting sand in my shoes. I glance back up at the road, can't see my car. Getting antsy about leaving it out there in the open. It's hardly likely that someone's going to steal a Geo bloody Metro with a dodgy door, but I'd like an easy escape route if things turn sour.

'I've seen beaches before,' I say.

'I used to run along here. Very bracing, good for the circulation. Really gets the blood going.'

'Look, like I said, I've seen beaches before. We have them in Britain. It's an island, so we've got plenty of them all around the coast, funnily enough. So if you've brought me down here to show me where dirt meets fuckin' water, you've succeeded and I'm unimpressed.'

Callahan smiles to himself. It doesn't flatter him, makes him look smug as fuck. He takes a few steps forward and points up the beach. 'You see that?'

I strain to see what he's pointing at: a large white house right on the sand.

'You know how much that place cost me?'

'I'm sure you're going to tell me.'

'No, that would be vulgar. But it cost a lot.'

'I heard you were minted. Must be if you've bought a house right in the middle of the sea.'

'*Ocean*,' he says. 'And it was just a wise investment, that's all. Sound business sense can get you a lot in this world. Of course, taking a chance pays off more.'

'Glad to hear you're a bit risky.'

'You'll forgive me for saying, but you don't look like a man with his toe in the property waters.'

I shrug. 'Well, y'know, there's the villa in the Maldives. But most of my cash is tied up in stocks and bonds right now, Mr Callahan. You know how it is.'

'You could use some money,' he says.

'I could always *use* some money. That's why it's called money.'

'You're being sarcastic.'

'Nah, mate – I'm having back spasms. And I'm cold. And I'm tired because it's stupid o'clock in the fuckin' morning. And I'm still wondering why you wanted to see me.'

'I think you have a good idea why I wanted to see you.'

'Do I? Cause I'm having trouble, I'll tell you. I can't think of a single reason why you'd want to drag me out of my pit and make me stand here freezing my bollocks off other than simpleminded sadism. Or maybe you just wanted me to see your house before a tidal wave took it away.'

'My boy's a good fighter.'

'I'm sure he is. Doesn't stop him being a prize dickhead.'

'I heard about the other night. The' – Callahan pulls a face as he gropes for the right word – '*altercation* in the parking lot.'

I nod. Here we go. Pull my jacket tighter until it feels like the material is cutting off what little circulation I have. 'I didn't touch your son, Mr Callahan. I was very careful about that. He says I touched him, then he's a lying wee fucker.'

'I know.'

'All I did was teach his mouthy mate a lesson.'

'I know,' says Callahan. 'Josh told me all about it. Came home smelling of bourbon with blood on him, I asked questions and he had to explain it somehow. Thankfully, and contrary to your opinion, Mr Innes, my son told me the truth.'

'He chop down the cherry tree, too?'

Callahan smiles. 'He cannot tell a lie. And I thought to myself, there's a man with intelligence.'

'You thought that.'

'Yes, I did. If you'd hit Josh, you must've known it wouldn't go unreported. You and your little lad would be out of the competition before you could blink. And, judging from last night, you didn't tell Mr Shapiro about it, either.'

'Didn't have anything to do with him.'

'I appreciate that.' The smile falters on his face; his mouth twitches it into an expression far more serious. 'You know Josh has a good chance of winning this competition.'

'I don't know that at all. I saw him fight last night, looked like he was mismatched to fuck. Or the other lad was off his face on something. Either way, I didn't see anything that made me worried. So if you're asking for my predictions about the forthcoming bout between Callahan and Wooley, I'd have to say your boy's going to get creamed.'

Callahan nods to himself. He takes a deep breath. When he looks at me again, he's all business. Same face the guy'd use in the boardroom, staring down the competition. 'I think you're right about that, Mr Innes. I really do. Which is why I'm offering you five thousand to see that it doesn't happen.'

That hangs in the air. I chew the inside of my mouth.

'Sorry?' I say.

'You heard what I said.'

'Nah, I don't think I did. You must've been talking into my trick ear or something, because I'm sure you just offered me a bribe.'

'That wasn't your trick ear, Mr Innes.'

I laugh. Once and sharp, comes out like a bark.

'You didn't tell Shapiro about what happened in the parking lot,' he says.

'That means I'm fuckin' corrupt, does it?'

'It means—'

'You're out of your fuckin' mind, Mr Callahan.'

I turn to go, start climbing the steps. Not as fast as I'd like, thanks to my back. It's not long before Callahan has my pace matched. I half-turn, hands dug deep in my jacket pockets, just to make sure he's not going to try anything daft like try to rush me. He's older than me, but that doesn't stop him from being powerfully built and fitter than me. But he doesn't try anything, just walks with me.

'I don't think we understand each other, Mr Innes.'

'Oh, I think we understand each other perfectly. You made me come out here to the middle of fuckin' nowhere because you're shitting it that Liam's going to mess up your pretty-boy son.'

Callahan shakes his head.

'Or you're just used to buying what you want,' I say. 'And

thinking back on Josh's fight last night, I wouldn't be surprised if you slapped down a wad on that.'

'Mr Innes—'

'Whatever it is, I'm not playing, mate. Taking my ball back and I'm going home. Tell you what, that five grand's burning a hole in your pocket, spend it on Josh's reconstructive surgery. He's going to need it after Liam's finished with him.'

'Excuse me?'

'You're excused.' I quicken my pace, get a short burst of speed. My back screams at me, but the air's turned close and sickly. It's all I can do to breathe. I need to get back to the car, back to the hotel, back to bed.

Callahan stops walking. His voice rises up far behind me. 'Mr Innes, your boy's a fish out of water over here. So are you.'

'Right . . .'

'You know what happens to fish out of water? They *drown*.'

I keep walking, shake off the fear and spit the taste of iron out of my mouth.

TWENTY-FIVE

When I get back to the hotel, Nelson's waiting in the lobby. He sees me coming through the doors and surprise flickers across his face. Checks his watch and the surprise turns into a smile. I don't have the energy or the inclination to match it. My back killing me, pissed off and tired, the last thing I want to do is be courteous.

'I called your room,' he says.

'I'm not there.' Nelson's another morning person. It wears me out even more. 'What're you doing here? I thought I was going to drop Liam off at yours.'

'I was in the neighbourhood,' he says with a shrug. 'Thought I'd swing by, see if you guys wanted some breakfast.'

'You know what time it is?'

'Seven?' He shakes his watch. 'It's an old winder. I don't know.'

'Only truckers and security guards have breakfast this early, Nelson. Let the lad sleep.' I walk to the lift, press the button.

'How did it go last night?'

I run a hand over my face. Of course, he wasn't there; he wouldn't know. I turn to Nelson and summon up a half-smile. 'Liam won.'

'That's great.'

'Yeah, you did a good job.'

'Hope you don't mind me saying this, but you look like shit, Cal.'

I press the lift call button again. 'Then I look how I feel.'

'You been out all night celebrating?' he says.

'Just an early morning.'

'Anything exciting?'

I look at him. He's here now, he might as well know the score.

And maybe he can point me in the right direction. 'Tell you what, let me pop to my room and we'll go somewhere, I'll tell you all about it.'

'Cool.'

'But we'll leave Liam in his pit. Let him catch up.'

Free refills on the coffee. What a wonderful thing. I take my pills, let my body settle into a dazed slump. Let the coffee keep the brain going. Our waitress is a hawk. I haven't finished one cup yet – she swoops in, tops me up and is gone before I get a chance to say thank you. We're at a smoking table, at least. Nelson's taken pity on me.

'You're sure you don't want anything to eat?' says Nelson. 'A muffin or something?'

'I gave up early morning muffins a while back. Besides, I don't think my stomach's up to it.'

I told Nelson about my meeting with Callahan and he raised his eyebrows, but that was it.

'If you had any doubts about this smoker being on the level, there's your proof. At least from Callahan's point of view. And now I've thought about it, Nelson, I could swear something was up last night.'

'How so?'

I shake my head. 'Caught the end of Josh's bout. The kid he was fighting, he didn't have much of an offence, even less of a defence. Like he was just standing there to stand there.'

'Like he'd been paid off?'

'Maybe him, maybe his coach. I don't know. Maybe the kid was defeated because Josh is a hell of a fighter. Like I said, I caught the end of the bout. Could be that Josh just made him that way.'

'But you don't believe that, do you?' says Nelson.

'I'm not sure.' I sip coffee, then: 'No, I don't believe it.'

Nelson lets out a long breath. 'I thought it was me, Cal. Letting my experience colour the situation. And I thought that having Alvarez's name attached to the competition might lend the thing some integrity, but then there's no guarantee about anything these days.'

I take the plastic off a fresh pack of Marlboros, light one.

'When I was talking to Liam about mismatching, I wasn't bullshitting him,' says Nelson. 'They've tried to clean up the sport, but there's still that thick stain of corruption they can't scrub out. It's a real pity. This used to be a sport, it used to *mean* something. See these kids from the Dominican Republic coming up now, just like the Latinos and the black kids, they're looking for a way out and boxing's the only way for some of them. As long as there's an underclass, Cal, there's boxing.'

'And as long as there's an underclass, there's someone looking to buy it out.' I tap ash.

'What did you tell him?'

'Callahan? I told him to fuck off.'

Nelson rubs his mouth, looks at the table. 'Good.'

'And I'm going to see Shapiro this afternoon, put it out in the open.'

'I don't think that's a good idea,' he says.

'You don't think he'll believe me?'

'No, I know he'll believe you. I just don't think he'll do anything about it except get mad at you. No reason to think Shapiro isn't involved, Cal. Especially with his record.'

'He dirty?'

'He went to prison. That's pretty dirty.'

'Depends on what he did.' The waitress tops up my coffee and I smile at her. 'He throw a fight or something?'

'No, but he broke a guy's hands because he wouldn't. Forced the situation.' Nelson moves his cup to one side and leans forward. 'He was a great fighter. I wasn't lying about that. But you know the deal, Cal. A guy makes his living with his fists, it gets so that's the only thing he knows how to do. And when you're pro, you learn things you don't want to learn. You can get like me and get out, do something else, scrub yourself and try not to look back. Or you can go the way Shapiro went and fall into line. Either way, this business has a way of throwing your mind out of whack.'

'Huh.' I stare at the end of my cigarette, tap stray ash.

'Jesus, man, you get hit in the head that many times, you hear one thing, you see something else, find out the people you respected and loved are setting you up because you're getting older and slower? You'd be a fucking saint not to let that affect you.'

'I see.'

'Sometimes the things that can push you out are the same things that keep you in. That's the only difference between me and Shapiro.'

'And he did time.'

'Aggravated assault, I think it was.' Nelson sits back, picks up his coffee and takes a drink. 'I don't know the legal jargon. It was a minor charge and nobody dug any deeper. Why should they? There's enough cash floating around to shout louder than anyone's conscience. It's free enterprise, Cal. There's no free enterprise without casualties, but that's the way of the world.'

'So there's nothing I can do about it.'

'Talk to Shapiro by all means. I'm just preparing you for what you might get.'

'Why didn't you tell me this before, Nelson?'

'Because nobody tried to bribe you, Cal. I didn't think it was important. I thought, hell, get the kid trained up, forget winning the smoker, Liam'll be good enough to beat anyone who crosses his path. And we'll deal with the other stuff when it happens.'

I stare at my coffee; there's a tidemark around the inside of the cup. I rub at it with one finger, wipe away the brown scum with a paper napkin. 'And you still believe in heroes, eh?'

'Yeah, I still believe in heroes. There's good guys in the business. But I believe in villains, too.'

'Well, you've got to have something,' I say. I finish my coffee, get the waitress' attention. 'You alright taking Liam yourself? I've got some business to take care of.'

'You gonna see Shapiro?'

'I'm going to have a nap first if the coffee lets me.'

'Then?'

'Then, we'll see. I don't know yet.'

I pay, we get out of there. Back at the hotel, I give Liam's door a knock. The lad's already up and about, changed and eager to get going. Wasn't so long ago, this kid was a fighting dog; now he's the Andrex puppy. He still doesn't really acknowledge me, though. Like Nelson's his golden ticket. It's good, keep Liam occupied while I try to find out exactly what kind of shite he's been thrown into.

I watch Nelson drive away in his people-carrier, Liam talking ten-to-the-dozen. Head back up to my room. The message waiting light blinks on the phone, but I walk past it into the bathroom, smoke a cigarette.

Callahan has my answer, for what it's worth. But he's a business-man in the Plummer vein. He doesn't take no for an answer, doesn't take any answer that isn't what he wants to hear. So he'll keep pecking my head until I give in. That's negotiation. But it's difficult to negotiate with a deaf man and that's what I intend to be until the bout. He can leave his offer out in the open until it grows fucking moss as far as I'm concerned.

I wrap the filter in bog roll and drop it into the toilet bowl, press on the flush. I should get some sleep, but the caffeine's kicked in. If I bed down now, I'll be staring at the ceiling with my skin twitching.

Pick up the phone, start punching in Paulo's number. Then I stop, put the phone down. Fuck it, what am I supposed to tell him? Better I get this sorted out on my own without the added pressure of Paulo going nuts in Manchester. Or else gather enough in-formation so I can pass it on without feeling that I'm making all this up.

And I need to get out of this room. Feels like I've been locking myself away when this trip's supposed to be a holiday. That's what I'm used to, though. Hole myself up in my flat in Manchester or the office at Paulo's. Or in my tiny car, watching the world grow drunk and insane. I'm used to it. I crave four walls and confinement, isolation. And this room might be a gilded cage compared to normal, but it's still a cage. Better than a prison cell, certainly: a telly, a minibar. Housekeeping for whom 'Do Not Disturb' translates into Spanish as 'Come On In'. A bathroom that doesn't stink of prison food farts.

Course, they let me smoke in my prison cell.

I don't want to think about it. So I head for the door before I get a chance to reminisce.

TWENTY-SIX

A transfer of cells to the Metro outside Shapiro's gym. I'm watching the entrance. It's still early and the place looks like it's getting the first influx of boxers for the day. I keep forgetting that there are other bouts taking place; I'm so wrapped up in Liam's future that it's difficult to maintain focus. I've seen Reuben out for a couple of smoke breaks. He hasn't seen me.

I don't know what I expect to see. Sometimes I wish surveillance was as simple as it's made out to be. Wait there long enough and something's bound to happen. Someone's bound to come out onto the street to do something illegal.

I reach into my pocket for my cigarettes. Then the other pocket. Nothing in either. And I realise I went and left them back in the hotel bathroom.

Shit.

Got loads left in the carton, but the carton's in my room and far too far away to nip back and retrieve. But I'll be buggered if I'm going to sit here smokeless. I get out of the car as a couple passes on the other side of the street. A blond bloke and his blonder girl – hair almost white. They're both tanned, young, and probably describe themselves as 'financially comfortable'. There's a black bloke heading towards them. He's built like a length of rope, a record bag slung loose over one shoulder, his other hand swaying by his side.

'Hey,' he says. 'You with a fine-looking woman, man.'

The blond bloke smiles. So does the girl. She is fine-looking. Nothing the matter with the black guy's eyes. But the couple doesn't seem keen on conversation.

'I'm just lucky, I guess,' says the blond bloke, his grip visibly tightening on his girlfriend's arm. They keep walking, the bloke looking like he'd use force if the black guy gets in his way.

'Lucky? Hell, no. Ain't no luck about it.'

The couple gets past the black guy, keep walking. They don't turn around.

'Ain't no luck. Ain't no luck at all. Luck's when you hit the right numbers on the lotto. I see a man with a fine-looking woman, I think that man's *blessed*. That woman there is a work of our Creator, man. Can't think nothing else.'

'Thank you,' says the woman over her shoulder. Her boyfriend tugs at her arm. 'Goddamn it, Scott.'

'Work of the Creator,' says the black guy, more to himself now.

I know there's a Shell round here somewhere; I passed it in the car. So I start following the couple.

'Where you going?' says the black guy.

I stop. 'Me?'

'Yeah.'

'I'm going to buy some cigarettes.'

'Cigarettes? They'll kill you.' He walks towards me, has his hands up. 'I don't mean any harm, okay? I ain't gonna mug you. And I'll even stay downwind. I know I got a funk coming off of me.'

'You're alright, mate.'

'Where you gonna get smokes?'

'There's a Shell up—'

'Hey, none of my business, but if you're gonna kill yourself, you may as well do it cheap. Don't go to White Hen. They charge you a dollar, two-dollar extra on the cigarettes. I dunno, they got high rent or something. So you want a smoke, you go further up, you hang a right and walk for a block, okay? Then you'll see a 7-Eleven. Probably a couple of fat old misery-asses sitting out front playing checkers, that's when you know you at the right place.'

'Cheers.'

'Now I don't smoke – I don't got that addiction hanging on me, man. I had plenty. The good Lord knows I had plenty. You know how it is. A man can't live in this world clean. But I do now. I got me a room at St Paul's. You know St Paul's?'

'No.'

'Bless 'em for what they're trying to do there, man, but it's a flea hotel. I got myself clean and I'm living in a dirty hole, you pardon my language. I'm forty-five tomorrow, can you beat that? I got my kids coming to see me, kinda like to get dressed up for it. I know they're gonna take me someplace nice.'

'How much d'you want?' I say.

The guy takes a step back, his hands still in the air. 'Didn't I tell you I wasn't gonna mug you? And when did I ask you for money, man?'

'You're building up to it.'

'You think I'm scamming you.'

I shake my head and smile. 'You're not scamming me. Way I see it, you saved me a couple dollars on my cigarettes, you deserve the difference.'

'I ain't panhandling you.'

'I know. You want to walk and talk, show me where this 7-Eleven is?'

His large eyes become smaller as he regards me. 'Now you scamming me. I told you I ain't panhandling. You got nothing on me for that.'

'I'm not a cop. C'mon.'

We walk, the bloke hanging back a step or two as if he doesn't want to be seen with me. Hang that right and I can see the 7-Eleven up the street.

'Yeah, and you thought I was scamming you,' he says.

'Nah.' I look at him. 'Okay, maybe. I'm new around here.'

'You don't got the accent, that's for damn straight, forgive my language. You British or something?'

'Something. I don't know the city very well. Don't really want to do the tourist shit if I can help it.'

'I don't blame you. This city'll skin a tourist. But you, man, you're a *traveller*.'

'Something like that, yeah. Listen, you know that gym I was just at?'

'Shapiro's?'

'Yeah, you know him?'

'Him? Shapiro's a dude? All I see is the sign when I walk past.'

Just like he said, there are two fat blokes playing checkers outside the 7-Eleven. Sitting on boxes, an upturned fruit crate providing them with a makeshift table. I stop as we get near the store, turn to my guide. 'You sure you don't know the guy who owns the place?'

'I look like I need to lose weight, man?' He rolls his shoulders. 'Or wait, what this is, you think I'm Huggy Bear, think I know the word on the street cause I'm a black man.'

'Okay,' I say. 'I'm sorry. How much d'you need?'

'I told you, I don't got no information on whatever guy own Shapiro's. It's a name on a sign above a door of a building that I pass. You want to dig, you find yourself another spade.'

I pull out my wallet, pluck a ten-dollar bill from the fold. 'It's me, mate. My head's up my arse. Sorry if I offended you.'

'Don't give that guy any money,' says one of the checker players, a man with rheumy eyes and a three-day white growth on his jowls.

'What the hell you know about it, Kelvin?'

'I'm saying, don't give this guy any money.' Kelvin narrows his eyes at the board. 'He's rolling in cash.' He moves a piece, sits back and points at his opponent. 'And fuck you, too.'

I push the bill into my guide's hand. 'Take it, man.'

'Bless you,' he says. He pockets the cash and walks backwards away from me, a big grin on his face. As he passes Kelvin, he leans close and shouts, 'You a nasty piece of work, you know that?'

'Yeah, and I ain't deaf, neither.'

'I know that, man.' He smiles, twists and starts walking further up the street. That same loping stride, head swivelling, looking for people to talk to.

'Son of a bitch,' says Kelvin. 'You shouldn't have given him nothing.'

I get my cigarettes from a guy who looks like he's seen better days and even they had sucked. He charges me tax on top of the price, which throws me for a second. I grab a bottle of Pepsi, too. Bigger than the British bottles and about half the price. I manage to guzzle half of it by the time I get back to Shapiro's.

Sometimes, there's only so much beating around the bush you can do. I've asked Reuben, I've asked Nelson, even asked a homeless guy – but hell, no, he's at St Paul's – and only Nelson's given me something to go on. And to tell the truth, it's taken me all this time to work out what I'm going to do next. I can't just hang around waiting for something to happen, don't have that kind of time to waste. I'd just get a little older, no wiser and the bribe hangs over the situation like a bad smell.

So I push into Shapiro's Boxing Center, fully intent on hearing from the big bastard himself. Reuben's straight across when he sees me.

'Where's Liam?' he says. Sweat running into his eyes, though it could just be the burrito he's shoving into his mouth as he talks.

'Eh?'

'C'mon, your kid in this thing or not?' He checks his watch. 'Y'know, I said morning, and we're running out of that. He can't get in the ring if he's not trained. I won't allow it. Phil won't allow it.'

'I already secured him another coach, Reuben.'

'When? Just now?'

'Yesterday. Thought it'd be easier on him. Don't worry, you're doing a great job as his second. Phil about?'

'Who?'

'Phil Shapiro,' I say. 'You know the guy.'

'No, who's the coach?'

'Doesn't matter. Is he in? I need to talk to him.'

'Why?'

'The fuck are you, Reuben, his secretary?' I push past him, head for Shapiro's office. I can see the big guy in there. He's on the phone, staring into the middle distance. As I cross the floor, I catch his eye. He doesn't look pleased. But what the hell, I'm getting used to that reaction.

'I find out he's done nothing, I'll throw it in,' shouts Reuben. 'I'm not here to see kids get hurt.'

I have to laugh at that one. I do the polite thing and knock on Shapiro's door before I push it open. He's still talking and looks at me like I just took a shit in the middle of the floor. The Chihuahua yaps at me. I crouch and hold out a hand. The dog trots up to me, shaking. Sniff my fingers, then retreats. I stand up and sniff my fingers. I can't smell anything awful, so I just put it down to me not being a dog person either.

Shapiro makes conversation-ending noises, like he's clammed up. When he puts the phone down, the dog skitters across the floor to him.

'You're not very polite,' he says.

'I knocked, didn't I?'

'You're supposed to wait.'

'I still knocked.'

He remains standing. I can hear the dog behind the desk, sounds like it's scratching at something. Shapiro says, 'What do you want?'

'I want to know if this thing's kosher.'

He blinks at me. 'Kosher?'

'On the level. This competition.'

Shapiro's face doesn't crack. He stares at me. 'Why wouldn't it be?'

'I don't know,' I say. 'I heard some things, that's all. Thought rather than sneaking about, I'd come to you with it, ask you straight out.'

'That's not what I hear from Reuben.'

'Ah, well . . .'

'Reuben says you were trying to pump him for information the other night. And that doesn't sound very "straight out" to me, Mr Innes. Sounds like you're digging.'

'You got anything to dig?'

Shapiro smiles. Shakes his head as he sits down. The dog jumps up onto his lap as he pushes his chair away from the desk. If I'm trying to read his eyes, I won't get much. Not only are they stone, but they're obscured by scar tissue and shadow. He puts his hand on the dog, another on the desk. Light from the office window slices across his face.

There's a flash on Uncle Morris and his grandson. Those same huge scarred hands. The quiet threat. Yeah, this bloke's got a past, and it's not pretty.

'So what did you hear?' he says.

'That's not the way it works,' I say.

Shapiro cocks his head, strokes the dog. 'What do you do for a living, Mr Innes?'

'Nothing much.'

'Because you're not police. You're definitely not the board. So what are you?'

'An interested party. I don't want Liam involved with a rigged comp. It's not fair on him.'

'And what makes you think this competition's rigged?'

'Like I said, I heard things.'

Shapiro lets out a sigh. 'So it's not just a hunch. You heard things, which you're taking as gospel. I hear things too, you know. I hear Liam's a troublemaker. I hear there was an incident in the parking lot the other night . . .'

'Liam didn't—'

'I know he didn't. You did. But you see about people *hearing* things.'

'Liam didn't start that. You want to keep an eye on some of the lads you've got coming here.'

'And you want to keep an eye on your fists.' Shapiro shifts in his seat. 'I know your type, Mr Innes. Been dealing with that type for a long time. You breeze in through these doors and you expect the world to stop what its doing and listen to what you have to say. Then you demand answers to whatever's currently bugging you. Am I right?'

I don't answer him. Looks like he's spoiling for a fight. His fingers flex on the desk, then fall still.

'That bump on your head,' he says. 'How'd you get it?'

'An argument.'

'You argue with people who like to use their fists?'

'I try not to. Sometimes it happens. And it wasn't his fist, it was his elbow.'

'Dirty fighter.' He smiles. 'I know all about that.'

'Did time for it is what I hear.'

The smile evaporates. 'So that's what this is about.'

'Part of it.'

'You heard I was in prison. You don't believe in rehabilitation.'

'I believe it in some people.'

'Let me tell you something, Mr Innes.' Shapiro pushes the dog from his lap. It lands awkwardly on the floor. 'Something you might be able to appreciate, coming from where you do. I did some stupid things in my life. I knew they were stupid at the time, but I still did them because I was a different guy back then. Then I paid the price. And it was a long time ago, despite what you've heard. I came out and had to work hard against the kind of prejudice you're wearing right now. People think, you've done time, you're beyond help even if you've taken your punishment like a man. You must get that. You did time.'

'Paulo told you,' I say.

'Paulo and I, we've become pretty good friends the last year or so. I respect what he's trying to do in Manchester. It's thankless work. He's a better man than me.'

'I'm sure he'll be glad to hear it.'

'And I told him my past, and he told me his. There's a moment when you have to stop hanging onto your history with both hands and start looking to something else. Drunks call it a moment of clarity.'

'Can't say I've had that.'

'With me, I found God in prison.'

'What was He in for?'

Shapiro's eyes spark for a second. He looks ready to lunge across the desk and make a torn arsehole out of my face. I plant my feet, make sure I've got a good head start if I have to bolt and pray that my back doesn't lock.

'This competition has Enrique Alvarez attached to it,' he says. 'You know who Enrique Alvarez is?'

'No.'

'You're not a boxing fan at all. Then I can't expect you to understand. Enrique Alvarez, Mr Innes, was a legend in the ring, a real gentleman warrior. He's a hero to a lot of these kids, showed you can get somewhere with a little determination and a lot of hard work. He came here one time, told them about his grandparents, they used to live out in Chavez Ravine in the fifties before they tore it down. Now he's out of the game, he's investing in low-cost, high-quality houses. Some of the kids in here live in Alvarez real estate, and it's a major step up from where they were before.'

I wipe away a fake tear. 'That's very sweet, Mr Shapiro.'

'You think this is a sob story?' Shapiro sucks his teeth. He shows me his hands. 'What do you want from me? I tell you this is a *kosher* tournament and you get sarcastic. You got your own ideas about this and about me, so I want to hear them. Because it doesn't seem to matter to you that the Alvarez name is synonymous with fair play, integrity and downright honesty in this city. It doesn't matter to you that I wouldn't be involved – wouldn't be *allowed* to be involved – if I wasn't one hundred percent down with that. There are gym owners who would've killed to host this competition, but they weren't legit enough to handle it. I take great pride in having it here.'

'I'm sure you do.'

'And if you think I'm going to let one man with a chip on his shoulder ruin this for a bunch of kids who want to do something with their lives, you've got another thing coming.'

'You threatening me?'

'I'm stating a fact. If you make me choose between having you call my every move – because obviously you feel qualified to judge how I'm running things here – and dumping you and Liam out of the comp, you know how I'm going to lean.'

'So you are threatening me.'

'No.' He pauses. 'But I'm not going to toe the line for you, either.

You look out there.' He points at the main gym. Outside, another crowd is beginning to develop. Amateur fight fans, other boxers. 'This isn't just about you and your boy, Mr Innes. Liam wins, that'll be great, you'll have my congratulations. He doesn't, then he's still got the potential to go far. No matter what you might think, though, there are boys out there who need this thing more than Liam does.'

Shapiro scoops up the dog as he gets to his feet.

'So if you haven't got any more insults, you'll excuse me,' he says. 'I've got a competition to run.'

TWENTY-SEVEN

'You're British,' she says.

Half-cocked Brit. What's it? Half in my cups, soused, stinking, however many sheets to the fucking wind, yeah.

'I'm Scottish,' I say. '*Scottish*. There's a difference. Romans built a wall to *maintain* that difference. And Britain's not a country.'

'Sure it is.'

'Doesn't have a patron saint.' And I start singing, 'It's just an economic union, that's past its sell-by date.'

She smiles. She's pretty enough. Very American. Good teeth, blonde hair that looks natural, decent skin. Certainly not the usual type who talk to me in bars. But it's a whole different class over here.

I don't go looking for female company if I can help it. Call it having a gay bloke for a best mate, whatever you want. Whatever keeps me from digging too deep. Truth is, the situation doesn't arise.

Yeah, you can say that again.

Celibate by circumstance. I could've stayed in my room, had a nap, woke up to my duty free booze and see if I could find a porn flick. But those are the actions of a non-functioning member of society. And besides, I could do that at home. Here, this is my tourist time. Getting shitfaced is about the closest I can manage to a proper holiday.

I just wish people would leave me the fuck alone.

'I'm Sherry,' she says.

'Like the drink or the fruit?' I try to draw myself up straight on my stool.

'The drink.'

'Good. I'm Callum. Cal.'

'Unusual name.'

I want to tell her it's not that bloody unusual. Probably was when my mam named me, but now you can't meet five people in Britain without hearing Celtic or Gaelic names, people so fucking ashamed of being English they have to plunder Scotland and Ireland for their children. My dad would've said it was par for the course; the English were always trying to steal the good shite for themselves.

'You know what it means?' says Sherry.

'Didn't know it meant anything.'

'It means "dove".'

I squint at her. 'You're not kidding, are you?'

She shakes her head once. 'It's a hobby of mine.'

'So what does your name mean?'

'It's Hebrew. It means "beloved".'

'And are you?'

'I have my moments.' Sherry gets off her stool, moves to the one next to me. I catch a whiff of something sweet. Could be her perfume or the alcohol on her breath. Either way, it's better than my own smell. I've taken enough showers since I got to this country, but I always find a way to sweat. Up close, Sherry's older than I thought, a lot more make-up, the kind of woman I'd describe as a stealthmoose if I was being unkind. But I'm not in the mood to be unkind. She still looks okay, a little frayed around the edges, smells better than she looks, and she's obviously interested in me.

Which means if she's not already drunk, she should be. I point to her half-empty glass. 'Get you another?'

Another smile. Something about her perfect teeth tugs at my chest.

'Why not?' she says. 'Rum and Coke.'

I order two. It's been a while and I remind myself that rum's a good drunk, a lazy, mellow headfuck. And I'm sick of bottled beer. About time I kicked it up a notch, feel like a poetic tramp. Isn't that what LA's all about? Tom Waits, Charles Bukowski country.

'So where are you going after this, Sherry?'

'You're right in there with the lines, aren't you?' she says, turning that smile on the bartender as he sets down our drinks.

'I didn't mean it like that. Just, I look around this place, I don't see many people dressed up. I thought maybe you had a party or something later on.'

'That's very sweet, Cal.' She sips her drink. Very ladylike. I see tiny wrinkles around her mouth. 'But no, I've got nowhere to go. I'm all yours.'

'Well, isn't this my lucky night.'

'What do you do, Cal? For a living.'

I think about it. What I'm going to tell her, whether it's worth telling the truth, exaggerating and embellishing, or just tell an outright lie.

'I'm a security guard,' I say.

'Really.'

'Yeah, I used to be a brain surgeon, but then I got my hand caught in a revolving door trying to save a small dog. Kind of put an end to my career.'

'Aw, that's sad.'

'Tell me about it. The dog was okay, though.'

'Good.'

'Yeah, you looked worried.' I pluck the straw from my glass, drop it on the bar, and drain half my run and Coke. 'What do you do?'

'I'm a writer.'

I look at her.

'What?' she says. 'That so difficult to believe?'

'No. I just wasn't expecting writer. I was thinking, actress, singer, something like that. What do you write?'

'I have a screenplay I'm shopping around.'

'What's it about?'

'You don't want to know.' She looks at her drink, half-smiling now.

'You're right,' I say. 'I don't.' My brain's tired. Done way too much thinking today to fake an interest, and the beer and rum are slowing me down. When I glance at Sherry, she almost looks relieved. Look up at the bartender and he's watching, but pretending not to.

I get it.

'What do you really do?' I say.

'Sorry?'

'I'm just wondering. You don't have anywhere to go and you get dressed up for it?'

The smile on her face becomes mouth-only. 'A girl can't get dressed up for no reason?'

You're not a girl, love. Haven't been a girl for a long time.

'Maybe it's different over here,' I say. 'Maybe people dress formally for fuck-all.'

'Yeah, maybe it is.' There's an edge to her voice.

'But in Britain, you see a woman on her own and she's all dressed up and chatty, you start thinking maybe she's not the lady she's trying to be.'

It takes a moment for that to sink in. Another moment for her to make her decision. And one last quick moment for her to throw that six-dollar drink I just bought her in my face.

'The fuck you get off talking to people that way?' she says. She gets much angrier, she'll crack her foundation.

'I'm just thinking out loud.'

'You need to watch your fucking manners, pal.'

'Okay.'

As I'm wiping the rum from my eyes – and by Christ, it stings – I think if she's any kind of lady, if she's truly been insulted and not just fucking rumbled, she'll walk out now. That's what happens. I've been here before. The shock, maybe some tears, but it ends with a slammed door. Call a woman a whore, or as good as, expect them to want nothing to do with you. Sometimes it's the easiest way to cut short a relationship that'll go nowhere.

But Sherry's a piece of work. She slips from her stool, starts shouting at me like I'm the worst shitheel on the face of the planet.

Like nobody'd ever mentioned to her that all that slap she's wearing might push her status from looker to hooker. That's all I said, meant it as a joke. I think. And if it was, well, it's plain that Sherry, for all her smiling, hasn't got a sense of humour.

Ach, it wouldn't have lasted anyway.

'Sherry,' says the bartender. 'How about you go cool off?'

'You heard what he called me?'

'He didn't call you anything, Sherry. You heard him wrong.'

'He called me a fucking hooker, Jim.'

'Sherry.' Jim the bartender stands firm.

She stares at me.

'Don't make me come around there,' says Jim.

'Fuck you,' she says. Storms to the door. 'You stay here, Callum, you fucking *fag*.'

'Oh, that's nice.'

And she's gone, heel-clicking into the night. The door hisses closed on its bracket. When I turn back, the bartender's in front of me. Big forearms folded across a bigger chest.

'I think you better hit the road, Jack,' he says.

I point to myself. 'Callum, mate.'

'Then hit the road, Callum.'

'Yeah, I got you.' I dab my face with a napkin, a big patch down the front of my shirt. I'm glad she managed to get half her drink down her before she got it down me. I place my hands on the bar, push myself off the stool. My legs give way for a second until the blood returns. I hang onto the bar, raise one hand like I'm okay, I'm alright, just give me a moment. Then I down the rum and Coke. Hey, I paid for it. Waste not, want not. A couple of steps before I have to stop.

'Here, mate,' I say. 'Was she really a hooker?'

'Sherry's a drunk,' he says, moving to mop the bar. 'But she does extra work every now and then.'

I nod. 'Yeah, like screenwriting.'

'Get some sleep, pal.'

I raise a hand, then turn and stumble out of the bar onto the street. Take a deep breath, let the night air clear out my lungs, wipe my mind. Then I light a cigarette. I knew it. I had my chance six months ago. The more that's happened to me since then, the more I know I had my chance and I fucked it up. And hindsight's a crystal-clear kick in the head. Keeps me awake most nights, or else caught between extremes, my own private purgatory.

I push my hands deep into my jacket, head down, trying to put one foot in front of the other. All I've got to do now is find the hotel. I've been lost sober, but never drunk. Alcohol kicks in the survival mechanism, almost unconscious. And I thank the Lord for it, I really do.

Because it's that same survival mechanism that tells me I'm being followed.

It's a car, drawing close to the kerb, the engine purring.

I keep walking because I'm not sure. Try to concentrate on my feet, but it's not needed. There's nothing like paranoia to sober a bloke up. So I walk quicker. Look up the street, think about crossing over just to make sure. I cross, they cross, then I'm onto something. Probably a beating. It's darker on the other side of the road. Means I could slip into the shadows if I'm careful. Or it could mean they'll panic and leap in after me. If there's any bodily harm to be done, I want it out in the open where there are potential witnesses.

The car keeps coming. Crawling after me.

Wondering who it is. Thinking it'll be Shapiro. He wanted to do me damage, I know it. But if he's in this position of trust like he says he is, he won't get personally involved. Which means, what? Hired guys?

'Mr Innes.'

The bloke has a voice like a cartoon snake. I don't turn.

'Mr Innes.'

He won't leave it alone. I want to run, but they're in a fucking car. How far am I likely to get?

So I stop. The car eases up next to me. In the back seat, a skinny guy has the window buzzed down. He's the one with the vocal chords. I don't see the driver, hidden behind tinted glass.

'What?' I say. Take a few steps back, maintain some distance so if there's a gun in that car, I'll notice it before I notice the pain in my stomach.

'You're Mr Innes,' says the skinny guy.

'I answered to my name, mate. You want to see some ID?'

'You talked to Mr Callahan this morning.'

I smile. So it's not Shapiro. It's Callahan. Should've guessed. 'Yeah, I got talked at.'

'He wants to know if you've had time to consider his offer.'

Look up and down the street – nobody. 'Funny you should mention that, actually. I was mulling it over in the bar just now. Had a few cocktails, thought about corruption, you know how it is.' I take a better look at the guy, try to commit his face to memory, but his features are so bland it's hard to hook him into my brain. That voice, though. I'll remember that voice. Especially if I get him to say 'inconceivable'.

'So you've thought about it,' he says.

'You a lawyer, mate? You look a bit like a lawyer. Nah, hang on, you're an *employee*, am I right?'

'Do you have an answer?'

'Whoa, you're a pushy fucker. You and Mr Callahan.' I sniff and spit at the pavement. Still can't see the driver, but I'm betting he's a skinny wee prick, too. 'I'll tell you, like I said, I've had the chance to think about the offer. And I have to say, my mind hasn't changed. I'm afraid I'm still replying in the negative.'

And I turn my back and start walking. After six feet or so, I can hear the car door opening, the skinny guy stepping out. I turn around. He's got a hand inside his suit jacket.

'I'll warn you right off the bat, pal,' I say. 'You shoot me, there's people who'll miss me.'

The skinny guy walks towards me. As he does so, his hand emerges with an envelope. 'I've been instructed to push the price up to seven thousand.'

'You don't catch on too quick, do you?'

'And I've been instructed not to leave until you've accepted.'

'Well, it's going to be a long fuckin'—'

He reaches forward, stuffs the envelope into my jacket. I pull my hands out of my pockets, ready to take the bloke on if need be, my arse clenching like an epileptic. Before I know it, he's back in the car. And the engine makes a slight revving sound. My reactions fucked – not as sober as I need to be – I stand there with the weight of the cash on my chest.

I should pull the envelope out, throw it to the ground, spit at it. Make a show of turning him down. But by the time my brain gets to that thought, all I see is a pair of retreating brake lights as the car disappears at the top of the street.

'For fuck's sake . . .'

TWENTY-EIGHT

I didn't just accept a bribe. I didn't do that. No, what happened was I had a bribe *forced* on me. That's not an acceptance, there's no culpability in that.

'Because Liam's not going to throw the fuckin' fight,' I say to nobody in particular.

The balls of the man. Callahan thinking, what the fuck, if he's *given* the money he'll just take it and do what I say regardless.

No, no way.

I checked the contents of the envelope before I chucked it onto the desk. The skinny bloke hadn't been lying: seven grand in a hefty wedge of used notes sitting there. I have to deal with it, but I don't want to right now. Been carrying that around with me all the way back to the hotel. And now I'm carrying the Smirnoff like a rosary, twisting the cap on and off. Alternate chewing the inside of my mouth to ribbons and burning it with vodka. My back's started to hurt and I really should sit down, take a pill, but I'm in the middle of a whirling drunk. The time for passing out and letting the world drift is long gone now. I've surfed over that hump into a mess of bad thoughts and worse outcomes.

I took the money.

I'm fucked.

Liam's fucked.

But, the way it seems, we're fucked anyway. Because for all of Shapiro's 'I found God' shite, he's still dodgy. Nelson wouldn't steer me wrong on that. What would he have to prove?

Last time I had money like this, I was thankful to be out of jail. And that kind of cash – the kind sitting right there, Benjamin fucking

Franklin giving me the evil eye – could put me right back. Except it wouldn't be none of your Strangeways bullshit. Talking American penitentiary now. The harsh Eddie Bunker stuff. Animal factories.

I drop to the bed, kick off my shoes. Set the bottle on the bedside table and look at the phone. That message light is still blinking.

'Fuck off,' I say.

But I pick up the phone anyway, check the message.

It's not Callahan.

'Cal, it's me. Just wanted to see how you and Liam were getting on,' says Paulo. He pauses, sounds like he's struggling with something. 'Uhh, what we talked about, about Mo? He's been back, thought you should know. Wanted to know where you were.'

Please tell me you called the police, Paulo.

'I sorted it.'

He sounds drunk. But when you're drunk, everyone sounds drunk except you.

'Just thought you should know,' he says again. 'I told him he wasn't welcome. That I knew he didn't have any protection from his dad. And, well . . .' He clears his throat.

And a long pause this time.

'It doesn't matter, mate. Look, give us a ring back, let us know how Liam's getting on. Don't worry about the cost, alright? I know it's stupid money, but it's good to know, eh? Sorry.'

Then the disconnection click.

Sorry? Fuck does sorry mean?

I check my watch, try to do the maths. Adding eight to one shouldn't be difficult, but the answer's doing its best to remain elusive. Then I try calling Paulo's place, get four digits in and realise I'm punching the wrong number.

Fuck, Cal. Think.

That old smiling comment: 'Well, I never call myself, do I?'

I tug my wallet out of my jacket. I know I've got some business cards in here somewhere, back when I used to be something other than a caretaker. Find one, alternate concentrating on the card and the phone keypad.

Listen.

'The number you have dialled is out of service.'

I disconnect the call. Try again.

Same result. Blah-blah-blah, out of service.

Maybe it's a misprint on the card.

Maybe my fingers don't work.

Or maybe something's happened.

I push the thought from my mind, dump the wallet on the bed and reach for the bottle again. No point in worrying about someone six thousand miles away. Concentrate on the here and now.

The here: a progressively shitty-looking hotel room in Los Angeles.

The now: getting drunk. Again. The drunk-hangover wheel pelting around like the old days. Falling back into old habits.

No. Think.

Use the money to bribe Shapiro.

Why?

'Because he can be bought,' I say.

I don't know that, though. I *think* that. But I can't be sure.

Forget the cash. Leave it. Give it to that homeless guy next time you see him. Probably be tomorrow, tell him, 'Happy birthday, mate. Get yourself a nice suit. Put a deposit on a flat or something. Live your fuckin' life.'

The bottom line, and say it with me:

'Liam's not going to throw the fuckin' fight.'

Spot on. Callahan just paid me to . . . what? Keep my mouth shut about the original bribe?

Throw the bout. Keep the money. Give the money away. Tell Shapiro. Keep my mouth shut. Don't do anything. Let nature run its course. Don't get involved. Take the money, I need it. Tell Nelson. Ask him what I should do.

Don't think so much.

I look at my wallet, see a small piece of paper sticking out from one of the billfolds. I should've screwed that paper up ages ago.

Should've binned the fucking thing. Left in the back pocket of my jeans and set the machine to a boil wash, pulp it.

I pluck the paper out now. A mobile number written down.

I call it.

A familiar ring tone brings me back to Britain, a crackle on the line that reminds me where I am.

And then she picks up.

'Hello?'

It hurts. I didn't expect the sound of her voice to hurt. What's that they say? Whatever it is, it's probably bullshit. Christ, I've got Jim Croce playing in my head now. I cover the mouthpiece with my hand, take a deep breath, try to steady the shakes, like some fucking twelve-year-old and his first girlfriend.

'Hello?'

That's all I'm going to hear unless I say something. And say something quick before she hangs up. But I can't think of anything.

My mind's a blank.

I've stopped thinking so much.

There's an irritated sigh at the other end.

And I say, 'Thank you.'

But Donna's already hung up. Money well spent.

TWENTY-NINE

I sleep like a dead man. None of the usual drifts in and out of consciousness. No pained and panicked visits to the bathroom for water and pills. No, I'm sparked out. And nothing can wake me up except shock.

I open my eyes. Looking at the door to my hotel room, standing open. I blink, look at my watch and the time swims into focus. Ah fuck, I'm late. Which means Liam's late and he didn't have the balls to wake me up. It doesn't surprise me, the way him and Nelson are all best friends and that. The lad probably just caught a cab. But I peel myself from the bed and knock on his door just in case.

Nothing.

That's fine. I left my door open. I must've passed out with it open. Liam came in, saw me well out of it, made his own way. That's okay. That's great. I did want to see him slaughter Josh, mind. But Liam's probably had enough of me. Let's face it, we were never on the best of terms.

So I wash my face, brush my teeth, realise I don't have time for a shower and head down to reception. Before I leave, I ask the guy behind the desk if Liam's taken a cab to the gym again. I get a shrug in reply.

Don't mean nothing, drive on.

My stomach growls, and not through lack of food. In fact, the whole idea of food is enough to make me a little sick. Maybe later, after Liam wins. Treat the lad to a slap-up. I've got plenty of cash to drop on him and he'll probably get off on the idea of a bloody steak after all those carrot sticks. I get in the Metro and sack the no-smoking rule by dragging the nicotine out of two cigarettes on the way to Shapiro's. When I get there, I park up and hurry through the doors. Looking for Liam, knocking into people, pushing further and I can't see him anywhere. I do see Reuben, heading my way with a face like thunder.

'Reuben, you seen Liam?' I say.

'The hell you talking about?' he says. 'You're supposed to be his driver.'

Not good. I pinch the bridge of my nose. 'The fight is today, isn't it?'

'You got fucked up.'

'Is it today?'

'Yeah, it's today. When'd you think it was?'

'And you haven't seen Liam.'

'No.'

I shake my head. 'Where's Shapiro?'

'Hang on there, man. You don't need to talk to Phil, you need to find your fighter.'

'Like fuck I don't need to talk to Phil.'

Reuben makes a grab for me as I head for Shapiro's office. His hand touches sleeve, but I shrug him free. Small fingers don't grip that well.

I push open the office door, hear it slam against the wall. Shapiro turns to me, glaring. 'You didn't even knock this time.'

'Where's Liam?'

'You're asking me?'

'He's not here,' I say. Stating the bleeding obvious. And trying not to panic but I have the feeling I should.

'No, he's not here.' Shapiro looks at his watch. 'And you've got two hours before he forfeits.'

'You're fuckin' joking.'

'I'm not joking, Mr Innes. Boxers need to be here three hours before the bout for weigh in. And I thought we discussed this yesterday. Your boy isn't the only boxer. I make concessions for him, I make them for everyone. I'm not running a charity here. There are rules and those rules have to be followed.'

'I don't know where he is.'

'Then he forfeits. The bout goes to Josh.'

'You can't reschedule?'

Shapiro sucks his teeth. 'No.'

I cross to his desk. Shapiro's a big guy, but a broken nose is a broken nose and I'll dish it out. 'How much did he pay you?'

His eyes become slits. 'Excuse me?'

'I saw Josh Callahan's father yesterday. He offered me five grand to throw the bout. I told him no. Then a bloke comes up to me in the street last night like he's been *following* me and he offers me seven, *gives* me seven, and I tell him no. So what I want to know is, what's your fuckin' price, Phil?'

'You took a bribe,' says Shapiro. 'That what you're telling me?'

'I didn't take a bribe. The guy shoved a bribe in my jacket and fucked off.'

'You took the money. Why would this man give you money if he didn't think you were going to do something about it?'

'I was drunk and that's not the fuckin' issue.'

'I don't have much use for people who turn to drink under pressure, Mr Innes.'

'How much did he pay you?'

'I don't take bribes.'

'You took plenty in your time, Phil. You were a fuckin' leg-breaker.'

Shapiro draws himself up to his full height, his shoulders back. Trying to put the wind up me, but it's not going to work. I'm too scared and I'm too angry and I couldn't give a shit.

'How much?' I say.

'Nothing. I don't take bribes. Or have them forced on me when I'm drunk. Now I'm going to be the good guy here, Mr Innes. The way you're acting, you're probably still half-drunk and you smell like you slept in your clothes. You're confused, you're not with it mentally, so I'll make this slow and clear for you. I don't know where Liam is. I don't know where he's been for the last couple of days, considering he's supposed to be training here. And I don't want to see him forfeit this bout because he's followed your lead and gotten drunk somewhere.'

'Liam doesn't drink. He's a good lad.'

'Yeah, he's a good lad who isn't here. Look, I'll try to hold off on the weigh-in as long as possible. He doesn't get back here in three hours, that's it. He's forfeited. That's all I can do.'

I resist the temptation to slam the door on the way out. But I know I'm being played here. If Liam had been at Nelson's, he'd be at the gym right now. Or there'd be a message waiting for me. Something. Nelson's not the kind of guy to leave me hanging like this. Which only makes me think the worst.

Why would Callahan insist on giving me the money if he didn't think I'd do something?

That's a good fucking point. I hadn't thought of that.

Callahan made sure I had the money because it implicated me. It set the blame at my door. Because he already had a back-up plan. And kidnap's an ugly word, but it's the only one that springs to mind.

I get to the parking lot as a Lincoln pulls up. I stop by the Metro, and I can make out Josh in the passenger seat.

Callahan gets out, a bag in his hand. His son gets out the other side. Josh looks startled as I approach. His father regards me, tightens his grip on the handle.

'Where is he?' I say.

'Who?' he says.

I slam both hands into Callahan's chest. He drops the bag, bounces off the side of the car. His face turns red, his arms trying to fend me off, but I push him back, harder this time. 'Who the fuck d'you think I'm talking about?'

'Get your hands off my dad,' says Josh, his voice hitting a whine.

'Josh, don't make me knock you out, son. You might be a nippy wee fucker in the ring, but I'll put my boot in your arse if you fuck around with me.' I keep a hold on Callahan. 'Where's Liam?'

Callahan's eyes are wide and blue. I can see my reflection in there, leering close.

'You're crazy,' he says.

'I think I've got to be,' I say. 'Because I seem to be asking the same fuckin' question over and over and I don't hear an answer. Where is he?'

'I don't know what you're talking about.'

'You don't know what I'm talking about. You tried bribing me, you fuckin' twat.'

Callahan shakes his head: deny, deny, deny.

'Yeah, you did. I got seven grand sitting in my hotel room that says you did. And I turned it down. Where's Liam?'

'I don't know.'

I hit Callahan in the side of the head with an open hand. Callahan flinches, his skin blossoming pink under his ear. My fingers ache, but I throw the pain out with a shake of the hand. 'Don't lie to me, mate.'

'I really don't know,' he says.

And I hit him again, this time with a fist. The crack and sudden yield as his nose breaks, the cartilage grinding against my knuckles. I take a step back, one hand still spread on his chest. Something clicks in Josh; he goes apeshit, running over to me. I hold out my free hand, blood on the knuckles. 'Don't, Josh. Your dad didn't pay me to take a dive for you so I can do what I like to you. Pick your fuckin' battles.'

Josh looks from me to his old man. He doesn't say anything, but his teeth are clamped together, his lips working. Water in his eyes. Matching the tears in his father's.

'You're the hard lad, Josh. You wanted Liam out of the competition. Don't tell me you didn't know anything about this.'

He didn't. He does now.

I pull Callahan from the side of the Lincoln, swing him round and let him go. He staggers a few steps before he collapses to the ground. His nose is dribbling red. Not a bad break, but enough to make him think he's got a six-inch nail in his sinuses and an ocean in his eyes. But then the fucker likes the ocean, doesn't he?

I catch my breath. 'You tried to bribe me. It didn't work. You took Liam.'

'I didn't do anything like that.' When he talks, blood bubbles appear through Callahan's fingers. 'I don't know where your golden boy is.'

'You took Liam.' I kick him, aiming for the face, but connecting with his right shoulder. Callahan doesn't drop; he sways in a sitting position, twisting. 'If you didn't take him, one of your *employees* did.'

'You don't know who you're dealing with.'

'I know exactly who I'm dealing with, Mr Callahan. I'm dealing with a knobhead who thinks he can buy his son a future. Someone who thinks cash equates to intelligence.' I turn to Josh. 'You believe me or not. Your dad tried to sway the bout. Didn't think you had the fight in you to pull off a win.'

'He didn't—'

'You're making a mistake,' says Callahan.

I start walking to my car before I get any more ideas. 'I made 'em before, mate, and I'll make 'em again.'

As I slide behind the wheel of the Metro, I glance at the pair of them.

'Help me up, Josh,' says Callahan.

Josh stands there.

I turn the key in the ignition and the lad looks over at me.

He really didn't know the first thing about this.

And part of me feels bad about it. But that won't last long.

I've got more important things to take care of.

THIRTY

That temper flash. That's what keeps me running headlong into the shitpile. If I'd learned to control it in prison, it was only because routine dulls the nerves, wears you down to the point where you don't have to feel anymore. All you have is monotony, that same grey existence day in, day out. It turned scarlet every time some hard bastard gets a face on or a mealy fucker's looking to graduate, but mostly it was a grind. What brought it out in the real world was confusion, chaos and bad luck dogging me like bog roll on the heel of my shoe. And I've got a horrible way of taking that personally.

Knuckles white and spotted brown on the steering wheel, thinking Nelson's the only person I can trust. Hoping to fuck he's seen Liam, panic gnawing away at me, but all hope's not lost yet. Control, focus.

If something's happened to the lad, I don't know what I'm going to tell Paulo. I know I was supposed to be here to relax – and what a fucking joke that's turned out to be – but the least I could've done was keep an eye on Liam.

If he fucks this up, it's his fault, Callum.

That's not true. If Liam fucks this up because of something I've done or something I haven't done, that's *my* fault. And the road to hell is paved with good intentions.

As I pull up outside the hotel, I can see Nelson standing out front. Get closer, and his face is white.

Christ. Something happened. I stop the Metro by Nelson, wind down the window. 'You seen Liam?'

'Where've you been?' he says. He blinks at me. Could be the sunlight, but his shoulders are tight.

'Where d'you think I've been? I've been at Shapiro's. Liam's not there. He's got his bout with Josh in about an hour or something. I've managed to get it postponed for a wee while, but Shapiro's not going to hold it forever.'

Nelson is shaking. If I thought it was bad before, I know it's worse now.

'Nelson, mate, what's the matter?'

'I know where he is, Cal.' He takes a deep breath, his shoulders dropping a little. His hand strays to his jacket. Looks like he's got a stomachache or something, the way his hand moves under the fabric.

'He alright?'

Nelson nods. 'I think so, yeah.'

'He in his room?'

'No.'

'The fuck's the matter with you, Nelson?'

'He's not in his room,' he says. He opens his mouth, presses a back tooth with his tongue and breathes out sharply. 'He's not in his room.'

'But you know where he is. You've seen him.'

Nelson nods.

'The fuck is he, then? I'm on a clock here—'

Nelson snaps at me: 'He's somewhere else, okay?'

'You need a lift? Can I drive it?'

Nelson removes his hand, squints up the street, then back to me. 'Yeah.'

'Then whatever you've got to say, you can say it when I'm driving. Come on.'

At first, I think we're heading to Nelson's house. The city drops away, becomes desert on either side of the car. Blue skies above, tattered anorexic clouds. Nelson gives me directions and I'm doing my best to follow them as I keep tabs on the clock in the dash. Been driving for an hour now, time's running out and I don't know what the fuck's up with my passenger. Nelson's been pale as hell and trembling in his seat. When he speaks, it's as if he's playing ventriloquist's dummy.

'My mother loved Willie Nelson,' he says. 'That's why she called me Nelson. She loved Willie Nelson.'

'What happened, mate?'

Nelson shakes his head, looks at his lap. In such a state, he hasn't buckled up. Just sitting there, this twitching mess. And I hope to Christ he snaps out of it soon, because I need answers and all this crazy shite is just making me fear the worst.

'That kid's got potential,' he says. 'He had a lot of potential.'

'Had?'

'He shouldn't be screwing his life up like this.'

'Like what? Christ, Nelson, you're scaring the shit out of me here. What the fuck happened to him?'

Thinking now Liam got drunk, Liam got robbed, Liam ended up on a D and D or assault charge because he let his temper get the better of him. Picturing him sweating cobs in a jail cell. The heat of this place, the strangeness of it all, part of me is surprised it didn't happen earlier. Thinking that if Nelson didn't see it coming, I should have. And kicking myself for it. But then, he was with his coach most of the time. What the fuck was he doing when Liam was getting himself into trouble?

'Liam called me from the hotel this morning, Cal.'.

'He was there this morning?'

'Bear right,' he says, gesturing with his left hand. The right stays on his hand, clenched in a ball.

I bear right.

'He was at the hotel this morning and he called me up and said could I drop him off at the gym. So I drove to the hotel and I saw Liam there.'

'Is he at your place now? cause if he's at your place, Nelson, I need to know. I'm running on a tight fuckin' deadline here, and I'll need to step on it if I'm going to get out to Palm Desert and back in time.'

Nelson leans back in his seat, closes his eyes, flexes his right hand. 'It doesn't matter.'

'What?' I watch the road, put my foot down. 'No, we can make this.'

'You left your door open,' he says. I hardly hear it, sounds like he's sighing at the same time. 'I saw the money.'

'What money?'

'The cash. On the desk.' He faces me. There's sweat on his forehead and the air conditioning's on. 'You took the bribe, didn't you?'

'I didn't take any bribe, Nelson . . .'

'You took the money.'

'I didn't take anything. They put the cash on me. Last night—'

'All this time, Cal, I've been *telling* you . . . I told you how corrupt the sport could be. And you told me you didn't take it—'

'And I didn't—'

'I went in your room and I saw the cash. That means you took the bribe.'

'Nelson—'

'You fucking *did*,' he yells. 'Don't tell me you didn't take the money, Cal. I *saw* the fucking money. What the fuck else was it going to be? You come into some cash that quickly? What was it, your fucking holiday money? Don't tell me I didn't fucking see something when I *did*. It was there—'

'Calm down. Let me explain.'

Nelson's voice drops low, almost to a whisper. 'You know, everything in this world has a dollar sign attached to it, everything can be bought, I thought there were actually guys out there who wouldn't sell out at the first fucking opportunity and I thought there was some fucking decency in you, I did, I thought there was some integrity left in this—'

'Don't start that white-hat, black-hat shite with me again, Nelson. Listen to me.'

'You sold him out.' Hard, flat. A statement of fact. And there's a rage in his eyes that I haven't seen since Liam was messing him about.

'I didn't sell anyone out, man. I sold him out, why the fuck am I looking for him now?'

'So he can take that standing count for you.'

'Fuckin' stop it, alright? Stop it. I sorted that out with Callahan. You want to see his face, I'll find him when we get back. *With* Liam. Now where are we going?'

I glance across at Nelson. His mouth is tight, his eyes narrowed. Hand laying under his jacket. He looks like whatever problem he had with his stomach has moved to his heart.

'Nelson. Talk to me, mate. Where are we going?'

Nothing. He blinks. Mouthing something I don't catch.

'You alright? You feeling okay? You look like shit.'

'Shit,' he says.

'C'mon, give me directions. I'm just driving here. I don't want to be stuck out in the middle of fuckin' nowhere.'

I look back at the road. There's nothing out there. Bleak.

'Tell me where I'm going,' I say.

Nelson's hand clamps on the steering wheel. Holds fast. I turn in my seat. His right hand is under his jacket. He brings it out, a gun in his fist. I jerk my head as the metal brushes my cheek.

'You're fuckin' jok—'

The gun goes off, the smell of what I suppose is cordite in the air, billowing into my face, and I can't hear anything apart from a high drone in both ears. Shattered glass down the back of my neck. I lash out. Forget the fucking car.

Lash out.

The world flares once, bright as the sun.

Then crashes into grey.

PART 3

A Satisfied Mind

THIRTY-ONE

Pastel shades on the walls, designed to keep your temper in check. Clean, reflective floors or thin stain-resistant carpet: any flooring that can repel blood, urine, vomit and – in some extreme cases – shit. The kind of hush that makes the air thick, taste like furniture polish or bleach at the back of your throat. The men here are wearing short-sleeved shirts, loafers and slacks with razor-sharp creases in them. Buzz cuts and the beginnings of beer bellies. These men are all clean-shaven. Some of them look so young, so fresh-faced, that a five o'clock shadow's about as foreign to them as a bloke with part of his ear missing, covered in blood, and talking with an accent that belongs six thousand miles away from here.

They've asked me to repeat myself a few times already. Mainly because they can't understand what I'm saying, sometimes because they want to see if I stick to my story. If I repeat it word for word, I've been prepped and I'm lying. If I change my story too much, I'm not prepped and I'm still lying.

Nice to see that some things are the same on both sides of the Atlantic. But at least it looks like I'm going to be spared the kind of am-dram DS Donkin's so fucking keen on. So far, I've been left pretty much alone, questioned by a couple of cops, left with one of them, then left alone again.

We ride this merry-go-round because the two cops – Munroe and Wallace – don't know what's going on. I'm giving them more questions than answers. So they go off, have a conference, come back and try again with their verbal sleight-of-hand. They haven't waded in hard yet. No need to. They don't know I'm an ex-con.

Sitting now, alone in a room that's only a little bigger than my kitchen, there's a part of me that thinks I've got it made. After all, this is a step up: an American police station. Something to be said for an interview by Los Angeles' brightest and best. I still want a cigarette and they took my codeine from me. Oh, and a Sprite or a Coke would go down well right about now. Or a Mountain Dew. Can't get that in Britain anymore.

A long mirror takes up most of the wall to my left, and I wonder if Munroe and Wallace are in there, muttering to themselves, 'What the fuck are we gonna do with this bastard?'

They can do what they want. I'm past caring. I made it out of this afternoon alive, and that's about all I can hope for. Inevitable that I'd end up here. But I had more important things to take care of – Nelson, Liam, Shapiro. Tick 'em off.

I adjust my position in the chair, feel my spine click. No pain. Too tired to feel much of anything. They'd offered me coffee earlier, but I declined after seeing the dishwater they had. And I was polite about it. I was polite about everything.

Play it like they've already beaten you down, and what comes out of your mouth will sound like the God's honest truth.

The door to the interview room opens. Munroe enters first. He's a tall, gangly guy with gingerish-blonde hair and invisible eyebrows. Ruddy face, more likely brought about by the sun than the booze.

'Mr Innes, sorry to keep you waiting,' he says.

Wallace follows him. Another strapping lad, looks like he might've played rugby or American football at one point in his life. But he's older, or *looks* older, a sprinkling of grey in his sideburns.

'Not a problem,' I say.

Munroe pulls up a chair and sits opposite me; Wallace closes the door and leans against it, his arms crossed.

'You're not going to sit?' I say.

'No, thanks,' says Wallace.

'If we could go through your story one more time,' says Munroe. 'Just a few things I want to get absolutely clear.'

'That's fine.'

'Just to nail the facts down,' he says.

'Yeah.'

Munroe laces his fingers together, looks down at my statement so far. 'You were in the car with Mr Byrne, is that correct?'

'Yes.'

'And you were heading where?'

'I don't know. He didn't tell me.'

'But he was giving you directions,' says Wallace. Obviously got this committed to memory.

'Yes.'

'Did you ask him where you were going?' says Munroe.

'A couple of times, yeah.'

'And what did he say?'

'He didn't answer me.'

'How was Mr Byrne's mood?' says Wallace.

'Homicidal,' I say.

Wallace smiles and nods; Munroe's mouth twitches as he says, 'You knew he was going to shoot you.'

'I take that back.' I shift position again, wonder what the hell these chairs are made out of. 'I didn't know he was going to shoot me. He was edgy, though. Something was bothering him.'

'Did he tell you what that was?' says Munroe.

'Before he shot me, yes.'

'And what was bothering him?'

'He thought I'd taken a bribe.'

'A bribe.'

'Yes.'

'What kind of bribe?'

'The money kind.'

'What was the bribe for?' says Wallace.

'I had a fighter in an amateur competition. The bribe was supposed to make him lose.'

'This would be . . . Liam Wooley?' says Munroe.

'That's him.'

'And the . . . Alvarez competition.'

'Yeah.'

'You a coach?' says Wallace.

'No.'

'But you've got a fighter,' he says.

'What did you tell Mr Byrne?' says Munroe.

'I was chaperone to Liam.' Wallace nods, scratches his chin. 'And I told Nelson he was out of his mind.'

'And what happened then?' says Munroe.

'He pulled the gun and fired it.'

Munroe waits for me to continue. I don't.

'You're saying he shot you,' he says.

I point to the side of my head. 'I'd say that was a pretty solid description.'

'But that was . . . the *second* shot?'

'Yeah.'

I dropped my hands from the steering wheel after the first shot. Couldn't hear anything, blinded by smoke and fear. I lunged at Nelson, felt my open palms connect with something solid, the seatbelt lock. The only thing I could do, instinct taking over. Then Nelson pulled the trigger again, took me out, threw my head back.

But before I tapped out, there was something. Nelson grew smaller all at once, sucked out of the car like it was a plane and I was flying low. As he dropped out of sight, the rest of the world followed suit.

And then it was a dull, aching grey. I don't know how long.

I heard something.

Someone telling me that *blue skies* were smiling at me . . .

It was Ella Fitzgerald.

. . . telling me I couldn't see anything but *blue* skies . . .

It was that bloke who did the theme tune to *Moonlighting*.

. . . and those bluebirds were singing a song . . .

And it was Willie Nelson. He caught the tune, stayed with it, pulled me out a little so I could feel my heart beating again, thumping hard against my ribs. Good job your parents called you Nelson, Nelson. Can't imagine how tough your life would've been with a name like Willie Byrne. There were worse folks to be named after, too. At least Willie had the soft, lilting voice, as if he didn't really care about the song, but he made *you* care with his braids and his shining perfect teeth. Another job to get the IRS off his arse, but to me, right then, it was like the heavens fucking well opened wide.

. . . and there were nothing but blue skies from now on . . .

Out of the murk, the song continued, dropped in volume and the sound of bubbling, hissing, like water running over the music.

Yeah, water in the middle of the fucking desert. Give your head a shake, Cal.

Then the voices. More than Willie Nelson. One male, one female, both American. Muffled at first. Became clearer as the temperature dropped.

'You think he's really dead?' said the female.

'I don't know. Leave him,' said the male.

'We can't leave him.'

'Leave him. Get to town, we'll call the police.'

'We can't leave him here, Ed. What if he's still alive?'

'Then he'll still be alive when the cops come.'

'You have your cell?'

'I can't get a signal out here. I tried already. We can't get a signal out here, and there's nothing here, it makes me wonder why we got the thing.'

'For emergencies,' she said.

'Yeah, like this one?'

'You really think he's dead?'

'I think it's hotter 'n Hades out here and there's nothing we can do for him. We'll call the cops in town.'

'I don't know . . .'

'Marie, I'm not discussing this anymore. You want to stay, stay here with your new boyfriend.'

'Ed.'

'You want to get out of the sun before your brains fry, you get in the vehicle and we head into town.'

And I tapped out again.

I came back like a match struck behind my eyelids, light flaring. The pain flared at the same time, made sure I was back and stayed back. I couldn't move my head. Didn't know of any way to do it without hurting myself. Opening my eyes was a struggle – they felt stuck together. I pulled out eyelashes as I pulled myself back to reality. My head was glued to the seat. The passenger door to the Metro hung open, the car leaning to one side and down. I tried to move my head, heard a wet sound as I peeled my face from the head-rest.

The air conditioning was still on in the car, cool air digging into my cheek. It hurt my lungs as I took as big a breath as I could manage. Felt like someone gone to work on my chest like Liam and his heavy bag. I tugged at the seat belt, but it wouldn't budge.

Telling myself, don't pass out again. If it wasn't for the air-conditioning, you'd be dead by now.

There had to be a limit on how long the battery in this shitpot Metro could last.

That shitpot Metro just saved your fucking life.

I remembered the way Nelson dropped out of sight, the passenger door swinging wild. That one snapshot of his face, pure panic.

But I needed to get out of the car, assess the damage. I touched the side of my face; my fingers came away bloody. I pulled the rear view mirror towards me. My face was wrecked, a deep gash in the left side of my head, digging under my cheek and leading to one tattered ear. Behind me, I could see what was left of my earlobe stuck white and speckled reddish-brown to the driver's door.

One inch further, and I wouldn't have been looking at anything.

I fumbled with my seat belt, managed to click it open. Felt the belt dig in as it crossed my chest, like it had dug deep there. Better that than ending up on the road somewhere. I gave it a few minutes, let my lungs take in more air.

One hand on the driver's door, pushing it open, and I threw my arm out onto a pile of dirt. Sunlight burned my eyes. I dragged myself out of the car, dropped facedown. Rolled over, planted one foot against the side of the car and pushed myself towards the road.

Forget the fucking car, eh?

And that's where it got me, tumbled and torn in a ditch. It could have been worse. Yeah, it could have been a lot worse.

Shooting someone because you thought they'd taken a bribe. That was fucking harsh. Not letting them explain or at least try to lie their way out of it. To be that solid in your convictions that you'd play judge, jury and executioner. Jesus, for a guy who *looked* centred, Nelson had a lot of pent-up aggression.

I didn't need to check my watch to know that Liam was out of the comp. Hours had flown by. Shapiro would've called it. So it didn't matter if I managed to get the Metro out of the ditch, got the engine running and started driving, because it was all over already. One bullet and my low threshold for pain just sealed the deal.

I tried to think of something good about my situation. I was alive. Tick that box. And that was it.

I could walk back to Los Angeles, or I could keep walking somewhere else. That was if I knew which way Los Angeles was. And if whatever brain damage I'd suffered didn't cut me down, the heat and blood loss would. After all, it was hot-hot-hot and the weatherman was wearing a suit. They'd find me roasted by the side of the road, pity the poor wee Brit who went out for an afternoon stroll.

'Didn't he know the meaning of desert?'

'Nah, man, they don't have deserts in Britain. It's all fields and shit.'

'But it's hot out there. He should've stayed in the damn car.'

That's what I intended to do. But then thought twice about it. I'd have the air conditioning, maybe a bottle of water, but I'd be sitting there waiting for help that might not come. And I'd be tortured with daydreams of beating the ever-loving shit out of Nelson bastard Byrne.

And where *was* Nelson?

Somewhere in the wilderness, vultures were circling. I couldn't see them or hear them, but I could sure as fuck feel them.

C'mon, *move.*

You fucking lazy bastard coward. Get moving. Get up. Get walking. Do something.

Get the fuck *up.*

I twisted round, dug my hands into the dirt and pushed myself up to my hands and knees. Stuck there in the middle of a girly push-up until I caught my breath. Then I tried to stand up. It was all baby steps, took far longer than it should have, but then baby steps were still steps forward. No sense in rushing it.

I stood by the side of the road on watery legs. Shielding my eyes from the glare, I could just about make out the scarred asphalt. Black streaks gleaming where the tyres tried to grab before I careened off the road. It looked like it had been a short drive to the ditch. I didn't have the momentum to go through the windscreen, just enough for my seat belt to lock and slam me across the chest.

Squinted up the road, thought I should've seen something other than brush and desert. Nelson should have been visible. Twisted in a heap somewhere. I hoped to Christ the fall from the car hadn't killed him, because I didn't need that on my conscience. I was a lot of things, but I wasn't a murderer.

So I started walking. Followed the ditch. My right leg gypped me worse than the left, and my back kicked in with every step.

Just like the old days.

Wishing I had the codeine.

Wishing I had the prozac, the diazepam.

Knowing they were all back at the hotel.

Wishing I had a beer.

Wishing I had . . .

I stopped, pulled out the battered pack of Marlboros and slipped a bent cigarette into my mouth, fumbled some more for my Bic. I didn't care about dehydration, didn't care that smoke scratched at my throat. Nicotine was the closest thing I had to a painkiller. And I was hellbent on smoking the rest of the pack just to see how far it got me.

A hundred yards, and the energy slipped away.

A hundred and fifty, and I saw where Nelson had hit the road. A fine spray of blood.

Two hundred and Nelson was still nowhere to be seen.

He was gone. The bastard had had a back-up plan. He hadn't acted spur of the moment, he'd had it all worked out. Nelson Byrne really wanted to kill me.

Realising something like that, it can take the wind out of your sails in an instant.

I had one more glance up and down the road. Nothing. Dropped to the ground and plucked the cigarette from my lips, held it out in front of me. The smoke plumed straight up.

No breeze.

Dead.

'So you just laid down?' says Wallace.

'I just laid down,' I say.

'Why?' says Munroe.

'I was waiting around to die. Not a lot else I could've done. I was miles outside of the city.'

'But you didn't die,' says Wallace.

I look at the big guy for a long time, then smile.

'No, that's right,' I say. 'I didn't die.'

THIRTY-TWO

I woke up freezing, drowning and grabbing at air.

'There you are, son. Coughing and choking just like the rest of us.'

I knew that voice.

'Don't be mean, Ed.'

And that one.

I tried to pull myself to a sitting position, my face stinging and wet. Wiped at my eyes, water caught in my nose. I coughed up something solid. Red, stringy phlegm hung from the back of my hand.

'I told you he wasn't dead.'

'Guy manages to get himself out of the car, sure he's not dead. I got eyes, Marie. I got a brain. I can use the two of 'em in tandem, y'know.'

I squinted at the new arrivals. My saviours were a couple in their early sixties. Ed was tall, looked even taller. One of the reasons I was feeling the cold was that his shadow fell directly over me. He wore a crumpled sun hat, had a cigarette in his mouth that was either menthol or filterless. From the gravel in his throat and the deep rattle of his breath, I guessed it wasn't a menthol.

'Ed thought you were dead,' said Marie.

'I didn't say that.'

'You said that.'

'I said he was *probably* dead. Probably.'

Marie was a plump woman, short. A patterned blue dress filled to the brim. She looked like a grandmother, and a good one at that. The kind of face you see smiling at you above a selection of baked goods at a church market.

'You okay?' she said.

'Yeah, he's fine. Look at him.'

I wanted to say something, but my throat felt like it'd been scraped raw. I waved my hand at them instead.

'You caught the sun, kid,' said Ed.

Marie pressed a bottle of water into my hand, closed her cold fingers over mine to make sure I held onto it. I nodded at Ed, brought the bottle to my mouth and guzzled the water. It hurt going down.

And it hurt even more coming back up.

Marie grabbed the bottle from me as I twisted to one side, coughed and spewed water.

'Yeah,' said Ed. 'You definitely caught the sun.' He waited for me to stop heaving, then put his hands in my armpits. 'We need to get you inside, son. You need to cool off.'

'I told you,' said Marie, her voice rising. 'I told you he wasn't dead.'

'Yeah, and I told you to get in the damn vehicle.'

The 'vehicle' was a motor home idling by the side of the road. One of those amazing flats-in-a-truck that you could live in for the rest of your life, as long as you didn't mind shopping at petrol stations. I pawed at my mouth, wiping away a thick string of spittle. Marie opened the door to the motor home and Ed helped me into it. The bliss of real air conditioning hit me.

'Get a towel,' said Ed, pulling me over to the couch. He helped me lie down. 'Goddamn it, Marie, get a wet towel.'

I could hear Marie fussing. Not too keen on Ed's choice of words, by the sound of it. I caught '. . . no need for that at *all* . . .'

'I'll tell you right now, you're a lucky guy,' he said.

I looked up at him. Ed looked like a groomed mountain man. A voice that belonged in a Peckinpah western and a face that had the texture of a saddlebag.

'You're lucky my wife's a damn nag.'

'I heard that,' said Marie over the sound of running water.

'Of course you heard it. You hear everything in this thing. Not like we can go in separate rooms.' He looked at me. 'Two rooms: inside and outside. It was her idea. "See all those places you wanted to see all your life, Ed. It'll be an adventure. We need an adventure . . ."'

Marie brought a sodden towel over to me. She pressed it against my head, water running in icy streams across my cheeks. 'You were going to stay in your garden and murder crickets, Ed.'

'This is your adventure.' Then, to me: 'Way I saw it, son, we should've left you where you lay. Too old to be getting involved in that kinda business. You were dead.'

'I said you weren't,' said Marie. 'I *knew* you weren't.'

'The hell with it. You just wanted another gander at the corpse.'

Marie made an O with her mouth. 'I did not. I had faith. I made him turn the RV around. He was grousing, but I had faith.'

She pressed the towel again. My head started to clear. Just a little, the fog lifting at the edges, but it was a good start.

'Yeah, my wife has more faith than I do. I know when to steer clear. This country, it's no place for old men, so I got to look out. My wife, she thinks she's one of God's only women, a real saint.'

'I don't think that.'

'You don't think that. You're closer 'n me. Because I said no, we drive on, we're on vacation, for Christ's sake.'

Marie's face turned to stone. 'That's enough of that.'

'That's what I said.'

'There was no need for it then and there's no need for it now.'

Ed shrugged what could have been an apology. Marie accepted it.

'What I say is, I say there's no *good* way a car ends up in a ditch. When I see you, I say there's no *good* way a guy ends up shot. Which reminds me . . .'

Ed put one huge hand on the side of my head, turned my face away and puffed smoke at my mangled ear.

'It hurt?'

Course it fucking hurt. I nodded.

'Ah, it's a flesh wound. Won't even need stitches. You'll be fine.'

Marie flipped the towel on my forehead, patted it down. 'I need to freshen this.'

When she got up, Ed leaned in and said, 'How'd you end up out there.'

'Let the boy rest.'

'I want to know. Hell, I *need* to know, Marie. Yeah, he's weak right now, but who's to say this kid isn't a serial killer or something?'

'I'm not a serial killer,' I said. Then coughed. One cough led to another, then a full-blown fit. I had to sit up, bend double. Ed shifted along the couch, obviously worried that I was going to throw up again.

'So you got a voice,' said Ed. 'Beginning to think you were a mute.'

I nodded slowly, tears streaming from my eyes. At least there was *some* moisture left in me. Ed took the cigarette from his mouth, gathered up a small ashtray from the side and stubbed out what was smoking. He waited for me to breathe deeper, then placed his hands on his knees.

'So what happened?' he said.

Marie stopped where she was, folded the towel over her arm. I looked well enough to do without it, then. She moved to a seat opposite Ed and me. I glanced at her, at those large brown-cow eyes and felt sick again. She was so desperate for me to be a loser, a kid knocked black and blue by life and dumped by the side of the road, it killed me. Mostly because at that moment I was so grateful to her for being such a harpy and making Ed drive back.

'A bloke I thought I could trust . . . He flipped out and shot me.'

'Why?'

I stared at Ed. 'It's a long story.'

'Were there drugs involved?'

'Ed.'

'Drugs are involved, I want to know about it.' Ed frowned. 'I got all the time in the world to hear this story, son.'

'We need to get going,' said Marie.

'No, we ain't going nowhere until I hear what this boy has to say.'

Marie started to protest, but Ed had final say.

'I mean it,' he said, looking directly at me. 'You tell me what happened, son. You tell me from the beginning, don't leave nothing out, right through to your ass out there in the desert. And tell it straight. I been alive long enough to recognise the smell of bullcrap.'

I looked across at Marie, thinking she'd have to say something to get me out of this, but she was too busy watching her husband, the towel between her hands. When our eyes met, I could see her mind was made up. The RV was going nowhere until I spilled my guts and made it convincing. My first instinct was to lie, make it up and see what stuck.

But then I thought, fuck it. Tell the truth.

It's the easiest thing to remember.

So I started talking.

THIRTY-THREE

'So did you tell the truth?' says Munroe.

'I told them most of the truth.' I lean forward in my seat, put my elbows on the table. 'Some things I had to keep out.'

'Like now?' says Wallace.

'Sorry?'

'Are you telling us the truth now, or are you leaving some things out?' He crosses his arms the other way.

'I'm telling you the truth,' I say.

Like fuck I am. Replace the facts with plausible lies. I've had time to polish my story so it hangs together like the truth. Got so I almost believe what I'm telling the cops.

'Then what happened?' says Munroe.

'They dropped me off in the city and I went back to the hotel.'

Munroe nods. 'Okay.'

I wish they'd just dropped me off at the hotel. Wish it was that easy.

Wish Ed didn't listen to my story and say, 'I'm sorry, Callum. But I don't believe a damn word you just told me.'

'Ed . . .'

'I don't, Marie. I may be getting suspicious in my old age, but I don't believe a damn word.' He pushed himself to his feet. At full height, the top of his head brushed the ceiling. 'That's not to say what you just told me was all lies. But there were lies in there. A lot of 'em. I can't point to which one's truth and which one's lie, but I asked you to tell it straight and you didn't.'

Ed ducked as he made his way to the front of the RV. He slumped painfully into the driver's seat and said, 'C'mon up, Callum.'

Marie blinked. 'We're going?'

'Yeah,' he said. 'Callum, get up here.'

I got up, moved to the passenger side as Ed checked the mirrors. The engine already running, a throbbing undercurrent that went through the entire vehicle. I sat down, buckled up.

'A man doesn't shoot another man unless he's done something wrong,' said Ed, throwing the RV into gear. 'That's the way the world is.'

As he drove, he reached for a soft pack of Lucky Strikes on the dash. He held the pack out to me; I took a cigarette. He lit both, puffed smoke as he continued. 'Look at it this way: there's two guys in a bar, they ain't talking to each other, just drinking. One of the guys gets up, he moseys over to the juke, sticks a quarter in the slot and puts on a song. A couple bars in, the other guy goes crazy, starts beating on the music lover. Now what do you think?'

'Bloke didn't like the song?'

'Maybe. Your thinking is it's the song that set him off. But it's never just the song. It's what the song means. Maybe he didn't like the tune because the music lover stole his girl a long time ago and that was her favourite song, or it was the song playing on the radio when he found the two of 'em in bed together or it was the song playing when she told him she didn't want to be with him anymore. Or it could be the singer reminds him of his father or his mother who used to beat on him. Or maybe it's just that this guy's had too many beers and reckons this is a fine time to start a brawl.'

'Okay.'

'Now, when it's all over, are you gonna ask the guy why he beat the crap out of the music lover?'

'No.'

'No. Exactly. That's what I'm saying. I'm saying there's a reason things happen. You don't always have to know the reason, just accept that there is one. That's what started it, that's the reason. You got yourself shot up, and you deserved it.'

Marie made a disapproving noise. 'Ed, that's not fair.'

'Don't take offence, son. That's just the way it is.'

I took a drag from the Lucky Strike, blew smoke. Looked out at the road and watched the lines on the asphalt break as they passed under the RV. 'I deserved it.'

Ed nodded. 'You're damn right you deserved it. You don't get shot if you don't deserve it.'

'What about that poor guy in Tulsa?' said Marie.

'That guy in Tulsa, he did *something* in his life.' Ed's hands loosened on the steering wheel, then flattened as if he was trying to shake out pins and needles. 'He must have. I mean, Marie, you're a God's honest Christian, you believe He has a plan.'

Marie started to say something, but stopped herself.

'And part of that belief is knowing when to question and when to accept. You don't question God's will, you accept it. But you, Callum, I question.'

'That's okay.'

'I have to question. I sold insurance too long *not* to question. You go to someone's door, you ask yourself, "Can these people afford what I have to sell?" and then, then you ask yourself, "Can these people afford to pass me by?" You understand what I'm saying?'

'You question,' I say.

'But I don't always ask the *right* questions. I'm not always blessed with the intelligence to ask what I need to ask. Sometimes you need someone who knows what they're doing. Sometimes you need a professional.'

'I see.'

'So you get it.'

I narrowed my eyes at the sun. 'Yeah.'

'I know you're not keen on the cops,' said Ed. 'But if any of this story is as serious as you made it out to be, then the authorities need to be notified.'

'It's for the best, Callum,' said Marie.

'I'm sure it is.'

These two rescued me, only to throw me back to the lions. I nodded. They thought I was agreeing when I was twisted up inside.

'I'm glad you understand, Callum. And this ain't to say I didn't believe *everything* . . .'

'You just didn't know the questions.'

'Yeah. We're helping you.'

'Helping you help yourself,' said Marie.

I ran through it over and over in the silence that followed. As much as I wanted to get this sorted – find Liam, hop on the next plane out of LAX – it was just a pipe dream. An abandoned car was one thing. But an abandoned rental car in my name, fractured with bullets and covered in blood, that wasn't going to stay unreported. The police had to be involved. Telling Ed and Marie the story so far just crystallised events. I didn't have an ending. And I thought, let the police handle it, clean up the mess. But I still needed to find Liam. Nobody else would. If he was still alive, that would be enough. If he wasn't . . .

Well, I'd have to play it by ear.

The city started to close in on me, the blur of the desert turning back to civilisation. I closed my eyes for a moment, opened them and familiar-looking streets came into focus. At second glance, I didn't recognise the places other than the usual brand chains. Starbucks, 7-Eleven, Dunkin' Donuts. Mangle it into one solid movie memory and dust with the fear of going to prison. Because American cops were movie cops. They wore mirrored sunglasses, pointed a gun with half a hot dog hanging out of their mouth. The police stations were clean and sterile. Or else the sweaty heave of an overcrowded cell, packed with *pendejos* and perverts. Chucked in there until the cops could work out what to do with a Brit who came right in and 'fessed up to . . .

What? I hadn't done anything.

Not that Ed believed it.

There was a reason for everything in Ed's philosophy. It was all part of God's big plan.

And Shapiro found God in prison. Maybe it was this kind of bullshit He was locked up for.

I saw a street sign: E. 6th Street. Downtown. I looked out of the window and there was a police station, large gold letters hammered into a red brick wall. A stars and stripes fluttered outside. The message was clear enough: *we are going to fucking incarcerate you.*

Ed eased the RV over to the side of the road, a manoeuvre that made him grunt with the effort. Motor homes aren't built for urban driving, which made me wonder why he'd taken me all the way to the middle of the city. Ed let the engine idle as he turned in his seat.

'You know what you have to do,' he said.

I clicked off my seat belt, stared at the station. Yeah, I knew what I had to do.

'You want us to come in with you?' said Marie.

'Nah, you're alright,' I said. Then, to Ed: 'You got another cigarette?'

'Yeah, sure.' He handed me another Lucky Strike.

I stepped down from the RV and lit the cigarette. The smoke closed my chest, rose up and into my eyes. I realised how dry my mouth was. Looked at myself in the side mirror of the RV, got a dusty and bloody look in return.

I walked around to the other side of the motor home as Ed buzzed down the window.

'I wanted to say thank you,' I said.

'No problem.'

I spat tobacco at the ground. Turned, dropped the cigarette and began to walk to the police station.

And because I had plenty of self-discipline, I waited until I got to the front steps before I broke into a run.

THIRTY-FOUR

'They dropped you at your hotel,' says Wallace.

'That's correct.'

Sorry, Ed.

Sorry, Marie.

I'm not that kind of bloke. You want to call it being brave and facing my responsibilities; I call it fucking myself too early in the game. And maybe I'm a coward, but I couldn't just walk into a police station and start spilling my guts. My story so far, it wasn't for the police. If it wasn't good enough to pass the Ed Test, then it certainly wasn't good enough to put in front of the fucking 5–0.

You guys might believe in the almighty power of the authorities, but I've seen too much to hang onto my faith.

I ducked into a side street, melted into a hurried walk, then down to a stroll. Tried not to look behind me, but I kept listening for the RV rumbling around the corner. My back prickled, but it was nothing compared to the ache in my neck and the painful itch of what used to be my left ear.

Sorry, Ed.

Sorry, Marie.

You guys were the ones I'd face on a jury. Mr and Mrs White-bread Middle America. Twelve of you. Because something like this led to a jury, ended with a cell. Nelson tried to shoot me and it was my fault? That's what the survey said, and there was no reason to think the cops would believe otherwise.

I couldn't do time. Not again. I was scared as I walked, my heart thumping with something other than the exercise. This was a strange country and I was a stranger in it. The one thing I'd learned:

you couldn't trust anyone. That bloke you thought was a friend, the bloke you thought was looking out for you? He was a liar. Worse than that, he was a fucking security guard or something and he was one wrong comment away from shoving a gun in your face.

The stroll became laboured, my legs seizing up. I took a breather by a newspaper vending machine, leaned on it and looked back up the street. No sign of the RV. I laughed. Scared out of my mind because of an elderly couple in a fucking motor home.

A guy in a suit quickened his step as he passed me.

There I was, fitting in after all.

Another crazy bastard.

I found my way back to the hotel, grabbed my pills from my room.

The cash was gone. Nelson must've taken it. Or the maid. I pulled open my wallet, found a stack of notes in there, the last of my holiday money.

Bollocks to it. I didn't need to eat and I didn't have time to hang around here. No doubt Ed and Marie had done their civic duty and called the cops themselves. As I got to the foyer, I spotted a middle-aged woman getting out of a white cab. She was loaded down with shopping bags, the paper-and-rope deals you got at the classy boutiques. I hurried through the doors, out and slipped into the back seat of the cab before she noticed me. I dug out Nelson's directions and passed them forward to the driver.

'Reckon you can get me there?' I said.

The driver looked at me in the rear view. 'It's way out of my way.'

'But you could get me there.'

'I don't mean to be rude or nothing, but this'll cost you.'

I held up a fistful of banknotes. 'More than this?'

'I got you, sir,' he said, screaming the cab out into traffic. I watched the diehard shopper frown at the taxi as we left her in our dust.

'She doesn't look too happy,' I said.

'Fuck her, and pardon my French, but those ladies, they think a cabbie's their fucking houseboy.' He shook his head. 'Not this cabbie, no sir. Got me some dignity left, kinda like to hang onto it as long as possible.'

'Too right.'

Most of the journey, the driver kept his mouth shut. Not like I wouldn't have talked to him, but I liked it that he didn't feel the need to chat about nothing. I just wished we had more of that in Britain. It'd be a far happier place if people knew when to shut the fuck up. And the silence gave me time to think. I swallowed a fistful of codeine to make up for lost time, caught the cabbie watching me in the mirror.

'They're for my back,' I said.

'I ain't judging.'

'Good. Because I was starting to like you.'

Two hours on, I pointed to Nelson's house and we pulled up outside. I got out of the cab, paid the guy. The fare was a gouger.

'You free to wait?'

'How long you gonna be?'

'As long as I need to be.'

'I got other calls, man. I can't be—'

'And I've got plenty of money. The exchange rate's shitty. You want to stay out here, I'll chuck in another hundred on top of waiting time and whatever you're going to stiff me on the way back.'

He looked like he was thinking about it, his bottom lip stuck out. He reached out for the Tex Avery wolf figurine on the dashboard and flicked its head. The wolf bobbled. I watched him.

'Yeah, why not?' he said.

I didn't expect Nelson to be home and he didn't disappoint me. I went round to the side of his place to look for a back yard. An awkward hop over a small picket fence and I was there, crossing in front of a small pool. The water feature – which looked like a pipe chugging water – was in full flow, which put me on edge for a moment. But after a quick recce of the living room through the patio doors, I suspected that all the running water was a permanent thing.

I wished I had my cricket bat.

I kicked at the patio door instead. The glass shook but didn't break. Obviously made from some double-glazed, hard-as-nails substance. At least I hadn't seen Nelson. I could afford to be a bit noisier. So I went back round to the front of the house. The cab was still there. Good. I marched up to the front door and aimed my foot at the lock. Bounced back, almost went on my arse. Tried it again and a vibration went through my leg so hard I had to take a moment to myself. Looked up at the cab driver and he was smiling.

'Enjoying the show?' I said.

He raised his hands and applauded in the car.

Fucker.

I charged at the front door, bounced again and wrecked my shoulder. Lost my temper and started kicking all over the door, finally aimed a kick that prompted the sound of splintering wood. That was the ticket. Spot fucking on. I felt good enough to try it again, so I did, aiming at the same place. Another crack. Then the lock.

It took a solid five minutes for the door to give way. I know that because the cab driver leaned out of the car and shouted my time at me.

I pushed inside the house, the sweat I had immediately cooling on my skin as the air conditioning brushed my face. The living room was deserted. I could hear the gentle hum of the refrigerator in the kitchen. Kept listening for any other noise. Nothing. If I was wrong about Nelson being out, he was being quiet about it.

First things first, I pushed open the door that led to the base-ment. Took it easy on the steps going down, hearing the wood creak underfoot. At the bottom, I fumbled for the pull-switch, grabbed it with one shaking hand and yanked hard. A light clicked on, throwing a pool of yellow about five feet, fading fast. The exercise equipment carved harsh shadows against the concrete walls.

'Liam?'

If he was down here, I couldn't see him. More to the point, I couldn't hear him or *smell* him. If he was dead and anywhere in the house, that would have been a major giveaway, air conditioning or no air conditioning.

Of course, he might not have been in the house. Nelson could have taken him somewhere else.

I didn't want to get on that train of thought.

I climbed the steps, took them as carefully as when I'd descended. Still nothing doing upstairs. I walked through to Nelson's bedroom. The uniform was still lying on the bed, but the gun was long gone. Checked out the shirt, it had a logo on the right pocket: a golden lion hanging onto the bars of a cage, the words REGAL SECURITY curled above it.

Hadn't had a job-type job in years, my arse. Suppose it was a fancy dress costume I was looking at. And that fucking gun wasn't real with real fucking bullets.

I went over to the closet thinking, if he had anything to hide, it'd be in there. I slid the door across, came face to face with more uniform shirts. Some of them were Regal Security, others with different logos, different company names. A few casual shirts, a couple of pairs of casual trousers, but nothing like the amount a guy normally had. This was a bloke used to wearing a uniform, spent most of his life at work. This wasn't someone who used to be in the fight game, not as far as I could see. At the bottom of the closet, a pile of trainers, some more formal but scuffed shoes. And next to the pile, shoeboxes, stacked one on top of the other. I bent down, grabbed one of the boxes and flipped off the lid.

Nelson Byrne was divorced. This is what he told me. He'd also said it wasn't a sad story.

The photos in the shoebox said different. There were loads of them. Photos of Nelson, grinning and bearded. Then a moustache. Then clean-shaven, but haggard. The glasses appeared in all of the pictures, different frames in each until I found a clutch of photos that shared the same pair. Nelson standing with a pretty brunette.

Her smile shone from the photo; his seemed forced. There they were, holding up a hot dog in a *Lady and the Tramp* pose. Behind them, I could make out the front of Skooby's.

You really know how to show a girl a good time, Nelson.

But something else I'd noticed, I had to double check.

Yeah. Nelson Byrne was a chubby bastard at one point. Check the next set, and he'd lost a little weight but not much. Had that puffy face of an inveterate drinker. I knew that face only too well – seen it enough in my bathroom mirror.

'If you were pro, Nelson, where's the fuckin' proof?' I said.

Because there should have been something. Boxers were just like everyone else. They got their name in the paper, they'd cut it out. A good review would be framed. And even betting that Nelson was modest – which he wasn't or he wouldn't have mentioned his pro status – where was the proof?

All I saw was a divorced guy who couldn't let go of the past. And someone I'd trusted to look after a kid.

A sound, like a creak.

I turned, listened hard. Put the box on the bed carefully and crept to the door.

There it was again.

Through the kitchen, and the creak got louder. I stopped in front of a closed door at the back of the house. I didn't want to open it. Felt my gut tighten, wanted to puke badly. Knowing there was something behind the door that I didn't want to see, but had to.

I pushed down on the handle, opened the door.

And there was Liam, the bribe sitting on the table next to him.

THIRTY-FIVE

Silence in the interview room. Wallace looks at the floor. Across from me, Munroe has steepled his fingers.

'You didn't check the guy's credentials?' says Wallace.

'Whose, Nelson's?'

'Yeah.'

'No, I didn't feel the need.'

'When you talked to Mr Byrne in the bar, when you first met him, did you mention boxing first?' says Munroe.

'Anyone in their right mind would have checked his credentials,' says Wallace. 'It's the first thing you do. At least *Google* him or something.'

I hold my hands up. 'I didn't know the guy from Adam.'

'You hadn't heard of him,' says Wallace.

'I'm not a fight fan.'

'You know how to use a computer, don't you?'

The cop's got a point. A quick search would've turned up nothing on Nelson Byrne.

'Mr Innes, would you answer the question?' says Munroe.

'What question?'

'When you first met Mr Byrne, who instigated the conversation about the amateur competition?'

'I don't know,' I say. 'How the fuck am I supposed to remember that?'

'Calm down,' says Wallace.

'I am calm. Obviously the guy was a fuckin' con man or . . . *deluded* or something because he wasn't who he said he was. I think that's a fact now, yeah? I mean, we've got that particular fact nailed down, Detective Munroe?'

'Yes.'

'So there's no need for me to answer that daft fuckin' question.'

'You broke into Mr Byrne's house,' says Wallace, moving from the wall. He's heading for me. 'You want to tell us about that?'

'I told you about that,' I say.

'You went in through the front door. Seems like an odd way of breaking into someone's house.'

'You want to get the cab driver in here to corroborate?' I say. 'And I think I had a bloody good reason for doing it, don't you?'

'We're not here to judge,' says Wallace.

'Course you're not.'

Munroe taps on the pad, leans back in his chair, his chin up. 'And then you found Liam, that's correct?'

'Yeah, that's correct.'

I found Liam on a single bed. He was fully clothed. Looked like the same clothes as the day before, but I couldn't be sure. He was coming out of something that resembled a deep sleep, but he let out the groggy moan of a lad either drunk out of his mind or on a severe downer. I talked to him, said his name, tried to pull him out of it. When that didn't work, I dragged the lad out of bed and shook the fucker till he sat up. His head lolled on his shoulders, eyes half-closed, the whites visible.

'Liam, we've got to go, son,' I said.

He didn't seem to hear me.

'Snap out of it, man. C'mon.' I kept talking to stave off the panic that I knew would be coming up the pike. 'C'mon, Liam, snap out of it. Snap out of it. Get up, man.'

And there it was, creeping in.

'What we're going to do, Liam, we're going to get up, we're going to walk outside, we're going to get into a cab and we're going back to the hotel.'

What the fuck was I thinking, a hotel? A *hospital.* The kid was drugged. If it'd been booze, I'd have smelled it. No, this was a whole prescription of something fucking serious.

I threw Liam's arm over my shoulder, wrapped my arms under his ribs and tried to stand up with him. Grabbed the money from the bedside table – I'd need it for the cab ride back. The lad was stringy, but he was a dead weight, not the easiest thing in the world to drag to the door. I had to adjust my grip, kept my mantra going, kept talking to him even though it was more for my benefit. 'Going to get you to a hospital, Liam. Going to get you out of here.'

Nelson had a gun. He came in now, he'd kill us both.

I managed to get Liam into the kitchen, then into the living room before I gave up. I couldn't carry him anymore, had to ease him onto the couch with shaking arms. I rubbed at my face. I couldn't do this by myself. I needed help.

And help had just hightailed it out of there. When I got outside, the cab was gone. The driver'd obviously had enough with waiting, or else got himself a fare that was peachier than mine. Or didn't want to be an accessory to a housebreaking.

Fuck.

I shouted it.

FUCK.

Sheer panic now, all the mantras in the world not going to hold this back, tearing through me. Giving me the all-over sweats when the temperature was way down. Back into the living room, staring at Liam. The lad had thick drool in the corner of his mouth. Christ, what if he was having a reaction? I needed help, but there was no one I could trust.

Except maybe Shapiro. The guy might've been corrupt, but he wasn't going to let a lad die, was he? I crossed to the phone, picked it up and rifled through my jacket pockets for the comp invitation Shapiro'd sent to Liam, see if there was a phone number on it. There was. I punched it in, waited.

Thinking, call a fucking ambulance or something. Don't drag Shapiro into this.

Also thinking, yeah, call an ambulance, get the authorities involved. Kid's drugged up, who's the first person they're going to point the finger at?

'Shapiro's Boxing Center.'

'Phil there?'

'Who's this?'

'Is that Reuben?'

'Who's *this*?'

'Reuben, get Phil.'

There was a loud cough at the other end. 'This Innes?'

'Yeah, Reuben, how many other Brits you know? Get Phil. I need to talk to him now.'

'Phil's busy.'

'This is a fuckin' emergency, *Rube*. Get him.'

'What'd I say about—'

'Fuckin' *now*. Fuck's the matter with you, you fuckin' twat? English your second fuckin' language?'

Reuben grumbled, dropped the receiver onto a solid surface. I looked across at Liam. It didn't look like he was breathing. I moved closer. He was, but only just. Jesus Christ.

'Mr Innes,' said Shapiro.

'Phil, I need help. I'm at Nelson Byrne's place—'

'Who?'

'It's in Palm Desert. How quickly can you get here?'

'Nelson Byrne?'

'It's Liam, Phil. He's . . . I don't know what he is, but it's not fuckin' good.'

'What happened?'

'Drugs or something. I don't know. I need help here, man.'

'What's the address?' he said.

I gave him Nelson's address, moved the phone to my other ear and wiped sweat from my palm. 'You know what to do?'

'Yeah, I know what to do. I'm calling a paramedic.'

'I can't wait that long.'

'And you can wait a couple hours until I get out there?' he said.

Shit.

'I can call,' I said. 'I'll call an ambulance.'

'No, you call, you'll have to pay for it.'

'*Pay?*'

'Let me call,' said Shapiro. 'You hang tight. I'll see he's okay.'

And that's when the shouting started.

'You have a way of making an entrance, I'll give you that,' I say.

And they did. A blue suit with a gun in his hand, yelling that he was armed police. I should put the phone down slowly and then put my hands behind my head. I almost shit myself, got it arse about face.

'Put the phone *down*,' he'd shouted.

His partner cuffed me.

'You were on private property,' says Munroe. 'We could bust you for that.'

'But you're not going to, right?'

'We haven't decided yet,' he says.

'Hey, I came quietly.'

'Yeah,' says Wallace. 'You've been very cooperative.'

'You being sarcastic?' I say.

'You haven't asked for a lawyer.' Wallace points at me. 'I'd say that was cooperative.'

'Or dumb,' says Munroe.

'Do I need a lawyer?'

'You haven't been charged,' says Munroe.

'I hope I'm not, too.'

'If you don't have one, legal counsel can be arranged,' he continues. 'You know, there's no shame in asking.'

'You what?' I lean close. 'Are you reading me my rights?'

'No,' says Munroe. 'Just telling you the way it is.'

Munroe gets out of his seat. Wallace moves to the other corner of the room.

'I'm telling the truth,' I say. 'I was there to help the lad.'

Munroe's behind me when he says, 'You know what he had in his system?'

'No,' I say. 'Something strong.'

'Flunitrazepam. Did I pronounce that right?'

I watch Wallace nod.

'What's that?' I say.

'Roofies,' says Wallace. He scratches the palm of his hand. 'Rohypnol.'

'Date rape drug.' I take a deep breath.

'You know it.'

'We've had it in Britain for a while.'

'Then you know what it does,' says Munroe.

I twist in my seat. 'Liam wasn't . . .'

'Doesn't look like it,' says Wallace, bringing my attention back to the front. 'Kid was fully clothed, like you said.'

'Where is he now?'

'In hospital.'

'How's he doing?'

'We don't know,' says Wallace. 'We'll find out, but it's not our concern at the present time.'

'You know roofies aren't prescription medication over here, Mr Innes,' says Munroe. He crosses back in front of me.

'They're not in Britain.'

'But they're a sedative. Like diazepam.'

Wallace frowns. 'A *lot* stronger than diazepam.'

'I don't follow,' I say.

There's a pause. Munroe takes his seat again, sorts through my notes. Wallace regards the palm of his hand. He scratches it again. Something must've bitten him.

'Where do you think Nelson went?' says Munroe.

'I told you, I don't know.'

'Guys don't just vanish into thin air when they get pushed out of a car, Mr Innes.'

'I didn't see him out there on the road. He must've walked somewhere. Or he had another car waiting.'

'Pretty precise spot to have a car waiting. How do you hide a vehicle in a flat landscape? It's all brush and dirt. You see any cars?'

'I didn't notice any,' I say. 'But it doesn't mean there wasn't one.'

'You're saying Nelson walked,' says Wallace.

'Yes.'

'In that heat?'

'He wasn't in his right mind,' I say.

'You didn't see any evidence of him walking,' says Munroe. 'And you didn't see any evidence of another car.'

'I wasn't looking for it. I was busy trying to work out how the fuck I was going to survive.'

'Guy hits the road from a moving vehicle, he's going to break something,' says Wallace. 'Or he's going to smash his nose, skin his knee, leave *something*.'

'There was blood on the road. I did tell you that.'

Munroe checks my statement, pulls a surprised face and nods. 'Yes, you did tell us that.'

We sit in silence. Munroe gathers up his notes. 'I think we'll take a break.'

Wallace nods.

'Could I have my pills back?' I say.

'Which pills?'

'The codeine.'

They look at each other. Munroe says, 'We won't be long.'

'Don't go anywhere,' says Wallace.

'I won't.'

They leave. And it feels like the walls are closing in on me.

THIRTY-SIX

Nelson Byrne and rohypnol. I'd ask why the hell Nelson had a date rape drug knocking around his house, but I don't think I'd want to know the answer.

Liam's okay, though. He didn't touch Liam. As far as they know. Liam's at the hospital now. He's in good hands.

As the over-excited blue suit ducked me into the back of the car, I watched the paramedics turn up. They hurried into the house. But I didn't see them bring Liam out. By that time, we were on the road to the station. At least he's being seen to. That's the main thing. And he'll be treated better. Victims of crime tend to be treated better than your average drug-induced coma case, I'm sure. There's the question of who's going to pay for the ambulance. Of course, I've got cash, but I don't know. Maybe the travel insurance'll take care of it. I can't be thinking about the fucking red tape at a time like this.

I lean on the table, rub my eyes.

They've left me alone for a reason. They know I'm lying. They know Ed and Marie came in probably just after I did a runner. There was me thinking Ed would take it on the chin and carry on his way. After all, he didn't want to get involved. Why should he, if he's got a perfectly good reason to mind his own business? Especially if it's going to put a crimp on his holiday.

I should've seen this coming.

Who the fuck could see this coming?

Me. I should've. I should've called Nelson on what I saw. Told him to offer up some credentials. Asked him about the uniform. Done something instead of take a back seat while it all conspired to blow up in my face.

I swear to God, if he's touched Liam . . .

No reports filed, no charges brought against me. Which means I'm here of my own free will, telling my story and trying to get it over with. But they keep pausing this interview to go dig.

Wallace is surprised I don't want a lawyer. He's on my side.

Munroe thinks I should have one. Makes me think he's got something on me.

I thank God I've signed off on my probation. Something like this could've meant a recall. Just being pulled in by the police makes some POs skittish.

I lean back now, wishing they hadn't taken my pills. Doesn't look like they're going to give them back to me, either. I mean, they're prescription, it should be in my rights to have them. Doesn't matter that I stole the prescription. Still my medication.

The door opens and Munroe steps into the room. He's carrying a cup of coffee, looking at me with a new expression on his face. I can't work out if it's pity, disgust or just plain confusion.

He stands there, takes a sip of his coffee and pulls a face. I don't think it's just the taste, either.

'Did you hear about Liam?' I say.

'No.'

'Is he okay?'

'I didn't hear about him,' he says. 'I didn't ask.'

Wallace enters. He's wearing a jacket now.

'Look, I'd kind of like to see Liam, make sure he's alright,' I say. 'And I appreciate you guys've got questions to ask, but I think I answered them all as well as I could. I've given you my statement. And if there's no charges being brought against me, then I'm a free man, right? I can go?'

'We got a couple more questions for you,' says Munroe.

'What?'

'Something came up,' says Wallace. He tugs at the lapel on his jacket.

'What?' I say.

'We found Nelson Byrne.'

'And you brought him in? What, he telling you a different story to me? I'm the fuckin' victim here. He *shot* me.'

'He's dead,' says Munroe.

The way it played was this. At least, this is the best I could come up with in the resulting two hours' worth of questions, answers, running around.

Nelson didn't have a back-up plan. He took it spur of the moment. That's why he grabbed the steering wheel. He didn't want the Metro spinning out of control. He wanted that car on the road so he could dump me and drive back to his place. It was just me he wanted out of the way. And he couldn't control that impulse. Thinking back to the way Nelson looked at me outside the hotel, the way he surveyed the street, I realise that if he'd had his way, he would've shot me right then.

When he fell out of the car, he fell on his head. He was lucky his neck didn't break. But there was concussion, according to pre-liminary medical reports. Crime scene indicated he hit the road, lay there, then got up and walked back to the car.

I listen to that and my mouth goes dry. Because I start thinking all the things I'm supposed to think. What if I'd come to when he was staring at me through the shattered glass? He'd probably have put a bullet in my head as I lay there. Or what if the car hadn't gone into the ditch? He'd have dumped me out, probably done the same. But with the Metro fucked and me half-dead, Nelson realised he'd have to get a wriggle on if he wanted to walk.

'You're lucky to be alive,' says Munroe.

'Uh,' I say.

Nelson walked past the car, checked the damage, decided he couldn't get the Metro out of the ditch by himself. That kind of concussion, he'd have thrown up, been dizzy as fuck. And so he decided to walk it. Munroe seems to think it's entirely possible he was trying to walk back to the city, but he didn't know which way he was going and ended up lost. The throwing up dehydrated him, the concussion slowed him down, the blood leaked from him and the heat did the rest.

I have a vision of Nelson dropping to his knees and choking out. For a second he's David Caruso in Miami.

I shake my head. This isn't right.

'What?' says Munroe.

'He's not dead. You can't die from the heat.'

'Mitigating circumstances.'

'Somebody picked me up. They must've seen him on the road too.'

'You said they thought you were dead. And there's no guarantee they even saw him. Only reason they saw you was because of the car.'

'Believe us, Mr Innes,' says Wallace. 'He's dead.'

'You've seen him?'

'Seen the preliminary.'

'There's no chance it could be a mistake.'

'No,' says Munroe. 'We don't make mistakes.'

I lean back and stare at the ceiling. 'So are you going to try and pin this on me?'

Wallace laughs. I lower my head and look at him. Munroe has a half-smile on his face.

'You want to tell us something else?' says Munroe.

'I told you everything I know.'

'Then I don't see how we can charge you,' he says.

'What about the breaking and entering?'

'You had a good reason,' says Wallace. 'Could be, you saved that boy's life.'

Munroe raises his coffee cup. 'Yeah, you're a hero, Mr Innes.'

I snort a laugh.

THIRTY-SEVEN

'Fuck's *sake.*'

Wedged into a booth, the phone stuck between my ear and shoulder, and I'm trying to figure out just exactly how much change I've got in my hand. Coins in this country don't follow any pattern, like bigger's more valuable. Nah, that would be too easy. So I have to hold the coins up and squint at what's written on them.

That there's a dime.

Okay, now what the fuck's a dime? Five, ten? A quarter's twenty-five. That makes sense. Quarter of a dollar. My mam didn't raise any stupid kids.

I stick a bunch of quarters into the phone. Follow it with the rest of my change – balls to it. This is an international call, after all.

Stab in Paulo's number. I've looked it up now, double-checked, and the number I had on my business card was right. Definitely the Lad's Club.

But every time I call: 'The number you have dialled is not in service . . .'

'Fuck's sake.'

I put the phone down, wait for the change to come clattering back to me. It doesn't. Then I go outside for a smoke.

The hospital has a cafeteria, one of those places that's supposed to feel light and airy, but it just takes me back to the airport in North Carolina. I get a wilted ham salad sandwich, a bottle of water and a cream cheese muffin, retire to a table at the back and stare at my food. No appetite, but I should eat.

'Anyone sitting here?'

I look up. Shapiro towers over me. I'm surprised I didn't see him coming, but then my mind's been elsewhere. I look back at my meal. 'Help yourself.'

He sits opposite, places his hands on the table.

'How'd you know he was here?' I say.

'I didn't. I just kept phoning around the hospitals when I heard you'd been taken in. Had to hit the right one eventually.'

I nod. That'll do it. I tap the muffin. 'You want a muffin?'

'No thanks.'

'I don't blame you.' Tap some more. It sounds hollow and stale. 'I should've squeezed it first. Seen better muffins in service stations. Cheaper, too.'

'You're a captive consumer here,' he says, looking around the cafeteria. 'Where else are you gonna go?'

I sniff. 'Thought I saw a Starbucks up the street.'

'You want me to get you something?'

When I look at him, Shapiro's deadly serious. 'Nah, y'alright. I'll be fine with water. Don't have much of an appetite. Don't think coffee would do me much good, either.'

'How is he?'

I take the top off the bottle of water and drink; it's warm. Wipe my mouth and say, 'He's stable. At first they thought there might be some respiratory trouble, he was breathing that shallow. They kept talking to me about brain damage. I don't know. They want to keep him for observation.'

'He awake?'

I shake my head. 'Not that I know of.'

'You been in to see him?'

I angle the bottle toward Shapiro. He holds a hand up, shakes his head. Waits for my answer.

'No,' I say.

'Why not?'

'I've been through the mill already. Been asked questions all over the shop. I don't need it from you as well.'

'I'm just interested,' he says.

'You're interested.' Take another swig of water and gaze at the café counter. A fat man is loading up his tray. 'I didn't see him. Didn't think he was up to it yet.'

'Uh-huh.' Shapiro doesn't believe me any more than I believe myself.

'What the fuck am I going to say to him?' I keep my voice low, but I want to shout. 'Sorry I got you hooked up with a psycho?'

'That'd be a start. And you know, Cal, you could've come to me in the first place.'

'Yeah, you,' I say. 'You with your record and Callahan chucking bribes at me. Put yourself in my shoes, *Phil*. What would you have done?'

'I would've talked to me.'

'Yeah, well, hindsight's a shitter, isn't it?' I take a swig. 'Definitely twenty-twenty.'

'Liam had Reuben and me looking out for him. You didn't need to bring Byrne into it. The guy never coached in his life.'

'Oh, you know him?'

'Yeah,' he says. 'I knew him on sight. When a guy comes round my place talking to the kids and telling them he'll get them in the pro circuit, I tend to take an interest. Do a little fact-checking. Byrne's a fan, but that's all he's ever been. Tried amateur once, as far as I know, and got beaten to a pulp because he thought he didn't need a coach, thought he could do it himself.'

'I don't know,' I say. 'He seemed pretty quick when he put that fuckin' gun in my face.'

'You think a real slugger would use a gun? Someone like you, he'd throw a cross that'd put you out cold.'

'He wanted to kill me.'

Shapiro thinks about it, says, 'He didn't, though, did he? If you'd come to me, I could've set you straight. Because I see guys like Byrne all the time. They had a shot, or *thought* they had a shot, many years ago. And they still think they've got the know-how to play at the big time, but they're deluded.'

'Well, Nelson's dead.'

He cocks his head at me. 'How?'

'I didn't kill him.' I pause. 'No, I didn't kill him. I pushed him out of the car. He went off walking in the desert. Heat got to him. Or concussion. Or something. I don't know. I don't fuckin' care.'

'I see.' Shapiro looks at the table.

'Ranting on about me being the bad guy,' I say. 'That I was the corrupt one.'

'You took the bribe.'

'And Callahan must've thought it'd do something, right? Which puts the ball in your court.'

'Mr Callahan's seen too many bad movies,' says Shapiro. 'Truth is, there's corruption, but I'd be surprised if anything was going on at an amateur level. Even if there was, I wouldn't be a part of it. I can't afford to be a part of it. I got a bad past and I'm doing my best to make up for that.' He taps the table. 'Most fighters don't make it. I know that. I didn't make it and I was good. They either get cut down by better fighters or they lose their mind with the glitz of it all.'

'Which was it for you?'

'Both. I couldn't fall hard or fast enough, Cal. And the best thing I can do with my life now is try to get these kids right in the head before they think about turning pro. So they're connected. So they don't fall as hard or fast as me, so they're prepared.'

'How very fuckin' noble of you,' I say.

'Why'd you call me?'

I don't say anything.

'Because I was the only one you had left,' he says. 'That's why. Because somewhere in there you trust me to do the right thing. And I come in here and you give me a kid's face when I try to talk to you like a man. That's a right-hand lead, Cal. It's an amateur jab. You show no respect with something like that.'

'Right, I've got to show you respect now?'

'You have to show *yourself* some respect. Pull yourself together, look at the world with a clean pair of eyes and realise it doesn't revolve around you, that not everyone is out to get you. You shake yourself off, you battle on. I swear, you could learn a thing or two from Liam, if you ever get the guts to talk to him. He's got his brain wired right.' Shapiro gets up. 'You want to sit here moping, you go right ahead. But there's got to be a time when you get off your butt and go talk to the kid. He can't stay here the rest of his life, and neither can you.'

I suck my teeth as Shapiro brushes the crease back into his khakis.

'There's no point in getting another rental car. So when you need a lift to the airport, give me a call. I'll be glad to drop you.'

And he walks away from the table. I stare at my sandwich, push it to one side. I'm not hungry.

THIRTY-EIGHT

I pass by Liam's room so many times, I start to look like I've slipped off the mental ward. Each time I go by, I can't get my fingers on the handle. Hand shaking, I still haven't figured out what I'm supposed to say to him. Been through speeches in my head, none of them sound right. And anyway, I don't even know if he's awake yet. Opening the door might disturb him.

I should wait.

But then he's had enough sleep, hasn't he? Been dozing for the last day and a bit. About time someone woke him up.

I stop in front of the door, turn the handle and step inside.

There's a lamp turned on by the side of his bed. Liam's eyes are closed. I watch him for a moment, then look around the room for somewhere to sit. A chair by the window. I walk over and ease myself into it, stretch my legs out. He doesn't look too bad. Pale, dark circles under his eyes, but really nothing more than the kind of pallor anyone gets in a hospital. He'll be fine, I tell myself. Then practise telling Liam that.

He moves a little. Exhales through his mouth, like someone letting air out of a balloon. Takes another deep breath, sighs it out. He sniffs. Something catches, turns the sniff into a cough and he wakes up. Smacks his lips, that thick sound of dehydration. His eyes open to slits and his arm moves to the water cup by the side of the bed. His fingers don't close at the right time, the cup slipping out of reach, tottering before it drops to the floor.

I get out of the chair. Pick up the cup and the straw that was in it. Water pools on the floor.

'Cal,' says Liam, his voice cracked.

I pour water into his cup, plop the straw back in. 'How you doing?'

'Headache,' he says. He tries to pull himself up on the bed as I hand him the cup. He starts sucking on the straw right away. Gulping so fast, I get worried he's going to choke.

'Ease up on that.'

He takes a breath. 'You didn't know he was nuts, did you?'

'No, Liam. I knew he was mental as. That's why I thought he'd be a good influence on you. Christ knows you need more insanity in your life.'

Liam swallows. Smiles. But only for a moment. He blinks as his eyes adjust to the light, then stares at the end of the bed.

'You want to tell me what happened?' I say.

'I dunno. My head's all mashed up.' He drinks some more water, clears his throat. 'He came to pick us up at the hotel, took us down to the car. Then he said he was going to knock on your door, get you up and about. You were drunk. And when he came down, he said that you were dead to the world.' He pauses. 'You took the cash.'

I don't know if that's a statement or a question.

'He told you I was bribed,' I say.

'He told us you took the cash. Were you going to tell me about it?'

'I didn't take the bribe. They forced the bribe on me.'

'So you weren't going to do anything about it.'

'I had ideas,' I say. 'I just didn't get to follow through with them.'

'Right.'

'I wasn't going to force you to take a dive, Liam. You know me better than that. And it's not like I could've persuaded you for seven grand, is it?'

'Seven?' He shakes his head.

I reach into my pocket, pull out the bottle of water. Swill the last bit before I swallow it down. 'He's dead, y'know.'

Liam stays quiet. For a second, I'm not sure if he heard me at all. Then he moves his head.

'You kill him?' he says.

'No.'

'He give you that?' Liam points to the side of my face.

I touch where my earlobe used to be. 'Yeah. He tried to shoot me.'

'Looks like he did more than try.'

'It's been a rough day.'

'Inch to the left . . .'

'I know. I thought about it. Been thinking about it non-stop, you want to know the truth. But I'm alive. And so are you.'

'Doesn't feel like it.' Liam shifts in bed. He seems stiff. 'Feels like I've been out for a while.'

'You have.' I jerk my thumb at the wall. 'They were worried about you. Said you weren't getting enough oxygen to the brain.'

'Huh.'

'I said it'd probably make you smarter.'

Liam gives me a sick smile. 'I'm not the one who got in the car with a fuckin' nutter, Cal.'

'Right enough.' I look at my shoes; they're scuffed and dirty. 'Should've known better. But you live and learn, eh?'

'You'll know better for the next time.'

'Suppose.'

The room falls into silence. I nod, because I can't think of anything else to do. Don't know what I can say to him. Sorry, maybe. But I think we're past that now. Liam keeps staring at the foot of the bed, his eyes at half-mast. I look around the room for a bin, find one by the chair and drop my empty bottle in it.

Turn at the sound of Liam moving down the bed, getting himself comfortable on his pillow. I take the cup of water from him and put it back on the bedside table.

'The smoker's fucked then,' he says. A yawn fights its way out of him.

'For this year, yeah.'

'Think what Nelson said's right?'

'About what?'

'About me not needing to win.'

'Probably,' I say. 'Always next year, mate.'

Another yawn. 'I won't be eligible next year.'

'I wouldn't let it worry you. There'll be other comps.'

'Right.' Even with the fatigue, that was a sarcastic one.

'Get some sleep,' I say.

'Nah, I had enough already.'

But Liam's slipping fast. He keeps talking. Tells me about a weird dream he had when he was under. He was in the ring and the canvas turned to quicksand. Pretty obvious to Liam what it meant, but he thought he'd share it with me anyway. Have to admit, I'm clueless, don't know the first thing about dream interpretation. But it doesn't matter. His eyes are already closed, movement under the eyelids. He'll drop out of consciousness in a minute. I watch him for a while, make sure he's not going to do anything horrible like cough or scream or throw himself off the bed, then I see the notebook on the table. I pick it up, go back to my chair.

It's a work diary. Details his training. Complete with little diagrams, charts of footwork and motivational slogans. It's the last thing that gets me. I don't know where he's taken them from, but there are quotes in here from Sugar Ray Robinson, Jake La Motta, most of them from Muhammad Ali.

This from Rocky Marciano: 'What would be better than walking down any street in any city and knowing you're a champion?'

And from Sugar Ray: 'To be a champ you have to believe in yourself when no one else will.'

It's all stirring stuff. If you'd asked me a week ago why Liam needed this, I wouldn't have been able to give you an answer. I thought he was one of those kids who knew how good he was, didn't need nuggets from champs to keep his eye on the prize. And looking at him now, even with that hospital smell in the air and the atmosphere of intense sickness, Liam's a lad in charge of himself.

This one rings true, prefaced by the words 'Muhammad Ali Statement after losing his first fight to Ken Norton, March 31, 1973':

'I never thought of losing, but now that it's happened, the only thing is to do it right. That's my obligation to all the people who believe in me. We all have to take defeats in life.'

If it's good enough for The Greatest, it's good enough for me.

THIRTY-NINE

'You sure you don't want to stay the week?'

'Nah, Phil, I think we're better off just going home. I got the money for the tickets, I might as well use it.'

Standing outside the Ramada Inn, bags packed. I already checked the both of us out. Left the duty free behind, packed the cigarettes. I'll be paying over the odds for the flights, but it'll be worth it. I want the plane back to be as direct and as fast as possible. No more changes, no more foreign airports than we need. They discharged Liam yesterday, gave him a cleanish bill of health and sent the other one to our travel insurance place. He's still shaky on his feet, pale, has the puffy features of someone who's spent too long asleep, but he'll get better. I don't want him hanging around Shapiro's gym, though. Nothing against Shapiro – he's been a diamond the last two days – but the atmosphere of the place might bring back a few unpleasant memories for the lad. No sense in torturing him with what might have been. Let it stay here in Los Angeles.

Right now, Liam's sitting in the back seat of Shapiro's car. He's chewing gum and staring out of the window, in a world of his own. He's been like that since he got out of hospital. If I think about it too much, I'll get worried, so I attend to the job in hand. Pick up the bags and put them in the boot of the car.

'He alright?' says Shapiro.

'Fine.'

'About Callahan . . .'

'We've been through it,' I say.

There wasn't a lot Shapiro could've done about the bribery thing because there wasn't a lot of proof – I'd already spent a hefty chunk of the money on cab fare and now plane tickets. Callahan tried to play the victim, swearing off his broken nose and threatening to sue me for the cash it'd take to have his beak reset by a professional. Shapiro had a quiet word in his ear. If Callahan didn't press charges, Josh was still welcome at the gym and it would go no further. Shapiro did tell me they were on their last warning.

'It's not what you would've done, I know,' he says.

'Well,' I say, slamming the boot closed. 'You're a more tolerant sort than I am.'

'I want you to know, you're both welcome any time you're in Los Angeles. I mean it, you want to come over, you can always depend on my hospitality.'

'That's a nice thought, Phil, but I don't know how often we're going to do this trip.'

'Just keep it in mind. Liam's a good kid.'

'I know.' We walk to either side of the car. 'I appreciate what you've done, mate.'

'Wish I could've done more.'

'Yeah, well, me too. But that's not the way it went, is it?'

He looks like he's about to say something, but keeps his mouth shut. We get into the car. I want to be in the back seat with Liam, but the lad still needs his space. It would be easier sitting back there, though. Then I could pretend Shapiro was a cab driver or something. Because I don't know, but there's still something about the man I can't get a handle on. Maybe it's that he's done time. No, that shouldn't bother me. Maybe it's the God stuff. Not that he rams it down your throat, but I've been around too many people who claim God saved them from booze, drugs et cetera, and they replace their vices with one virtue. Way I see it, even divine intervention can't change a leopard's spots. A leopard's born that way, has to see those spots every day at the watering hole and he's constantly reminded of his nature. There's no way around it.

So I watch the city dissolve again, feel my hands tighten in my lap. Streets become freeways, billboards proclaiming the latest hot movie.

I'm constantly surprised by the space in this country. Back in Manchester, there's no such thing as *this* much space. The city centre's become a shrine to high-rise buildings, people shunted into tiny apartments, paying over the odds to enjoy wooden floors and sky-high urban living. Students and young professionals everywhere, multiplying like a hostile virus. But here a man can live without seeing another individual if he wants to. It's a comforting thought, that kind of isolation. I've lived too long under people's feet, or with people under mine. Might be good to get away from it all out here.

It's a fantasy. A ridiculous fucking dream, but that's what this country's all about.

Liam's still staring out of the window, caught up in dreams of his own. He's stopped smacking the gum in his mouth. I wonder if he's thinking the same thing. Wonder what the hell he *is* thinking. Because I haven't seen the lad lose it once yet. If I'd gone through his last couple of days, I'd be a wreck. I just put it down to his sedation at the hospital, but now there's no reason for his mood. No tears, no recrimination. He's accepted Nelson's death with the blink of an eye, like it was most normal, logical thing in the world. Can't say I've had the same attitude. I wanted Nelson caught, tried, in jail. Or else shot down by the police. I wanted something dramatic for his death, but all I got was a whimper in the desert.

I turn away from Liam, concentrate on the scenery.

There's something not right about that lad.

When I come back with the tickets, Liam's standing by the bags looking bored.

'Bulk heads,' I say. 'Got some leg room.'

He nods. Shapiro's long gone. Dropped us off at the terminal and we said our goodbyes quickly and without sentiment. I was glad of it. I didn't want to be around Shapiro any longer than necessary and Liam looked like he wanted to be far away.

I pick up our carry-on luggage, head through to the waiting area. Liam picks up a boxing magazine from a newspaper kiosk, sits down a seat away from me and starts leafing through it. I half think about getting something to read myself, but realise there'll be plenty of movies to sit through on the plane. Besides, we need to talk.

'How you feeling?' I say.

He doesn't answer me.

'Liam.'

'You keep asking me that,' he says.

'I'm interested.'

'You asked us at the hospital. You asked us when I got out the hospital. And you've been asking us pretty much on the hour until now. You going to ask us on the plane, too?'

'If I get a straight answer out of you, no.'

'How am I supposed to be feeling?'

'I don't know.' I rub my nose. Could do with a cigarette, should've had one before we got in the car. 'I'm sorry.'

Liam stops reading. 'For what?'

'For Nelson.'

'You didn't know.'

There's a pause as Liam turns the page.

'They give you any medication?' I say.

'No.'

'Nothing?'

'Nothing.'

I reach into my jacket, wrestle with the lid on my pills. The noise bothers Liam. I smile at him. 'I can never get these things open on the first try.' I pop the lid. Shake out two pills and swallow them. 'I would've thought they'd give you something.'

Liam watches me, then turns back to his magazine. 'I'm not in any pain.'

'Not physical, no,' I say.

'Not any,' he says.

Silence between us. Goes on so long, I can't stand it.

'I'd be pissed off,' I say.

'Course you would.'

'Fuck's sake, Liam.'

'What?'

'Do something, mate. Take a fuckin' swing at me, anything. I got you in that position with Nelson, the least you can do is vent or something. You want to take a free swing? You'll probably kill me, but it's the least I can do.'

'The least you can do is leave me alone, Cal.'

'What's the matter with you?' And I'm honestly interested. Sick of this silent shite he's been playing since he came out of the hospital, the stoic wee prick. He thinks he's what? Above a little emotion? He's got every reason to be raging right now, tearing the place apart with his bare hands and me with it. Just had his dreams stamped on because of me, just had the light snapped off on his golden fucking future. So I've been expecting the cracks to show, but there's nothing. If anything, the lad's stonier than ever.

Liam closes his magazine carefully. 'There's nothing the matter with me, Cal. I just got out the hospital. Feeling fine.'

'Well, you look like a psycho.'

He narrows his eyes when he looks at me. 'The fuck you want us to do?'

'Anything you want. But don't bottle it up.'

'If I go nuts, Cal, what does that accomplish? If I get out of this seat and I knock you out for putting us in the hands of a guy who drugged us and fucked my chances at ever turning pro, what does that accomplish?'

'It makes you feel better, Liam.'

'No, it doesn't make me feel better. Because I do that, and nothing's changed except I've made the world a messier place. Fucked up some airport cleaner's day because she has to scrub you off the seat. It doesn't change the fact that I lost something without getting a chance to hang onto it. Doesn't change the fact that when we get back to Manchester, I'm going to have to explain what happened to Paulo.'

'I'll explain it to Paulo—'

'You'll explain nowt, Cal. You'll get a few drinks down you to pluck up the courage and by that time it'll be too late for you to slur out the truth. Fact is, I said that I'd walk if I wasn't confident with Nelson. You remember that?'

'Yeah.'

'So if I didn't want to do it, I wouldn't have done it. I'm my own man. I make my own decisions. You want to keep treating us like a fuckin' kid, I got no choice but to remind you I'm not.'

Yeah, this big man, eh? 'You're not a kid, why'd I have to come with you?'

'Because you needed a holiday. Everyone says you've been mental since you got back, y'know. Like you're sick, you need all those fuckin' pills.'

'It wasn't so long ago you were mugging grannies,' I say.

'Bad things happen to good people,' he says. He looks at the cover of his magazine. 'Bad things happen, you can't stop them. Best you can do is get up and battle on.'

'Shapiro tell you that?'

'I told him that.'

'When?'

'When he checked up on us.' Liam opens the magazine. 'That first night I was in. Which is more than you ever did.'

'I checked up on you,' I say.

'When you thought it was safe, Cal. You can guilt-trip yourself all you want. I don't blame you for what happened, and I'm not going to swing for you, either.'

That's the last thing he says to me. It boils my piss. I keep trying at him, but he's put a wall up. We get on the plane, the first thing he does is bury his nose in that magazine. When the plane's up, he fiddles with the arm-rest, brings out the wee TV screen and pulls it up so it's a barricade between us. Then he starts messing with the remote, trying to find something to watch.

I give up on him. Let him be a lairy little fucker if he wants to be. Fuck him if he doesn't want to talk this through like an adult. Bad things happen to good people. Too much time around Shapiro, he's gone all spiritual. You battle on. Doesn't sound like too much battling to me. Sounds like you take your punches and don't throw any back. Turn the other fucking cheek. And if he thinks that's the secret to the way the world works, he's dead wrong. Someone hits you, you hit back. Christ, that's the backbone of boxing. A hundred tiny revenges in two minutes. Then it's back to your corner to figure out how to score a hundred more. You keep going until one of you wins. That's the way it is. It's hardly fucking rocket science.

Battle on. Yeah, that's about right. But there's got to be a moment when the battles are over and the war is won.

I press the button in the side of my seat, recline and pull my own TV screen out. Nothing decent showing, so I listen to piped Yanni until sleep catches up with me.

Battle on.

FORTY

Liam and I take separate cabs from the airport. It wasn't my choice. I wanted to go back to the club first, get the explanation out of the way, but Liam darted for the first black cab he saw before I got a chance to stop him. Then the taxi took off into a typical Manchester summer landscape, drizzle slow-soaking everything in sight.

Looks like I'll have to explain the last week to Paulo myself. I hoist my bag to my shoulder, slide into the back seat of a cab and tell the driver to head for Salford. He grinds the car into gear and we head off.

I'd like to say it's good to be home, but the smell of plane sweat and damp clothes takes the shine off my arrival. Besides, there's still too much to do before I get to the flat. Trying to piece together the past couple of days, weave it into some kind of story I can tell Paulo that doesn't make me look like a complete arsehole. The usual struggle, trying to figure out where it all went wrong, then flipping back, branching out. What did I do right? Replay it until the image degrades and realise there's no way of telling the truth without accepting it myself.

'Can I smoke in here?' I say.

'Nah, mate.'

Figures. No reason to cut me a break now.

Bloody hell.

Not even a week and I'm talking like an American.

The cab drops me off on Regent Road. That's as far as my limited pounds sterling will get me. I pull my bag from the back seat, turn up the collar on my jacket and start trudging up towards Gloucester Street. Flanked on either side of the road by industrial parks with no industry. A hotel and a Sainsbury's. A casino and a couple of fast food places. If it wasn't for the signs, you'd swear they were all the same buildings housing exactly the same things. I cross, stare up the road at Paulo's club. The doors are closed.

As I get closer, I notice the large steel bar across the doors to the club, a brand new padlock securing it in place. Along with the rain, there's a smell of stale smoke in the air. I drop my bag on the ground, notice the blackened edges of the double doors, some of the paint blistered and chipped.

I head round to the back of the club, where what used to be my office overlooked the bins. The back window's boarded up, but someone's chipped away at the wood. I peer through the gap. The office is charred. Squint a little, and I can just about see the door to the office is open. Other than that, it's black. Someone gutted the entire building. The stench is overwhelming, carried out on a stiff breeze.

I take out a cigarette, light it. I couldn't bring a lighter on the plane going over there, but they weren't so bothered when I was coming back. Pull my jacket tighter and look around, cross back to the front of the club. Up the street, there's a gang of kids on mountain bikes coming this way. Shouting and whooping at each other. As they get nearer, I recognise Ewan. He's on a stolen bike. I say stolen, because his ride's too short for him and it's pink with a white plastic basket on the front. The way he's riding the bike, though, he obviously thinks it's a monster hog.

'Ewan,' I say.

The fat kid grins, rides towards me. Starts circling, then comes to a scraping halt in front of the Lad's Club.

'Where you been?' he says.

'Where's Paulo?'

'Tell you what, give us a ciggie, eh?'

'I'll give you a smack instead. How about that?'

The rest of Ewan's gang stop their bikes. One of them I know.

He's a bruiser from the club. The other two look like scally cousins. They can get to fuck. Ewan straddles the bar of his bike and looks hard at me.

'What happened to your ear?' he says.

'What happened to your hairline?'

Even his gang laugh at that one. Ewan's no leader.

'Where you been, smart arse?'

'I've been away,' I say. 'Where's Paulo, Ewan?'

Ewan looks at his cronies, sticks his tongue under his bottom lip. He always was a wee prick, this one. 'You missed all the fun, man. Paulo's back on the fuckin' sauce.'

'Commercial,' says the bruiser.

I jerk my head at the doors. 'What about the club?'

'Ask Paulo about that, man,' says Ewan. 'He's the one fucked with the wrong people.'

'Cheers.' I pick up my bag, walk away from them.

'Go pick up your fuckin' boyfriend,' shouts Ewan.

There are some catcalls, smooching noises. The fat balding bastard is still jeering when I hit Regent Road.

The Commercial's a pub pushing into Castlefield. There are plenty of pubs down there, catering for the off city centre drinkers, the new wave of yuppies residing in the canalside apartments, but the Commercial's the only place that looks like a proper pub. It's also decorated with boxing photos, the landlord being in the circuit in his younger days. Back when Paulo used to drink, he was a regular. So regular that he started getting chucked out on a nightly basis. I don't like the idea of Paulo drinking again, especially when I hear it from a scally like Ewan. Because if it's got to Ewan, it means it's out of control. Paulo's been the kind of ex-drunk who'll enjoy a couple of pints now and then, but that's his limit. And he's been good about observing that limit until now.

When I see him in the corner of the pub, I already know the two-pint limit's been thrown out a long time back. Check my watch and it's knocking on six o'clock. There are four empty pint glasses on the table in front of him. And it looks like Paulo's made a sizable dent in his fifth pint. He looks up as the door squeaks closed.

'Cal,' he says. He tries to smile, but it doesn't quite take.

I pull up a chair, drop my bag on the floor. 'What happened, mate?'

'No,' he says. 'No, you first. I haven't heard from you.'

'Paulo—'

'What happened in the States?' There's a slight sway to his head; he uses his mouth too much when he talks. 'Tell me what happened in America. Our boy do good?'

'I tried to call,' I say. 'You change the number?'

'Nah, the phone's off. What happened with Liam, man? C'mon, don't keep me in suspense.'

I shake my head.

'He fuck it up?'

'I did.'

Paulo lets out air, gazes into his pint. 'I should've gone myself. No offence, Cal, I love you like a son, but I should've gone myself.' He runs his hand over his mouth, his eyes widening. 'The kind of shite that's been going on round here, mate . . . He lost?'

'I'll tell you some other time. It's a long story. What kind of shite?'

'You been to the club?'

'There's a padlock on the doors.'

'Well, y'know, can't leave it open. All kinds of mess in there. Don't want kids looting the place, either . . .'

'What happened?'

Paulo pushes his pint to one side, leans both elbows on the table. He has to prop his chin up on his hands as he looks at the frosted glass window next to him. 'Someone like Mo Tiernan, Cal . . . Something needs to be done about that lad. He's a mess. Y'know, I thought he was a scally dealer, but he's . . . just . . . *messed-up* inside. Twisted. Time was, there'd be his dad to keep him in check. But now . . .'

'Now what?'

'Now he can go burning whatever the fuck he likes,' says Paulo.

'Did you call the police?'

'What'm I going to tell them, Cal? I don't have nowt in the way of proof. I barely got my club. Shit, the damage, man . . .'

He looks like he's about to start crying. His eyes are red. It could just be the drink, though.

'Go home,' I say.

'I can't go—'

'Go home. I'll deal with it.'

FORTY-ONE

Paulo's not the only one drinking. When I get to the Harvester, that skinny bastard Mo's at the back of the pub with his boyfriends. They're sharing some joke, something that makes Rossie look like he's about to piss himself laughing. Baz, the man-child fat lad, is having trouble holding his drink. Literally. His pint in both mitts like a fucking baby, his right hand a mass of bandages.

Because Baz is the type of daft cunt who thinks it's the petrol in a petrol bomb that burns, not the fumes. Probably stood there holding it with a pained look on his flabby features before he found the nous to hurl it into Paulo's club. He's lucky he didn't fry himself.

On the way over here, I could picture it. It didn't take much imagination. Had to be Mo's idea. A cheap burn like that, Mo was the only one who could've come up with it. It didn't take a mastermind, just the brain of a petty fucking vandal. It was a cowardly scally trick.

'It might not've been Mo,' Paulo said to me before he went home.

But who else was it going to be? Nobody had any grudge against Paulo. Paulo was an institution. He was hard, he was fair, and he was a fucking pillar of the community compared to the Tiernans.

Seeing Baz's hand is the only evidence I need.

I walk over to Mo's table. He doesn't see me until I reach forward, grab him by the Berghaus and haul him through a forest of empty pint glasses. He's a skinny fucker, but he's still heavier than he looks – it takes three good pulls to drag him over the table and onto the floor. Course, when that happens, Rossie's on his feet with his hand in his jacket. Baz doesn't know what to do. His hand's a mess; he's not going to start throwing punches.

Mo blows beer from his nostrils. It becomes bloody with a well-aimed knock to the face. Still hanging onto his jacket, Mo swaying under, I plant my fist against his nose again. And again. Hitting the same spot, feeling my knuckles ache. Keep at it, push my knee into Mo's chest to make him stay put on the floor. Blood spilling from his nose now, running in a sheet across his shattered left cheek, mingling with the beer, piss and sweat in the carpet. He hasn't had a chance to scream. Makes these yelping sounds, getting quieter as I grind my hand against what's left of the cartilage in his nose, wanting to push it up, into the brain. Kill the fucker. Make sure he doesn't ever get up again.

You hit me, I hit you. You fuck up a man's dreams, I'll fuck you up.

One more punch, one more wet thump against Mo's face and my hand hurts more than I can take. I stand up, use my good hand to steady myself. Let Mo drop to the carpet, watch him curl slowly, his hands cupped over his face. His knees come up to his stomach as he rolls onto his side, this low growling, crying noise escaping him.

I can't move my right hand. Hold it up in a frozen semi-closed fist. I've broken a finger, one of my knuckles. I can't work out which.

Look across at Rossie. He's stuck to the spot. Wants to do something. Thinks maybe he needs the word from Mo. He's not going to get any word. Not unless his sic command is a liquid moan.

'Keep your hands to yourself, Rossie-mate,' I say.

Rossie takes a moment to think it over, then removes his empty hand from his jacket. I didn't think it would work. But being covered in someone else's blood gives a guy authority, it seems. And maybe Rossie and Baz agree with me, that Mo's been cruising for a full-on hiding for a while now.

I turn my attention back to the shaking figure on the carpet.

'Listen to me, Mo.' I aim my foot at his cupped hands, kick them apart. His face is slick with blood, his eyes shining bright blue and scared. 'You look at me, and you listen to me, mate. Because this is the last time I'm going to say this. You stay away from Paulo's club. Stay the fuck away. This isn't a friendly warning like the last time, this is a fuckin' promise. Because I see you anywhere near Paulo, near the lads that go to his place, near the club, near *me*, I'm going to kill you on sight.'

I kick him in the side, feel something snap. Bring my heel down on the broken rib.

'You hear that alright, Mo? I'm going to kill you. I'll beat you to death or I'll stab you with a fuckin' knife. Or see if I can get a gun, I'll empty the fuckin' thing in your skull. I will murder you. Don't get any notions otherwise. Your time, you scally fuckin' cunt, is over. You get that? You hearing me alright?'

Mo opens his mouth, his teeth pink. Can't tell if it's a grimace or a grin. I swing my foot at it, anyway, snap his head back. He lies there. Still breathing. For now.

Then I take a few steps back, keep an eye on Baz and Rossie, make sure they don't do anything daft.

And I'm out the door, my right hand burning.

FORTY-TWO

I've fucked my hand. Thinking that all the way back to my flat, my left hand on the steering wheel, but I can't grip with my right; the fingers have frozen into a blood-spattered claw. I rest my wrist on the wheel, feel the throb travel from my knuckles up to my elbow. Use my wrist to keep the steering wheel in position as I wrestle with my prescription, can't get the bottle open. I end up throwing the pills to one side, the brown bottle bouncing into the crack of the passenger seat.

There are things you don't fucking do. What Mo did, you don't do. Probably a laugh to him and his mates, but robbing a man of his dreams isn't something that cracks my face. Paulo's the good guy. He's the guy in the white hat. Might've been sullied at one point, sure as fuck looking grey now, but at one time that hat was pristine.

I pull into the car park, struggle with my bag and the pills and the car door and my flat keys, finally manage to juggle them and get into the block. Up the stairs, my front door key and bag in my left hand. I get into the flat, drop the bag, dump the keys on the table by the door.

Home sweet home. And it's a tip. I realise I've left the telly on. It's muted, and the evening news is on. The presenters wear court clothes. If you look close enough, you can see the dandruff. Grab a towel from the bathroom, hack some ice from the overfrosted freezer and make a cold bandage, try to take down some of the swelling.

It won't work. I know my hand's broken. Went too hard into Mo.

Fuck that, I should've killed him.

Like I should've killed Nelson.

No, I did kill Nelson.

I bring a bottle of vodka back into the living room, sit on the couch and put the bottle on the coffee table. Wrestle with my pills again, finally manage to pop the lid and shake a couple into my mouth, wash them down with a swallow of vodka.

It'll take a while for the pills to kick in. Until then, my hand throbs out a beat.

I need to get to a hospital.

But not yet. First I need to sit. Drink. Get my head muddied.

I press the bridge of my nose with my left hand, catch a whiff of myself. Plane sweat again, damp clothes, Mo's blood. I pull myself off the couch. I need to get cleaned up. I bring the vodka with me into the bathroom. Twist the cold water tap and take off the towel. My knuckles are turning black. I run the cold water over my right hand as long as I can bear it, then replace the towel.

Bony bastard broke my fucking hand. I should've stayed away from Mo in the first place. I shouldn't have talked to him. It might have been Mo and Rossie and Baz with the Thunderbird bottle and rag wicks, but I set the flame.

You don't reason with a pillhead psycho. You don't try. You do what I just did – hit him as hard as you can and run the other way. And you hope you hit him hard enough that the battle's done and so's the fucking war. Hope you put enough force into those blows to make 'em count, put him down and keep him down.

I reach for the vodka. It burns my lips, but the pills are working now.

Mo's not going to give up. If he's got any brains, he'll leave it, but Mo Tiernan doesn't have any brains. If he had brains, he wouldn't have pulled the burn in the first place. Must've known that would get back to me sooner or later.

And why didn't Paulo call the police?

Because he needs to fight his own battles.

When I'm finished, I reach for the towel, catch a glimpse of my reflection in the mirror above the basin. The glimpse turns into a full vacant stare. Blood spots all over my face. A missing earlobe.

Battle on. That's what they say.

I rub the towel over my face, watch the blood smear in the mirror.

Yeah, you battle on.

I grab my mobile from the living room, walk over to the window and see the rain's turned from drizzle to downpour.

Punch in a number and wait.

I'll drive myself to the hospital in a minute. One more thing to do.

'Don? It's Cal. You still need me to do that eviction job for you?'

Acknowledgements

Thanks, as always, go to my wife for reading it until it stuck to the page. Sunshine and Leblanc for reading it second. Alison for allowing me to keep my gazelle. Neville and Team Polygon for not being twice shy. Marc and Sarah at The Agency Group for their L.A. insights and pimpage. Thanks also to anyone who picked up the first one, whether begged, borrowed or stolen. Indirect thanks go to: Mr Russell, Mr Cash, Mr Bukowski, Mr Fante (Snr), Mr Waits, Mr Rourke, Mr Lewis, Mr Bragg, Mr Stella, Mr Thompson, Mr Muller, Mr Thornburg and the bloke on the cover. Thanks also go to Tony Danza.